10/12

GRT.
06116

D0755101

www.**totallyrandombooks**.co.uk

C333165787

Also available by Karen Mahoney

The Iron Witch

The Wood Queen

Visit Karen at
www.**kazmahoney**.com

Falling to Ash

A Moth Novel

KAREN MAHONEY

CORGI BOOKS

FALLING TO ASH
A CORGI BOOK 978 0 552 56526 4

First published in Great Britain by Corgi Books,
an imprint of Random House Children's Publishers UK
A Random House Group Company

This edition published 2012

1 3 5 7 9 10 8 6 4 2

The Random House Group Limited supports the Forest Stewardship Council
(FSC®), the leading international forest certification organization. Our books
carrying the FSC label are printed on FSC®-certified paper. FSC is the only
forest certification scheme endorsed by the leading environmental organizations,
including Greenpeace. Our paper procurement policy can be found at
www.randomhouse.co.uk/environment.

Set in Adobe Garamond 11.5/15.5
Corgi Books are published by Random House Children's Publishers UK,
61–63 Uxbridge Road, London W5 5SA

www.**randomhousechildrens**.co.uk
www.**totallyrandombooks**.co.uk
www.**randomhouse**.co.uk

Addresses for companies within The Random House Group Limited
can be found at: www.randomhouse.co.uk/offices.htm

THE RANDOM HOUSE GROUP Limited Reg. No. 954009

A CIP catalogue record for this book is available from the British Library.

Printed and bound by CPI Group (UK) Ltd, Croydon, CR0 4YY

For Veej –
my sun and stars.

I have long ago lost my belief in immortality
— also my interest in it.

Mark Twain

Prologue

He raises his head and she looks into the eyes of a predator.

So dazzling . . . She almost has to look away from the blaze. They seem to drip silver – like liquid mercury escaping from a broken thermometer.

But even though she is transfixed by the terrible beauty of his eyes, it's his teeth that suddenly draw her fascinated gaze. Teeth that have extended inhumanly, the canines sharp and dog-like as he bares them and growls.

The spell breaks and she has the sense to struggle. She kicks and pushes at him, trying to make an impression on his strength. She bites the hands holding her down, her own teeth blunt and meaningless. Even as she begins to hyper-ventilate, she knows there is no escape. He's too strong; his arms feel carved from cool stone. Strange how, even in her terror, she can think about how bright he burns – his face, his eyes – and yet his body is cold.

Somewhere in a very dark place inside her mind she starts laughing hysterically, and she thinks: I have gone insane. Mad, crazy, like in the movies.

How can she be laughing in her head, but screaming on the outside?

Because she is screaming, loud and shrill and hopeless, a bird in the jaws of a cat that's been stalking it forever. Never getting bored. Endlessly patient.

Her screams in the face of the impossible are filled with the knowledge of blood – and death.

Chapter One

I knew my morning was off to a bad start when I sneaked home from an illicit night out to find two cops waiting at my apartment door.

It didn't take me long to figure out who they were despite the regular street clothes – I can smell a cop from a mile away. Once a police officer's daughter, always a police officer's daughter. For a split second I considered leaving again before they saw me, but it wasn't like I had anything to hide.

Apart from being a vampire, I mean.

It's not as though I'd killed anyone. Lately.

No, I'm kidding. I don't do that – not unless someone makes me really angry.

OK, now I really *am* messing with you. I may be a member of Boston's underground undead (that nobody is

3

supposed to know actually *do* exist, outside of colorful legends and the *Twilight* franchise, of course) but I like to think of myself as one of the good guys.

I took a moment to watch the man and woman as they knocked on the door again. One was white – the woman; the man was black, and actually the shorter of the pair, but I couldn't tell how old they were from here. My eyes are good, but even I can't see through the back of people's heads. Though now that I think about it, X-ray vision would be pretty cool.

The woman turned and I tried to look like I hadn't been hesitating. *Nothing to see here, Officer, just your average teen vampire. Totally harmless.*

'Hey,' I said, as I walked toward them. I flashed them a fangless smile (I might be inexperienced but I'm well-trained in this) and produced the door key by removing one of my chunky knee-high boots and shaking it upside-down.

Thanking God that I was still wearing my contacts to hide my vamp eyes, I grabbed the key off the floor, replaced my boot and tugged down the short skirt of my black dress. 'You want to come in?'

I set about making coffee, turning my back to the detectives and measuring grounds, taking my time, adding water and trying to remember if there was any-thing vampire-y in the kitchen that would give me away.

The clock on the microwave told me it was 7:55 a.m.

Noticing that made me think guilty thoughts about the microwave. That's where Holly and I heat up the blood we drink when we can't stomach it cold from the bag.

Pushing that thought hastily away, I swung around to face my unwelcome guests.

Detectives Alison Trent and Denmark Smith had introduced themselves and showed their ID before following me inside Holly's North End apartment where Theo had put me six months ago. They seemed surprised that I could afford to live in such a nice place, but I wasn't going to tell them about all the interesting ways that the vampire Family of Boston finances their affairs. Not that I know much about it myself, only what Theo or Holly see fit to share. In the year since my life changed forever, I'd been told very little. So little that I was reduced to sneaking in and out of the apartment while my roommate was at work or out socializing, and picking up scraps of information where I could.

Trent was probably in her late thirties and had shoulder-length blonde hair tied back in an untidy pony-tail, with lots of scruffy strands hanging loose. Her face was make-up-free and her blue denim jacket looked well worn, kind of like the rest of her clothes. She smelled of cigarette smoke and mints, and her wrinkled pants and fitted sweater were plain black. She also looked vaguely familiar in that really annoying way that sort of itches at the back of your mind. Maybe my dad knew her and I'd seen her at some kind of police social event, back before he'd been quietly retired off the force.

Detective Trent's intelligent blue eyes took in everything around her, cataloging and filing it all away for later examination. She seemed intense and direct. Way to make a girl feel nervous.

Denmark Smith on the other hand, the younger of the pair, was everything that his partner wasn't – at least in the sartorial stakes (no pun intended). He was dressed in a beautifully cut charcoal-gray suit, and his shoes were shiny enough that you could see your face in them. If you actually *had* a reflection. His black hair was close-cropped and perfectly sculpted and even his fingernails were neat and tidy. He was obviously handsome, but a little *too* handsome for me. I wondered that he even had time to solve crimes, what with all the personal grooming he must do.

I turned back to the counter and pulled down the only two clean mugs I could find. They were large and decorated with comic-book characters; one was Wolverine and the other Batgirl. I poured the freshly brewed coffee from Holly's secret stash and shrugged as I offered Batgirl to Detective Trent.

Smith raised his eyebrows, but accepted Wolverine without a word.

Trent stirred sugar into her coffee and watched me. 'You live here alone?'

'I have a roommate.'

'She wasn't out dancing with you?'

Dancing? I smirked, but let the old-fashioned term slide without my usual snarky commentary. 'No, she works nights.'

Of course she works nights. She works nights, parties nights, sleeps days. She's a vampire.

Smith took a sip from his mug. 'What does your roommate do?'

Drinks blood! 'She's a motorcycle courier.'

'And you? Work? School?'

I blinked at him, feeling stupid. I hadn't even thought about how I'd answer a question like that. Theo had me so sheltered that I never even thought I'd have to worry about it. What *did* I do? Good question, Detective.

The cops exchanged suspicious looks.

Say something. Anything!

'School,' I blurted.

Trent tapped short fingernails against the side of her mug. 'Which one?'

'U/Mass. I'm an art major.' That much had been true a year ago, at least.

She nodded, holding my gaze. 'Records show you dropped out last year – just after the course started, in fact.'

Crap. I scrambled to cover the lie. 'I didn't actually drop out. Not officially.'

'Marie, you haven't attended any of your classes for months. It's November now, but you haven't even gotten started this year.'

'Just don't tell my dad,' I muttered.

Smith quirked a smile. 'He doesn't know?'

What? That I got turned into a monster? That just as Theo had told me, I hadn't been able to go to school because every time I did try I got overwhelmed by the smell of humanity – all that hot blood pumping through veins, just begging to be—

I realized that the detectives were looking at me strangely. *Please don't say I said any of that out loud.* I swallowed, wishing I'd made myself a drink. Of *coffee*, I mean.

This was why Theo, my Maker, insisted I should stay tucked away; at least until I learned to control it: the bloodlust.

'Marie?' Trent leaned forward. She seemed genuinely concerned.

'I had some problems, OK? I'm going back. Maybe next year.'

She nodded, but didn't look convinced. They clearly had me pegged as a slacker. I hated that, but what could I do to change their opinion? All they saw was a young adult who'd dropped out of college, didn't appear to have a job, and was most likely living off her roommate and family hand-outs. What did they care about my dreams?

I'd always wanted to put my artistic talents toward a career drawing superhero comics. Dreams die, though.

I hoped the questions about my home life were over and that we could now get down to business. 'Do you think maybe we could get to the point? It's been kind of a long night . . .'

'I should have thanked you sooner for seeing us so early, Marie,' Trent said. 'I realize it must be something of a surprise, us just turning up like this.' This was said in a no-nonsense kind of tone that made it quite clear that she didn't care whether I minded or not.

I nodded, schooling my face into an expression of polite interest. I'd already gotten them to assure me that they weren't here with bad news about Dad or my sisters, but that didn't mean there wasn't bad news of a different kind.

And I have more than one Family. Theo will never let me forget that. Two names too: the old me – Marie. And the inner me, the vampire me that Theo had named Moth.

Smith tried a tentative smile. 'We're hoping you can help us with an investigation.'

The cops were taking up the only two chairs at the table, so I moved to the windowsill and sat down, removing my leather jacket and laying it down as a substitute cushion first.

'OK,' I said.

Trent took over. 'Do you know a boy named Richard Doyle.'

Who? My mind raced and I searched my memory. Life since being turned was becoming more blurry as each day passed. Especially when I was anxious.

I slowly shook my head. 'I don't think so.'

'You don't *think* so?' Trent gave me a cop stare I recognized well from my father. 'You either know him or you don't.'

'Sorry,' I replied. 'Can you tell me anything else? Something that might help me to place him?'

'You mean, something more than his *full name*?' Smith's tone dripped sarcasm.

'I don't have a great memory,' I replied, smiling sweetly and fiddling with my long black curls.

He didn't respond to my feminine charms. I was tempted to show him my fangs; perhaps *that* would get a reaction.

'Miss O'Neal,' he said, 'are you on any substances at this time?'

'What?' I didn't blush – couldn't blush, at least not until I fed properly, which was a good thing considering how guilty I felt and probably looked. 'What kind of substances?' *Like, blood? Do you mean blood?*

Trent pushed Batgirl away and scowled. 'Don't play us for fools, Marie. We're talking about narcotics. Do you take drugs?'

'Of course not, Officer,' I said sincerely.

'Detective.'

'Of course not, Detective.' I cringed. This wasn't going well. I already knew they were detectives, but I was suddenly nervous and couldn't think straight.

Authority figures do that to me.

Trent stared at me. 'Richard Doyle is dead, Marie. He was murdered, that's why we're asking you about him.'

I leaned back against the winter-chilled glass and shivered. *Murdered?*

'He attended the same art course at U/Mass that you dropped out of last year,' Smith said. 'Maybe that'll help you place him.'

I resisted the urge to give him the finger. Not because I have oh-so-much self-control, but because suddenly I *did* know who they were talking about. Of course I did. It's just that a lot can happen in a year (like, for example, being turned into a monster against your will), and those things take up a lot of space in your head and heart.

Sometimes, it's hard to remember your own name, let alone the name of someone you only knew briefly as the skinny dude with the shock of red hair who worked at an easel on the other side of the room from you.

'I'm sorry, Detectives, I really am. When you called him "Richard", I got confused. I knew him as Rick.' Which was true enough. 'Or Red.' Also true. 'Some of the guys called him "Doily".'

Trent raised blonde brows. 'Why would they call him that?'

'Um . . . his *surname*? Doyle? And the whole Irish thing. You know.' I shrugged.

Smith looked at me like I was from another planet. 'The "Irish thing"? You're going to have to explain that one to me.'

I tried to look like I wasn't crazy. 'Irish lace, you know. Doilies. Doyle.'

Smith's blandly handsome face was blank.

I sighed. 'I guess it made sense at the time.'

His partner came to my rescue. 'Marie, we need you to tell us everything you know about him.'

'I don't know much, I swear.'

Smith snorted.

I glared at him. 'I mean it. We just took the same class for a couple months and it's not like we stayed in touch. He had a twin sister, Erin. I talked to her once or twice, maybe. We were hardly BFFs.'

He still didn't look convinced and I wondered what else was going on here. For some reason these two cops thought I knew more about Rick than I was telling.

'What about others from your class? Even though you weren't there for long, did you stay in contact with anyone else?'

'No,' I said. I regretted that, but it wasn't like I'd been in a fit state to go out for coffee with friends. Not . . .

after. There'd been some girls I thought were actually OK; people I figured I'd have time to make friends with beyond those first weeks of getting-to-know-you. Rick's sister, Erin, might even have been one of them. But becoming a vampire changed you right down to the bone. People became prey. That's not a good basis for friendship.

I licked my lips. 'How was Rick killed?'

'I'm afraid we can't share that information at this time. There wasn't much evidence at the scene of the attack, and he died during emergency surgery, so we were really hoping you'd be able to give us something to go on.'

'But why would *I* be able to do that? I keep telling you, I hardly knew the guy and haven't even seen him for ages.'

'Because we found this on his body.'

Detective Trent produced a small, clear plastic bag from an inside pocket. She laid it on the table and I could see a scrap of white paper inside. On the paper there was a hastily scrawled note in a rust-colored ink that, to my suddenly feverish brain, looked like it could have been dried blood.

A note that consisted of my name and address.

Well, that can't be good, I thought.

Chapter Two

At least now I knew why I was getting the attitude from Detective Smith.

Alison Trent continued to fix me with her steady gaze.

The bagged slip of paper glared at me accusingly from the center of the table. What did it mean? Why would Rick Doyle, of all people, have my name and address on him when he died? We *hadn't* known each other well – there hadn't been time. And where would he have gotten those details from, anyway? The university's records department would hardly just hand them over to a fellow student.

'Considering you hadn't seen the victim in so many months,' Trent said, 'do you have any idea why he would have this in his wallet?'

I really didn't. I could count the number of people

who had my full address on one hand: Holly (obviously), Theo, Dad and my two sisters. That was it, apart from school. Theo didn't know I'd given the university my change of address when I officially moved in with Holly. He wouldn't like it, but I'd wanted to have those lines of communication open – just in case I could go back to the course. One day. When I got my bloodlust under control. *If* I got my bloodlust under control . . .

But there was nothing that would explain why a note of my home address had been found on Rick's body after he'd been murdered.

'Any romance between the two of you?' That question from Smith.

I shook my head. 'Rick's gay. *Was*, I mean.'

Trent and Smith exchanged a look. It was Detective Trent who spoke up. 'You're certain of that?'

'That he was gay?' I shrugged, trying desperately to make sense of this. Not for the police, I didn't care about them. But for an innocent kid who'd been murdered. 'Sure. From what I remember, he didn't run around announcing it but he didn't hide it either. It just . . . was what it was. You know?'

Trent tucked a stray strand of blonde hair behind her right ear, exposing even more of the side of her neck. My gums throbbed as my fangs tried to slide out. I saw her pulse jump and quickly looked away. Vampire fangs only fully extend when we need to feed or when a vampire's emotions are running high – both of which applied to me right now.

Being a vampire is about living in a constant gray area: the blurred space between human and monster. Between civilized and wild. It was like walking a tightrope between the two sides of my nature, and I wondered if I would ever learn to reconcile them.

Somebody's phone buzzed, making me jump.

Way to look guilty, Moth.

Smith pulled a sleek handset out of his seemingly wrinkle-resistant jacket and excused himself, taking the call in the hallway.

Out the corner of my eye, I watched Trent remove something from between the pages of her notebook. 'This is a picture of the victim, kindly provided by his family.'

She slid the photograph of Rick Doyle toward me and I was about to take a proper look when I heard Detective Smith's lowered voice talking from beyond the kitchen doorway. Adjusting to un-life as a vampire is hard in so many ways, but there are some benefits. I'm not going to pretend that's not true: increased strength, speed and agility, as well as enhanced senses – such as smell and hearing. Which meant that I could eavesdrop on Smith's phone call and hear every word he said. My natural abilities didn't extend to the person on the other end of the phone, but that didn't matter. What I heard from the detective in my hallway was more than enough to set alarm bells ringing.

'*A . . . what?*'

There was a pause as he listened, and I fiddled with the picture of Rick to buy myself some time.

'*You're telling me that a wild animal tore out his throat and is, potentially, on the loose in the city?*' There was a brief pause as he listened. Then: '*Exactly how much blood did he lose?*'

Holy crap! His throat was torn out by . . . a *wild animal*? Why did I think it unlikely that an *animal* was responsible for Rick's death? What kind of predators – capable of that sort of damage, causing that much blood loss – actually existed in a city like Boston? I imagined a giant red arrow pointing over my head: vampire! I wanted to leap off the windowsill and grab the phone from Smith, find out more from whoever he was talking to, but I forced myself to stay where I was. Had a vampire done this? I felt twitchy, wishing the detectives would leave so I could think about it properly. The note on Rick's body was bad enough, but now this . . .

It could hardly be a coincidence. But what did it have to do with *me*?

'*Let us know when the body can be moved from MGH.*' Smith wrapped up the call with a few technical details that I didn't understand, but I'd gotten enough. MGH is

Massachusetts General Hospital – or Mass Gen, as most people called it.

I thought: This is bad. This is really bad. This is *worse* than really bad. And while my mind kept up this super-intelligent monologue, I forced myself to stare at the photograph in front of me. I pretended not to notice when Detective Smith returned and told Trent he'd been speaking to the ME who had briefly attended the murder scene and then made an initial examination of 'the victim's' body after his death on the operating table.

'The victim's' photograph made me remember him all over again. Rick Doyle's bright hair was like a red flag against the summer sky and he had his arms around a girl and another boy. They were all wearing graduation robes. The ridiculous mortarboard that he should have been wearing was long gone, thrown into the air and trampled in the excitement of the last day of high school – the last day of being a kid.

But he had still been a kid when he died. He must have been my age – my true age, I mean. Around nineteen. I'd stopped ageing at eighteen, thanks to my Maker. I bit the inside of my cheek and studied the picture, wondering what Rick had been doing the day he was murdered. He would have been planning for a future filled with hopes and dreams. All gone in an instant, his life snuffed out like the candle flames Theo was so fond of.

'Yes, I remember Rick,' I said, my voice thick with sudden emotion. 'But I honestly can't tell you anything. I haven't the slightest idea why he'd have my address on him – I wish I did.'

Detective Trent glanced at Smith and nodded, almost imperceptibly.

'Thank you for your time, Marie. If you think of anything that could help us, anything at all – anyone who might have had a reason to hurt Rick, the name of someone he was friends with that we might not know about; boyfriends . . . *anything*. Please call us.' She produced a business card from somewhere and pressed it into my cold hand.

There was no way the police would drop their interest in me or my possible link to the case. If I was one of their only leads, they would surely be keeping tabs on me. I wouldn't dare tell Theo – anything that brought our hidden world into the light made him angry. Perhaps I could find out more without having to tell him anything? Maybe he didn't even have to find out that Trent and Smith had paid me a visit? I was sick of playing by his rules anyway. I stared at the flimsy piece of cardboard without seeing it. All I could see was Rick Doyle's joyful face in that photograph. All I could hear were Smith's words during the phone call I wasn't supposed to have heard.

A wild animal? I doubted it. There were a lot worse things than 'wild animals' living in Boston.

After letting the detectives out I headed straight to my room.

I didn't bother with the chair or the bed, just slumped to the floor as my legs gave way with relief. My hands were shaking, a fact that surprised me despite the visit from Detectives Trent and Smith. Or perhaps it was the news of Rick Doyle's death that had affected me.

Maybe I was just hungry. Vampires only need to feed once a week to sustain us, but more was preferable, especially during the first year and definitely if under stress. It was Friday, and I realized that I hadn't taken blood for almost eight days. No wonder Trent's neck had looked so yummy.

Ugh. I wished I didn't think such disgusting things. I hated that, since it made me feel no better than whoever – or *whatever* – had killed poor Rick. They'd left him in the sort of state that had police detectives talking like he'd been mauled by something other than a human. Considering that Boston, Massachusetts, has one of the highest vampire populations per square mile in the whole of North America, I figured that my gut feeling might be right.

Added to that, there was the not insignificant detail of my name and address found on his body – the name and address of a vampire. Though, of course, the police didn't actually know that. I'm not sure I really believe in coincidences, so either Rick really did want to contact me for some mysterious reason – which seemed unlikely – or someone wanted me to think that he did. And I couldn't say I liked that theory a whole lot better.

Whatever the case, I felt like I owed it to Rick to try figuring it out. Maybe he'd been trying to reach out to me, only he'd gotten himself killed before he could do it. Whether that was true or not, I knew what Theo would do if I told him any of this: he'd hand the matter over to his Enforcer, Kyle, and that would be the end of it. I'd never find out what happened and everything would be covered up.

According to that phone call Rick's body was being held temporarily at Mass Gen. That was good to know, but only so long as they actually kept him there. If I wanted to get a quiet look at his remains before he was moved on to wherever the cops would do their main examination, I needed to beat them to the body. There was probably red tape and stuff, especially as he'd died at the hospital rather than at the murder scene, but still . . .

I wouldn't have long. Maybe I could use my newly developed senses to find a clue that the on-scene examiner had missed? It was weird, but as a vampire I might be able to *scent* something on him.

I tried to tell myself I wanted to do this for good reasons. Unselfish reasons. But there was something sneaky lurking in my heart; something I didn't want to admit, although it was hard not to when I was so brutally honest with myself about most things. Tomorrow night was my official introduction to the Elders who oversaw the vampire Family of Boston – Theo's Family. He'd kept me pretty much on lock-down for the best part of a year, only meeting just a select few of the Family, but now he considered me 'ready' to face them. I wouldn't be the wild, half-crazed creature I'd been in those early days. Or the depressed, suicidal girl I'd become as the weeks and months progressed. I was, apparently, well-adjusted. Finally.

Meeting the Family meant a change in the status quo of my life. On the one hand, I welcomed change, because I was sick of spending most of my time hiding. I didn't even see my human family – my dad and two sisters – that much anymore, though Theo had approved some short visits so that no one would get too suspicious. On the other hand . . . I knew it could mean more restrictions of a different kind. There would be expectations of me. Maybe even responsibility. Probably those rare visits to my family would have to stop too . . . I shuddered. I could never have my old life back – the one Theo had stolen from me – but as I couldn't have that human existence, then I at least wanted to do whatever I wanted with this 'new' life.

And today, I wanted to figure out what had happened to Rick Doyle. Nobody had the right to stop me – not even the man who made me what I am.

I headed across the room to my closet. I needed more suitable clothes. Getting into the hospital through the front doors would be the obvious choice, but there were ways of getting around Boston that most people didn't know about. Sometimes, even vampires needed to travel during daylight – and that's where the tunnels came in. I grabbed jeans and a sweater – both black, natch – and quickly changed. I wanted to be out of here before Holly got in. She was late coming home this morning – her shift was over well before daylight. As she was now too 'old' to go out in full light, she could be in the tunnels – I'd have to make sure I didn't run into her.

My DMs were super-comfortable and made me feel ready for anything. I left them halfway open and tucked the laces inside. Looking up, the first thing I focused on, as usual, was the mirror attached to the old-fashioned dressing table that had been my mother's. I liked to remember her sitting in front of it, brushing her thick dark hair – before she cut it short. Before the first round of chemo.

When I first moved in with Holly, I'd painted the mirror itself with three coats of black paint. Holly keeps threatening to rip it from its brass fixtures at the back of the table. She says I'm torturing myself. I prefer to call it reminding myself of what I no longer have. I like to think that's a subtle-and-yet-significant difference. When I was first brought back to life as a vampire, my reflection had

23

initially remained intact – but it faded quickly during those first painful months of adjustment. I had felt sick with fear each time I saw a little more of myself slipping away, almost as though someone had taken a giant eraser and set to work rubbing me out of existence. I would sit in front of the gilt mirror in Theo's grand hallway, watching my flesh become more translucent as the light from the arched windows shone right through the ghostly girl looking back at me. It was like watching my own transformation: human Marie slowly dissolving and becoming inhuman Moth. A new kind of metamorphosis.

It was like watching myself die all over again.

Now, I'd gotten used to it. Not having a reflection, I mean. Dressing was never a problem to me – who needed a mirror to check out the effect of whatever ensemble I'd chosen for the day? Make-up was more challenging, though I only ever bothered with eyeliner and Holly would take great pleasure in telling me if I screwed it up. And sometimes – though I had never confessed this to Theo – I would catch a distorted, ethereal reflection of myself in a window, if the light was shining at a certain angle, or even in water if it was very still. I didn't know if that was normal and I didn't want to ask.

But mirrors were as much use to me now as trying to find my reflection in a brick wall. Some people say that mirrors provide a reflection of the soul, so what does that say about me? Do I even *have* a soul? I wonder about that a lot. My mom had been pretty religious – we're Catholics, and I still have family in Ireland, apparently – and Sunday was an important day when she was alive.

A full-length mirror mocked me now from its place on the back of the bathroom door. I stood and looked at the space where I should be and my stomach flipped over. It still made me feel nauseous. You try it: even though you know you're standing *right there*, the mirror reflects nothing but the room around you.

However, despite how unsettling it could be, a big part of me was relieved I no longer had to gaze at my mother's face every time I looked in a mirror. My father resented me for many reasons, but one of the most obvious was how much like Mom I looked. OK, and there was the not-so-tiny matter of how disappointed he'd been when I told him there was no way I was following in his footsteps onto the Job. No way did I want to be a cop. Can you imagine it?

My phone rang just as I was pulling my leather jacket back on. I checked caller display: Caitlín. My little sister (*not so little*, she'd tell me, now that she was sixteen). I sighed, briefly considering pressing the 'ignore' button. Cait had been on my back a lot lately, though I could hardly blame her. After Mom died I'd hardly been around. It wasn't like I didn't have a good reason for that, considering how I'd met Theo at the time, but how could

I tell my sister that? Honestly, she was the only person in the world who I'd even *considered* telling the truth to. I just had to figure out a way to do it that meant Theo would never find out. And, really, did I expect Caitlín to believe me? '*Hey, sis, guess what? I'm a vampire.*' '*Really? Cool!*'

I hit the answer button. 'Yo.'

'Yo, yourself. Where are you?'

'Home. You?'

'Same.'

'No school today?'

I could hear the pout in her voice. 'Why? Is your name Sinéad all of a sudden?'

I frowned, even though she couldn't see me. 'Are you ill?'

'Marie . . .' Her voice whined at me. I hardened my heart.

'Skipping?'

'Like you're one to talk.'

Actually, I'd never skipped high school. I had been a model student, once upon a time. Just because I was into Goth clothes didn't mean I didn't work hard. People and their crazy stereotypes bugged me.

I sighed. Caitlín had gotten more rebellious lately, and I couldn't help taking on some of the blame for that. Not that she wasn't ultimately responsible for her own behavior, but after Mom died I should have been there for her. Not left it all to Sinéad, our older sister. Caitlín was only three years younger than me so I was the one she really wanted around. Sinéad just didn't cut it for Caitlín.

I looked at the photographs on my bureau. There were just two of them – a small picture of myself with my mother, taken at my fifth birthday party. The other one, larger, of me and Caitlín from three years ago. It had been taken before Mom died, so we looked happy. I was sixteen in the photo, and Cait thirteen. We looked similar apart from the color of our hair: pale faces, big eyes, long wavy hair. My curls are black, inherited from Mom, and hers a beautiful autumnal shade of red. Dad's legacy to both of my sisters.

'Why didn't you go to school?'

'I just can't concentrate, lately.'

'Is it Dad? Is he . . . you know.'

We didn't actually need to say the words. His drinking had gotten worse, and that was yet another thing I wasn't there for – to help. Not that Dad would want me around.

'He's always . . . "you know". You know?'

I half smiled. 'Yeah. Sinéad's not there today?'

'She's been on a residential course. She gets back today – I told you that last weekend.'

There was no judgment in Caitlín's voice, but I felt the sting of her words all the same.

'Sorry, I forgot.' My memory really was screwed up.

When I told the cops that, I'd actually been telling the truth. Crap. Caitlín had been home alone with Dad for most of the week. I felt terrible. Not that he'd ever hurt her – she was his favorite, after all – but that didn't make his moods any easier to handle.

'Marie,' Caitlín said. 'Are you OK?'

'I'm always OK.'

'And I'm serious. I haven't seen you in ages.'

I ran my tongue across my fangs and remembered my last visit to the O'Neal family home. It had ended badly. None of us had coped with Mom's death well, and instead of pulling together, sometimes it was more like we were all intent on pulling each other apart. Except for Caitlín. She was the only one of us who tried – at least, she had done for a while – and although I knew it was wrong that the baby of the family should always be acting as peacemaker, I didn't think I'd ever get on well with Dad and my older sister, Sinéad.

'Sis?'

'Sorry,' I said, pressing the phone against my ear and trying to focus. 'I'm still here.'

'Are you coming to dinner tomorrow?'

Ah, yes. The Sunday dinners. We come from the standard, working to middle-class Irish-American family, hardworking, honest, all of that good stuff. Our family rituals still continued, despite everything going to shit. Despite the fact that Dad would spend most of the afternoon watching the game and drinking beer. Sinéad would treat it like a duty, complaining that she should be studying her law books rather than cooking for her ungrateful sisters; while poor Caitlín would look increasingly depressed and sneak gulps of wine when she thought I wasn't looking.

Those dinners are just grand. *Not.*

'I can't make it tomorrow.'

Caitlín blew out a frustrated breath. 'You said that last week.'

'I know, I'm really sorry.' I tried to sound sincere.

'No you're not.'

'I am! I hate letting you down.' Well, that much was true. But this time I really did have an excuse, albeit not one that I could tell Caitlín: just that not-so-small matter of meeting my 'new' Family. I swallowed. Oh, joy.

'Well, if you'd just come over more often you wouldn't have to worry about letting me down.'

I felt supersize guilt. 'That's low, sis. Even for you.'

'Yeah, yeah. Whatev.'

'Why don't you just meet me after school one day next week? We can hang out. Or go shopping.' Something normal and non-vampire-related would be nice and I could handle it for a few hours, I felt sure. If I didn't look too closely at the people . . . Nobody here had to know about it. Being such a new vampire meant I could still be out during daylight too – at least for another year or two.

29

If I was lucky. It got harder and harder. Like Holly, there'd come a time when I wouldn't be able to face sunlight at all.

'Maybe.'

'You know you want to.' I kept my tone light, teasing.

'We'll see,' she said. 'I should go. You have a good day, sis.'

'OK.' She was disappointed in me and I hated that. 'You have a good one too. Especially now that you have an unscheduled day off.'

She snorted. 'I'm sure I'll have a blast.'

'Bye then,' I said.

'How about dinner *next* Sunday?'

I laughed. 'You really don't give up, do you?'

'Nope. Well?'

'I don't know, Cait. It didn't go so well before . . .'

'That's because you spent most of the time arguing with Sinéad.'

'It's not just down to me.' I knew I was being petty, but my big sister brought out the best in me.

'Marie, can't you be the bigger person? Sinéad really would like you to come too.'

'Well, now I know you're lying.'

'I'm not,' she replied, way too quickly. 'So, you'll try for next weekend?'

'OK.' It came out as more of a sigh. Would Theo let me go? By next weekend, I'd truly be part of his Family.

'You *will*?' Her voice rose up at the end, genuinely excited. It just about broke my heart.

'Yes.'

'Really try? Don't just say it to blow me off.'

'I'm not. I promise.' I bit my lip, wondering if I was lying to her already. 'I really will try, OK?'

'OK.' Caitlín didn't sound convinced. I could hardly blame her.

'Hey,' I said. 'I love you. You know that, right?'

But the phone had already gone dead, and I knew that my sister hadn't heard me.

I shoved the phone into my jeans pocket. I felt utterly drained. I *did* want to see my sister, of course I did. But it was so hard to be among humans. I was no longer one of them. What if I hurt someone? What if I hurt *Caitlín*? I could manage these short visits this first year, but I knew that I'd have to break off all contact some time. Theo had explained it all to me.

But how could I explain that to Caitlín?

I zipped up my jacket and pulled my mind back onto Rick. I could hardly believe it was only just past nine. I wanted to sleep, but figured that the best thing I could do was take a look at Rick's body *now* before anyone moved it. It shouldn't be too difficult to sneak in there – sneaking was something I did pretty well.

I listened to the sudden silence in the apartment, inhaled the scent of coffee that had drifted in from the kitchen. A moment of peace before I took action.

Of course, Holly chose that moment to slam into the apartment, tossing her motorbike helmet to one side as she headed for the kitchen. I heard her hesitate there for a blissful moment . . . before clomping on through the tiny hallway. *Great.* She was coming in my direction. I rolled my eyes and prepared for trouble. She hadn't liked me ever since Theo insisted she let me share her space. So Holly Somerfield had inherited me as her roommate, and I'd inherited a love–hate relationship with a twenty-something bisexual bike courier with seriously dodgy taste in music.

My bedroom door banged open. Holly never knocked. She seemed to have lost the whole concept of 'personal space' during the two relatively short decades of her undead existence.

She posed in the doorway: all cobalt-blue hair, multiple piercings and attitude. The effect was slightly ruined by her T-shirt, which was purple with little black bats on it. Holly had a thing about bats.

'Who the hell's been drinking my coffee?'

I sighed. It was like living with my own personal member of the three bears.

Chapter Three

'We should make Theo buy us a dishwasher,' I said.

I was sitting in the kitchen watching Holly crash mugs around in the sink, supposedly washing up so that she didn't have to drink her coffee out of a shot glass.

'How nice for *you* that you can "make" Theo do anything,' she replied tartly.

Lines of small hoops ran the length of each ear. They weren't silver, of course. Vampires were violently allergic to silver, so if they had been silver Holly wouldn't have much of her ears left. All the piercings had been done pre-vampire. It was the same with her blue hair – she was stuck with it forever, which was a sore spot with her. 'You try looking like you belong in a sci-fi movie for all eternity,' she would snap if anyone dared to comment. I only made that mistake once.

I just needed to get Holly out of the way. Hopefully, once she'd finished clearing up the kitchen (she was kind of OCD at times), she'd go to bed. Or maybe she'd do some crafting. Seriously. That's just one more reason that she resented my being here: I'd taken the room she'd originally converted into a workroom. She made Goth-style jewellery (lots of bats, of course) when she wasn't roaring around on her motorcycle doing courier stuff, and ran her own little mail order business on Etsy.

'Hey, whose are these?'

I glanced up from lacing my boots to see what she was holding: an expensive-looking lighter and a crushed pack of menthol cigarettes.

Trent. 'Oh. One of the cops must have left them here.'

Holly had been horrified to hear about our visit from the police, though I'd kept the details to a minimum. I'd realized I had to tell her *something* – both she and Theo would be seriously mad if I hid something like this from them, and the police might be back. I told her they were just making routine enquiries about someone I might have known at college who'd gone missing, and that seemed to satisfy her. You never knew for sure with Holly, though. She could be more sneaky than me – which was probably the only thing we actually had in common. Maybe it was a vampire thing: Cunning. Wits. Guile. All of that good stuff.

Well, that and our mutual love of coffee. With my

reluctant roommate's help, I'd discovered that if you soak up enough caffeine you could actually cut down on your weekly blood intake. I was still experimenting with quantities, but it honestly seemed to work. At least, it seemed to help. Thinking about that made me contemplate joining Holly for another coffee before I made my escape, but when I saw her dig a bag of the 'red stuff' out of the refrigerator I changed my mind. She tossed the bag from one hand to the other.

'Now that I'm back, wanna join me for breakfast?'

Blood was the last thing I wanted after thinking about Rick's violent death. 'No, thanks.'

I slipped Trent's cigarettes and lighter into my jacket pocket and headed for the door.

'Where are you going?'

I opened the door and paused. 'What are you, my mother?'

'Theo doesn't like you going out when I'm sleeping.'

'Well, you're not sleeping yet, are you?'

Holly scowled. 'Don't be a smartass.'

Anger warmed my cold limbs. I knew I should feed, but I didn't want to delay any longer. Rick's body was at the hospital, but for how much longer? This was my chance to do something for myself – to play detective and figure out my own problems.

My roommate stalked toward me, a predator lurking in her silver eyes. 'Tell me.'

'I don't have to tell you anything.' I crossed my arms across my chest and tried to look like I wasn't scared of her.

'You really aren't cut out for this,' Holly said. 'You shouldn't go out alone. And it's daylight now.' There was no judgment in her voice. More like . . . sympathy.

I bristled. 'I can manage a bit of daylight.' She gave me a look that said, *Yeah-right-for-now.*

'Later, roomie.' I flipped her off and ran out the apartment, using my vamp-speed to sprint down the staircase.

I smiled to myself as I hit the street and almost ran through the maze of narrow lanes and redbrick buildings that filled the oldest neighborhood in Boston. I headed for the tunnels.

I was free.

Boston's abandoned subway network was mostly blocked off now: spooky tunnels filled with rats and long-abandoned areas where trains used to be turned around in specially built junctions. Theo liked to tell stories of how he'd been around when the tunnels were first built in the late nineteenth century: America's first ever subway system. The tunnels were pretty unstable, which was why most of them had been closed in the first place. I was happier down here in some ways. Strange, considering how pathetically grateful I was still to be able to walk about in daylight.

Crowds disturbed me, though. All those warm bodies, hearts beating and pumping blood: *prey*. Yet I still couldn't truly stomach the taste of blood taken fresh from the source. Sure, the bagged stuff we 'liberated' from hospitals had a strange aftertaste – like those disgusting artificial sweeteners people put in their coffee – but at least it didn't feel *alive* as it slipped down my throat. And it did the job. It gave me the energy and nutrients I needed to survive without any of the ethical issues.

I still got urges to drink from live donors; that constant gnawing hunger was hard to ignore, but I did the best I could and hadn't fed from a human since I'd survived the dark days of my transition. It made me feel sick just thinking about it, remembering it. One week after Theo had turned me, he'd been forced to hunt me through the city as I went looking for fresh blood.

The iron-rich taste of hot blood in my mouth, running down my throat. The pain in my body – the pain that I thought would last a hundred years, a thousand, forever – immediately passes. I feel as though I am hooked up to an IV filled with pure energy. Sunlight. The blood burns as it goes down, but it feels so good. It wakes me up and makes me feel powerful. I can have anything I want, anyone I want. I only have to reach out and take it . . .

I remember the expression on Theo's face as he pulled me

off my unfortunate prey. A homeless woman, middle-aged and alone and sleeping beside a dumpster in an alley. She wasn't dead, thank God. I'd only fed from her arm. Theo used his hypnotic gaze – his power over humans – to convince her that she'd been attacked by a large dog . . .

The scent of the tunnels was overpowering, bringing me back to the present. I sloshed through puddles in silence for a while, trying to orient myself beneath the hospital by memory. The tunnel came to a sudden stop around a sharp bend at a wall with a rusty iron ladder climbing up into the gloom. This was a narrow side tunnel, maybe a service access or something similar, though why it would be directly underneath Massachusetts General was a mystery to me. The lighting here also stopped completely and I was glad of my night vision. It wasn't perfect, but it was way better than regular human eyesight. I knew this part of the tunnels well; scaling the ladder was child's play, except that it always felt like it was going to break away from the wall despite how little I weighed.

I sighed and shimmied up the ladder, keeping my weight as evenly distributed as possible. The trapdoor in the roof at the top was made of rotten wood reinforced with steel hinges and a rusty bolt on my side. I reached for the bolt, intending to wiggle it free, but stopped with a jolt of surprise. *The trapdoor had already been opened.* The bolt was free of its crumbling moorings and the mechanism had clearly been forced. OK, this wasn't good. I thought for a moment. Abort the plan? But there could be a totally reasonable explanation for this. For one thing, I certainly wasn't the only person to know about this 'back door'. Plenty of the other vamps in the city were aware of it. Though come to think of it, surely anyone Theo had sent on a food run wouldn't have to force the bolt – they'd already know it wasn't half as rusty as it looked.

My Maker would be furious if he knew what I was up to, but I was determined now. Why? To prove myself to him – and to the Elders I'd be meeting tomorrow night? Or because I somehow felt I owed it to Rick to see what had happened to him? If I was being honest, I was also sick of being told what I could or couldn't do by Theo all the time. Just because he'd made me what I was didn't mean that he owned me.

Except, of course, he did.

I rolled my shoulders and pushed up on the trapdoor. A few centimeters was enough so that I could peek into the familiar disused storage room of the hospital. I couldn't see all the way around, but despite the lack of light it still looked empty. I'd never seen anyone in here before and had even begun to wonder if the stories the nurses told about it being haunted were true. Urban legend said that a ghostly presence was the real reason this particular storage area had been abandoned. It was possible, but I had a good enough sense nowadays for these things and had never felt anything dead in here. Well, no more dead-smelling than most parts of a hospital. No matter how much bleach you used, death was one of those impossible smells to erase.

I should know, I smell it on myself all the time.

Shivering slightly, I pulled myself up into the cluttered space and closed the trapdoor. OK, so maybe I *did* smell something out of place here – something that plucked at my memory and stuck out even above the familiar scent of death.

For one thing, it wasn't quite pitch dark after all. The windows were blacked out and the main door into the corridor had a blind drawn over it, so where was that cold sort of light coming from?

I turned in a slow circle and sniffed the stale air, focusing my eyes on the dim light that was coming from the far corner of the storeroom.

Did ghosts use cell phones? OK, it was a crazy thought, especially considering that I'd never actually encountered a ghost, but still . . . There was a lot of freaky shit in the world. My existence alone led me to believe that vampires couldn't possibly be all there is to it.

The light disappeared with a tiny click. I only heard it because of my freakishly good hearing, but there was something about the noise that made me think someone was over there, trying to be silent – and failing. I backed up half a step as a dark shape rose behind a stack of plastic crates and flat-packed boxes.

The figure stood to human height – a *tall* human male, by the looks of things – and I suddenly realized where I recognized that scent from.

'Crap,' I muttered.

A single, naked bulb flicked on overhead, flooding the space with an eerie yellow glow that danced off shadows thrown by boxes and other packaging.

'You!' exclaimed Jason Murdoch, vampire hunter-in-training. 'Moth! What the hell are *you* doing here?'

Chapter Four

I cursed as Jace looked me up and down. How could I be this unlucky? There's no way this could be a coincidence. I refused to believe that Jason Murdoch hadn't been following me, despite the logical part of my brain reminding me that *he was here first, so how could he have followed you*?

The wannabe hunter glared at me. 'I said, what are you doing here?'

Jason Murdoch . . . I'd hardly given the guy a thought these past few months, what with trying to get to grips with my new life and all. But six months ago, after Theo had sent me over to Jason's father's apartment, a real test for a fledgling young vampire, we'd fought. Jace had tried to kill me, and I'd repaid him with a busted leg and a kiss I still remember to this day.

Jace was the son of a hunter who'd been a thorn in Theo's side some months back. Thomas Murdoch had killed a number of vampires – including Maxim, a powerful master vamp who just happened to be a friend of Theo's. More recently however, Murdoch Senior had gone pretty quiet. Too quiet. And it didn't seem to have anything to do with the Family's attempts to shut down his operation. ('I'm going to rip his throat out,' were Theo's actual words, I seemed to recall.) No, the hunter had just dropped off the radar, and Theo seemed genuinely surprised by his disappearance.

But how had the hunter's son ended up *here*?

I took another step back and tried to slip the toe of my boot under the edge of the trapdoor. Last time I'd come up against Jace Murdoch I'd almost gotten killed.

I attempted a sunny smile, but it wasn't an easy trick to pull off when you were half terrified. 'Wow, fancy seeing you here.'

I made a big show of shaking my head as though it really was just a funny old world when you can run into the guy who might one day become your arch-nemesis. But only if this was a freaking comic book.

Much as I didn't want to admit it, Jace would make a damn good comic book hero. He was tall, with broad shoulders that had filled out even more since we'd last tangled. *Someone's been working out*, I thought wickedly. I could tell these things, despite the dark sweater and an army jacket. I mean, not that I was an expert. Theo had been my only real relationship, but that doesn't mean I didn't have an opinion on this stuff. Murdoch's waist tapered down to slim hips, and long legs clad in blue jeans and Chuck Taylors that had seen better days. His blond hair caught the light; it was shorter than I remembered, though still cute and spiky and—

Oh my God, what am I thinking? I wanted to beat the crap out of myself for even allowing that sly little thought any space in my severely screwed up psyche.

I was one sick puppy. And Jace Murdoch was not cute. No way. Not even slightly.

The voice of the object of my non-admiration vibrated with shock and anger. 'Don't tell me this is a goddamn coincidence, freak. Have you been following me?'

Wow, he really isn't happy to see me. He took another step forward. 'Answer me!'

I scowled. 'What makes you think *I'd* be following *you*? What is it with men and their egos? You're the only freak standing in this room.' I liked the anger that burned in my gut, making me feel ten feet tall. It helped to cover up my nerves as he took another careful step over scattered debris. Maybe if I kept him talking I'd think of a way out of this. 'And how would I know you'd be here, anyway? And wait a minute – why would I even care? *Duh.*'

Clearly unimpressed, Jace pulled a huge hunting knife

out of a scabbard hidden beneath the well-worn army jacket.

'Nice knife,' I said, trying to keep my tone light. 'You planning on dry-shaving with it? Maybe show me how manly you've grown?'

'Shut up, freak.'

'Oh, but I can see you don't really *have* any stubble yet. Wow, how many nineteen-year-olds do *you* know who haven't even started to grow their first beard?' I shrugged. 'Not that it bothers me – I still think you're super-sexy, even if you're not quite there yet. And you're a little too . . . *alive*, for me.'

All the while I was doing the fast-talking thing, I was still trying to get my toe under the edge of the trapdoor – but it wasn't working because of my stupid boots.

Jace came toward me brandishing the knife, the murderous look on his face still visible in the weird glow of the gently swinging bulb. Wavering yellow light spilled down in sickly waves, turning his brown eyes into pools of shadow.

But there was no mistaking the grim set of his mouth. I remembered those slightly-too-thin lips (*Oh, how I remembered them*), but back then they'd been mostly grimacing in pain after I'd broken his leg. He seemed to have made a full recovery, more's the pity. I should have kicked him harder. All I wanted was to get a look at Rick's body, and here I was having to deal with Van Helsing Junior.

I gave up any pretence at subtlety and made a dive for the trapdoor, jamming my small fingers into the even smaller gap and prising the creaking wood upward. But despite my unnatural speed, Jace was like an unstoppable force of nature. He lunged at me and I only just deflected the knife's progress in time, grabbing his wrist as we both went down beyond the trapdoor.

'Get *off* me!' I was half crushed, as six feet of furious young hunter tried to force the knife against my throat. If it was edged with silver, I was seriously screwed. The way the light caught the blade didn't fill me with much optimism, but maybe it was just really shiny.

The 'really shiny' knife nicked my throat and, *Oh shit, that burns*, I thought. My body spasmed as it processed the fact that a tiny piece of silver had entered my bloodstream. I was easily stronger than Jace, but the knife was taking up all of my attention, making it impossible to get a good hold on him. And now my freaking neck felt like it was on fire. I decided to try reasoning with him instead. My mom had always been all about the 'Make love not war' thing.

'Jace, let's stop this and talk. Maybe we can help each other?'

I gasped as the wickedly sharp silver edged close to my face and our arms waved wildly back and forth, wrestling for control. There was no way I should be having this much trouble subduing him – sure, he looked like he'd been working out, but this was crazy. Vampires had much more strength than humans. Was I weak from not having fed recently? I wished now I'd taken Holly up on her offer of blood before heading out here.

Murdoch Junior held my legs clamped between his, and I tried to remember which leg I'd injured six months ago. Maybe I could use that to my advantage. But with his full weight on me and the knife wavering close to my face, it was tough to get the leverage I needed to push him off.

Jace was panting with effort, both hands on the hilt now and his handsome face twisted with something dark and mean. 'Not so tough this time, are you?'

I stopped struggling and met his eyes with mine. For a moment I was distracted by the glint of a tiny silver ring in his left eyebrow; but then I focused, pushing all of my will onto his as I struggled to capture his gaze in mine. Vampires could do all kinds of impossible things, and those abilities increased the older they got. I was way too young to be able to do something as complex as mould another's will completely to mine, but if I could manage it for a few seconds – distract him . . .

I locked eyes with him, just for a moment, and it was enough. He froze and I grabbed his shoulders and rolled him over, pushing his body until we exchanged positions. I lay on top of him, not even caring when I heard the jarring clatter as the knife fell from Jace's limp fingers and hit the ground. He smelled fresh, like the city streets after hard rain.

I licked my lips, fighting the rising hunger in my gut, trying to stop the primal urge to bite into the soft skin of his throat as it lay exposed beneath me. My silver eyes glowed so brightly I could see their shining reflection in the brown depths of his. I was right there, reflected in his eyes; inside of him, gaining a precious foothold on his will and personality. His life and dreams and hopes and fears laid bare before me. This was better than I'd ever managed before.

Jace fell *in*.

His face went slack, empty. All that earlier rage just slipped away like drops of water sliding down glass.

The weight of his mind cradled within mine was too much for me, I wouldn't be able to hold it. How could I, when there was so *much*? I couldn't make sense of this mass of complicated pain and beauty that was Jason Murdoch. I couldn't . . .

A much younger Jace walks toward the door. It's a regular painted wooden door like in any suburban home. No glass, all solid. No way to see through it. But whatever's on the other side is scaring the crap out of him. He is so afraid, and as he reaches with shaking fingers and grasps the handle and turns it he knows what he will see.

'Say goodbye to her, son,' says a tall man, a man who

looks like an older version of the boy. His father. 'There's not long left.'

The room beyond is plain and simply furnished. Utilitarian, just the way the boy's father likes it. The bed in the corner holds a woman who might've once been beautiful, long before the approach of implacable Death. She is so pale, like bleached bones and the perfect moon in the sky outside the tiny window. Although she is slender, petite in build, her stomach is swollen beneath the covers and her white-knuckled hands clutch over the second life dying inside her.

The boy kneels by the bed and straightens the blanket, smooths back his mother's sweat-soaked hair. Tries not to meet her strange, shimmering eyes. The room reeks of something twisted and . . . wrong – sickness, death, mortality on the brink of slipping away. Slipping away like . . .

. . . like drops of water sliding down glass.

'What the *fuck*?!' Jace was choking, curled into a ball on his side, coughing and trying to catch his breath.

Somehow I was halfway across the room, as far away from the trapdoor as it was possible to get. I slowly pulled up into a sitting position. It was as though I'd been flung – presumably by Jace – with such force I'd landed in a crumpled heap against a pile of crates. They hadn't moved on impact; must be something heavy stored in them, because my back hurt like someone had stomped on it while wearing my best steel-toe-capped boots. The ones I save for special occasions.

Well, if that little *mind meld* had achieved anything, at least I was free.

Unfortunately, Jace was now between me and the hatch.

Everything seemed to slow down as we both rose to our feet, tentatively, like new-born colts testing their legs for the first time. My head felt full of splintered glass.

I was light-headed and yet strangely *energized*. Apart from the pain in my back, I was sort of OK. Jace didn't look like he'd fared as well from whatever had just happened. He stood facing me, empty-handed.

'You were in my mind. You bitch, you were in my *head*.' His voice was hoarse, almost too quiet to hear.

'I . . . I didn't mean to do that.' And I really hadn't. Not like that; not as deep or as *intrusive*. I shivered.

Jace rubbed his hand across his mouth, as though trying to wipe away a stain or the memory of something.

I shook my head, angry for losing control of an ability I still didn't understand.

He rolled his neck from side to side, breathing deeply and avoiding eye contact. I wouldn't catch him again, not like that. He was too smart. At least the rage seemed to have passed. Surely now I could talk some sense into him—

Jace grabbed a crossbow from behind some tumbled crates. A wickedly sharp silver-tipped bolt was already locked and loaded and he pointed it at me. The stock rested firmly against his shoulder, one eye squinting as he got me firmly in his sights. Literally.

The weapon was aimed directly at my heart.

I looked for the nearest exit or hidey-hole, anywhere I could gain some cover. I wasn't sure how accurate a shot Jace was but I had a horrible feeling he'd be pretty good. His hands were certainly steady enough.

'Don't move,' he said. 'I won't hesitate this time.'

'Neither will I,' I said, throwing Jason's dagger directly at his head.

'Holy fu—' Jace hit the floor and the flying dagger missed him. Which is exactly the way I'd planned it (go, me!).

Because, of course, I hadn't been aiming for him at all.

The annoyingly creepy light bulb shattered with a satisfying pop. Glass fell in a musical sprinkle, crunching under my boots as I ran toward the trapdoor.

Impressively, he had actually managed to keep hold of his crossbow and got trigger-happy from his position on the ground. But I was already miles away from where he was shooting. The crossbow bolt *swooshed* past my left shoulder and *thunked* into the wall close to the main door to the room.

'I hope you're going to collect that,' I said. 'We can't have any hospital staff finding crossbow bolts around here. That would be totally suspicious.'

51

I'd reached the hatch but Jace was advancing on me again, having tossed aside the now empty weapon. Maybe he intended to finish me off with his bare hands, but I didn't think he'd be stupid enough to believe he could take me in a fair fight. Even weakened from lack of blood, I was stronger than him. I think I'd been so shocked to see him earlier, that was surely the only reason he'd been able to match me.

I raised both hands in front of me. 'Stop right there. *Think*, Murdoch. I'm not trying to hurt you – I only want you to leave me alone so I can get on with my work.'

His step faltered. '*Work?* What kind of work would someone like you have to do in a hospital?'

'That's none of your business.'

'It wouldn't have anything to do with the kid they have down in the basement, would it?'

I couldn't help it. My mouth dropped open. 'Um . . . you mean the kid who may have been attacked by a *wild animal*?' What was the point of denying it?

Jace's eyes flickered toward the closed door that would lead back into the hospital. 'Yeah, that sounds like the one.'

'I'm investigating.'

He actually started to laugh. The bastard. 'Who do you think you are, Veronica Mars for the undead? I've got news for you: you're not blonde enough.'

'That's OK, you're blond enough for both of us,' I shot back. 'Have you had *highlights*?'

Jace narrowed his eyes. 'If you think I'm letting you go, you're dumber than you look.'

I glared back. 'If you think you can stop me, this time I'll break *both* your legs.'

Stalemate. We watched each other in the gloom. I had no problem seeing the anger and confusion etched into his face, but I wondered if the only thing he could see of me was my eyes. If I closed them, would I disappear into the shadows?

He ran a hand through the close-cropped spikes of his hair. 'So.'

'So.'

'Now what?'

I shrugged. 'If you can't bear to let me out of your sight, why don't you come with me?' *Hello*, was I completely brain-dead? What did I have to say *that* for?

His mouth lifted at one corner, but it wasn't exactly what I'd call a smile.

'I think I will.'

We made our way through the winding corridors that led to the basement space that served as Mass Gen's morgue. Not really a morgue; more just an interim place before bodies were transported to the real deal. It was a depressing fact that life as a vampire meant you learned these things about the city – things involving the dead.

Jace had ignored me all the way so far, which was fine with me except for the fact that I had plenty of things I wanted to ask him. I wanted to know what he was doing here, for a start; what did he know about Rick, lying dead in the hospital basement? But even more than that, I wanted to ask him something I had no right to: had the dying woman I'd seen in his head really been his mom? How had she died? I knew it was something bad, maybe even something unnatural. I could still smell the way that awful room had smelled. There was nothing natural about that. And her eyes – I didn't want to think about how horribly familiar that silver shimmer had been. Not that Murdoch Junior was likely to share his deepest feelings with me.

I doubted he shared those with anyone. You could see it written on his face – the grief and bitterness sort of locked in around his eyes. It made him look far older than nineteen.

Jace glanced over at me. 'So what's your interest in this kid?'

I met his gaze, knowing that my eyes would be shining brightly in the gloom. They always responded badly to stress. 'Why should I answer any of your questions? All you've done is attack me and threaten me. *Again.*'

'That's my job.'

I shook my head, frustrated that a seemingly smart guy could be so short-sighted. 'It's not your job. This is what your *father* does.'

'My father's gone.' His voice was low; something hollow echoed beneath the hard edge. There was pain hovering beneath the surface – a lot of pain – but I didn't have time to tread gently. Not that I could tread anywhere gently in these boots.

'He's dead?' I couldn't wait to tell Theo that the 'great' Thomas Murdoch had actually croaked. Last time we'd talked about him, my Maker had seemed almost disappointed that the hunter had been so quiet lately. It looked like Theo wasn't the only one missing Murdoch Senior.

Jace scowled. 'Try not to sound too happy about it. No, he's not dead – he just skipped town and I haven't seen him in weeks.'

Oh, well . . . 'I wasn't happy. Simply curious.'

He didn't sound convinced. 'You're not the only one. A lot of people are looking for my dad, but I can't tell them a damn thing. Anyway,' he continued, 'I've tried all the contacts I can think of – all Dad's old hunting buddies – but if they know anything they're not talking.'

'Maybe you're better off,' was all I said.

'You don't know anything about it.' Jace's voice had risen well above the respectable level you were supposed to use in a hospital. Not to mention the fact that we were supposed to be sneaking into a restricted area.

'Shut *up*! Do you want to get us caught?'

He slid me a sideways look from those almost too-pretty brown eyes, what with the long lashes that put mine to shame. 'What do I care? This is *your* stupid mission.'

'Then why are you even here? I thought you said you were here for the boy.'

'It sounded like a possible vampire attack when I heard about it over the police scanner and I wondered if Dad might be here,' he replied. 'He checks out anything with vamp-potential.'

I glanced around, suddenly worried that Thomas Murdoch could be creeping up on us at any moment.

The young hunter shrugged. 'Anyway, there's no sign of Dad and I don't care about the kid one way or the other. I'm only here now to keep tabs on you. Can't have an undead freak wandering around in a place where humans are sick and vulnerable.' He crossed his arms. 'I don't trust vampires.'

'Because you know so many.'

'Well, I don't generally spend time getting to know them, I leave that to my crossbow. That's the best way to deal with monsters.'

I narrowed my eyes. He didn't look intimidated, just gave me a slow quarter-smile. A lump rose in my throat.

I tried to swallow past it so I could give this self-righteous punk something to chew on, but it felt like nothing would shift the ache of wondering if he was right. After all, a year ago I would have agreed with him. And a part of me – the Marie part – still did.

We finally reached the door we needed. There was an orderly on duty and luckily he took a shine to Jace. I tried flirting with him until I realized I was wasting my time; the guy only had eyes for the tall hunk of brooding muscle standing next to me. One look into Jace Murdoch's soulful brown eyes – allied with his smooth talk of 'medical studies' – and the orderly was only too happy to allow us into the restricted area.

'He was totally hitting on you,' I whispered as we walked down a corridor that stank of disinfectant.

The corner of Jace's mouth quirked blink-and-you'll-miss-it fast. 'Yeah, I'm just irresistible.'

I leaned against the wall. 'OK, before we go any further I need to know something. Are you helping me or not?' I was pleased that my voice was steady.

'Sure, I've got nothing better to do.'

'Fine. Just don't get in my way,' I muttered. *And don't try stabbing me*, I wanted to add.

As we came to a stop, he suddenly looked at me with something other than disgust. 'Hey, listen—'

But I never did get to hear what he was going to say, because I suddenly realized that the 'secured' door was partly open and a gut-twisting stench came from the room beyond.

My stomach knotted. A thick coppery smell hit me like a fist.

'What is that *smell*?' Jace was visibly gagging. He drew the silver-edged knife from beneath his jacket.

No, it can't be . . . I stepped closer and peered around the edge of the door, trying to see through the narrow opening. The body of a large woman in green nurse's scrubs lay on the shiny floor, blocking the door from moving any further.

'Crap,' I whispered. I thought I'd said it under my breath but Jace was right beside me. I imagined I could feel the warmth from his arm as it rested against my rigid shoulder.

'What?' Jace caught sight of the nurse's body. 'Oh.'

The woman's dark blonde hair was spread behind her on the floor, trailing blood and something that looked like wet, glistening pieces of meat. I swallowed and tried not to choke. I could smell the blood. There was *so much blood*; it was intoxicating and nauseating at the same time. Something dark rose up inside me, and I don't mean vomit. I mean, something in my 'soul' – the part of me that I didn't want to admit was there.

The monster.

I growled, low in my throat.

Jace grabbed me by the arms and pulled me away

from the door. He shook me. Hard. 'Hey, get a grip. This isn't feeding time.'

I tried to block out the sickly sweet scent of fresh blood. It was almost impossible, but I had to do it. This was self-preservation: if I went vamp right now Jace wouldn't hesitate to turn that knife on me. In fact, I was pretty surprised he hadn't tried to kill me again already.

The room smelled like slaughter and I wanted to puke. It was so twisted, being hungry and nauseous at the same time.

Jace looked at me, a frown pinching his eyes into something more dangerous. 'No, seriously, what *is* that smell?'

I tried to steady myself as I experimented with a deeper breath. 'It's blood, Jace. What did you think it was?'

'Not the blood. I know what *that* is.' He shook his head, as though trying to brush off cobwebs. 'I mean the other smell. The one that's like . . . rotting meat.'

I cringed and remembered the stench that had hit me to start with; before the blood had taken over and gotten the better of my senses. I sniffed the air, picking out that raw-meat stink again. And something else; something that reeked of death and decay. If evil had a smell, surely this was it.

I didn't want to know what it was, but as I stuck my

head back around the gap in the door I had all the confirmation I needed.

Rick was sitting on a steel trolley swinging his legs and gnawing on something that looked suspiciously like an arm.

Swallowing hard, I looked back down at the nurse's bloody body. *Yep, it was an arm. That was pretty much the grossest thing I had ever seen.* I caught sight of a nametag: *Fox*. Poor Nurse Fox.

'Well?' Jace was trying to push me out of the way.

He so did not *want to see this.* I shoved him back, edging away from the door and hoping to God that the thing chewing on a human limb hadn't caught our scent. Apparently, vampires didn't have much of a scent to humans, but I was pretty certain Rick wasn't anywhere near human. Not anymore.

'What is it, Moth?' Jace was trying to muscle his way past me again.

'We need to get out of here,' I said, fixing him with what I hoped was a look that said: *Do What I Tell You If You Want To Live.*

He scowled. 'Did Rick go vamp? Is that it?'

'It's much worse than that,' I replied. 'I think he's a zombie.'

Chapter Five

I couldn't help taking childish pleasure in watching the color drain from Jace's normally golden cheeks. He licked his lips. 'No way, there's no such thing.'

I shook my head. What was wrong with this guy? His father hunted things-that-go-bump-in-the-night for a living.

'Zombies aren't real.'

'OK then, fine.' I gripped his arm and swung him toward the door. 'Let's hope you still feel the same way when one of them takes a bite out of your ass.'

'Cute. You're funny for a dead girl.'

Jace stumbled as I pushed him close to the gap, my hand squeezing his arm so tightly I knew he'd have a bruise there tomorrow.

'Hey,' he complained, trying to pull his arm free. 'Get off me!'

'Shut your mouth,' I hissed, right up close to his ear. I had to stand on tiptoes to reach. 'It'll hear you.'

The zombie – if that was what Rick had become – was still chewing, and I took great delight in hearing Jace gag.

Unfortunately, I wasn't the only one who heard him. Whatever was left of Rick turned its head and stared at the door. Its dead eyes were completely white, the iris and pupil swallowed up by a horrifying milky glaze that made it look blind. Maybe it *was* blind.

I tried to remember if Theo or Holly had told me anything about zombies. I was drawing a big fat blank, but it looked like zombies weren't one of the false myths – not if I was going to believe the evidence of my own eyes. Or, at the very least, we were facing something that seemed very much like what I'd imagine a zombie to be.

A deep growl came from the room as Rick tossed what was left of the nurse's arm into a far corner. I shuddered. Maybe I should concentrate on getting out of this place in one piece. 'Zombie 101' could wait.

Jace backed away, slowly shaking his head. 'No. Way. No. *Way*.' He repeated the same thing over and over, his voice strained and close to breaking. If the zombie apocalypse ever came, perhaps Jace Murdoch would lead

62

the resistance, whispering his new mantra under his breath.

I resisted the urge to roll my eyes. Now was certainly not the time to lose the plot.

'Hey, come on, man up! Whether you like it or not – whether you *believe* it or not – we're in this together. And frankly I don't care if you refuse to believe the evidence of your own stupid eyes, so long as you point the damn knife over in *that* direction and cover me.'

The 'zombie' slid off the table and landed silently on bare feet. It was still wearing Rick's clothes, which somehow made it seem even more like a bad remake of *Dawn of the Dead*. I couldn't help wondering where his shoes and socks had gone. It was weird seeing those narrow, pale feet sticking out from beneath black skinny jeans. He'd been wearing a KISS T-shirt when he died. Poor Rick, I thought. And not because he'd been into an ageing rock band.

He had been a living, breathing boy. A kid who'd been passionate about art and music. He could have done something with his life, but now we'd never know. His family would never be able to watch him grow into an adult and see what he would do in the world. My throat was tight, pity warring with horror and making me feel even more nauseous. This whole situation was even worse than I'd suspected. I *knew* there was something weird going on when I saw my name and address inside that evidence bag. It wasn't just that, though. There had been a growing sense of *wrongness* deep in my gut from the moment I'd seen those cops at my door.

Jace had regained his color – and some of his composure – and was holding the silver-edged knife in a more battle-ready stance. Thank God for small mercies.

I licked my lips and wondered how best to deal with the situation. I'd never seen a zombie before, and had no idea what would happen if we tried to 'kill' it. How did you even kill them, anyway? Cut off its head? Too difficult with a knife, even a hunting knife like the one Jace had his white-knuckled hands wrapped around.

I remembered something about fire being a good weapon against zombies but I wasn't certain, and maybe I was just thinking about movie zombies. Not that my speculation was any help without a handy incinerator that we could push it into. And what were we going to do about the fact that a newly risen flesh-eating monster was about to run rampant around a huge city hospital?

Zombie Rick took a few shuffling steps forward, staggering on uncertain legs.

Jace nudged me. 'So, is the silver on this knife going to be any good against that thing?'

'What are you asking me for? We're not *related*, you know.'

'Hey, no need to get defensive. I'm just asking, OK?'

'*Fine*. Silver hurts vampires, so maybe it's the same for

all undead, but I honestly don't know for sure . . .' I trailed off. 'Why didn't you bring your crossbow?'

He gave me a look that showed me exactly what he thought of such an idiotic suggestion. '*Riiight*. I'll haul a crossbow around Mass General. No worries, folks, just regular security for hospitals these days.'

I bristled under his patronizing tone. 'Hey, it didn't stop you bringing it inside in the first place.'

'Yeah, into a room that hardly even gets used, through a *secret entrance*.' He spun the knife between his fingers. At least he seemed to be getting his act back together.

Unfortunately, Rick seemed to be getting the hang of walking on reanimated legs. Zombie Boy staggered toward the nurse's body and crouched down by her feet. For one horrible moment I thought it was going to continue with its macabre meal, but instead it grabbed both ankles and pulled the body out of the way of the door. Clearing a path.

So it could get to us – and the *door*.

So zombies weren't as mindless as I'd imagined. It gazed at the exit, an expression of . . . *longing* on its face.

I had to do something. I had to stop it from getting into the main part of the hospital. I gritted my teeth and stepped into the room, Jace so close behind he almost bumped into me, but all I could think about was the . . . thing in front of me.

The zombie – or whatever Rick had become – gazed

at me from those dead eyes. Whether it could see me or just had a really good sense of smell, I wasn't sure. But I was certain of something: it was one of the scariest things I'd ever seen. Even though it seemed like nothing more threatening than a teenage kid in a baggy T-shirt, with bright red hair and a body that was all bones and angles, my knees trembled as we faced each other over Nurse Fox's remains. I tried not to look too hard at the mangled place where the poor woman's left arm used to be.

I had known this kid. I mean, I didn't *know* him, but we'd shared a classroom. Maybe I'd borrowed a pencil from him. Maybe he'd even held open the door for me on the way to class. Or, more likely, I'd held it open for *him*.

Either way, this was someone who had been in my life – my life before all this craziness. But there was absolutely nothing human left in the zombie's face and it broke my heart.

Jace closed the door behind us with a loud *click* that made me jump.

'What did you do that for?'

'We've got no chance of taking it down if it gets out of here. Too many casualties.' Jace's eyes had gone cold. It reminded me of that look he'd gotten when we'd run into each other in that storeroom. At least he was aiming that expression at someone else. I also liked the fact that he was thinking beyond the immediate situation; kind of reassuring to know Jason Murdoch had hidden save-the-world Boy Scout potential.

And now here we were, working together within half an hour of fighting. Yes, the world was indeed a crazy place.

I bit back a hysterical grin. Of course the world was crazy; I was a freaking vampire and that seemed almost normal compared to *this*.

The zombie stopped staring at the door and resumed its shuddering walk. I grabbed the metal door handle and twisted until the mangled shape I achieved didn't look like it would be opening anything any time soon.

Zombie Boy lunged and I dived to my left, leaving Jace out in the open. I twisted so that I fell on one shoulder and rolled all the way over until I was standing again. OK, so maybe my back was to the action now but the move got me out of the way – and it made me feel like Lara Croft. A clumsy Lara Croft.

I spun in time to see Jace wrestling with the creature, the glinting blade straining toward its throat as two implacable white hands gripped his forearms and easily held him away. Jace struggled to keep his footing as he was forced back, the knife trembling in his hand and his face creased with pain.

Wow, that thing looked *strong*.

I tackled the zombie from behind, getting both my arms around its throat and hauling backward as hard as

I could. Trying to choke it didn't make much sense – it seemed less alive than I was – but it was the best I could come up with. While I was hanging on, I got a good look at Rick's throat. Or what was left of it. Yep, there were the bite marks all right – still clearly visible against the blue tinge of his flesh. More of them punctured his pale, skinny arms, looking like an overzealous drug addict's track marks.

It was weird, but the kid didn't smell of anything other than death. Dead meat, with a ripe undertone of rotting flesh; almost like he'd gone *off*.

I swallowed bile as we struggled, and the thing made a weird trumpeting noise from somewhere deep in its chest. It tried to shake me off, blundering around and trampling Jace into the ground.

Colorful cursing came from somewhere below as Jace tried to get up, only to be kicked in the face by one of Zombie Boy's flailing feet. I hung on grimly and clamped my legs around the monster's waist, clinging on with all the strength I possessed. Was it wrong that there was a tiny part of me having fun? Only a very small part, I swear, but maybe that's the monster in me.

Jace was back on his feet, blood pouring from his nose as he spun the knife in his hand. 'What are *you* grinning about?'

I ignored him and tightened my death-grip on Rick, who had already figured out a neat way to get me off. The creature turned around and walked backward into the nearest wall, crushing me between it and the solid brick. It couldn't walk too fast, thankfully, but it still hurt. This dude was *smart*. It slammed me into the wall again.

I groaned as my lower back went numb.

Jace was aiming the knife and looked suspiciously like he was preparing to throw it. 'Hold on, Monkey Girl, keep it there another minute!'

'*What?*' I screeched. 'Don't you dare throw that thing. You'll hit *me*, you idiot!'

'Trust me,' Jace said.

'A minute ago you were trying to kill me – how am I supposed to trust you?'

He wiped blood off his face and took aim. 'When I say duck, duck.'

I was too busy hanging onto the bucking zombie to pay too much attention to Jace's showboating. Who the hell did he think he was? *Indiana freaking Jones?*

Jace yelled, 'Duck!' and tossed the knife in a spinning arc.

I dropped to the ground, sliding against the wall and bumping my forehead on Zombie Rick's bony shoulder as I went down. I crouched by jeans-clad legs for a moment, waiting for the colored sparkles to disappear from my vision.

The creature made an odd little huffing sound, as

though somebody had punched it in the stomach, and took a jerking step backward. *Had Jace hit it?*

I wriggled out from behind it and jumped to my feet, backing away while keeping the thing in clear view. Jace was looking pleased with himself, and when I caught sight of the hilt of his knife sticking out of the zombie's chest I could see why. It was a perfect shot – *bull's-eye!* – right through the heart.

If the thing had been a vampire, depending on its age it'd be dust by now.

But of course it wasn't a vampire. Zombie Rick staggered about the enclosed space, making a horrible high-pitched mewling sound as it clawed at the blade embedded in his thin chest.

Jace was out of weapons, and I didn't have any to start with. I scanned the room for something that might prove useful against the recently undead as the zombie succeeded in pulling out the knife. It made a disgusting sucking sound as it came free of fat and muscle tissue. 'God, that is so gross,' I said.

Jace looked at me and raised one of his golden eyebrows. 'What's the problem? You must see stuff like this all the time.'

I scowled. 'Oh, shut up.' There would've been a lot more venom in my voice if it weren't for the fact that the zombie had fixed its milky-dead eyes on me and was slowly advancing in my direction. Being in the hospital's restricted area had its benefits – we wouldn't attract much attention despite all the noise we were making down here. But it was also incredibly claustrophobic: stuck in a small room with no windows and only one door, and the dead body of a woman with one arm missing.

I leaped onto the steel table Zombie Boy had only recently vacated. The blue sheet that had covered his body was on the floor, and there was something creepy about seeing some kid's shroud lying on the ground while his body walked around like it was the most normal thing in the world.

I watched carefully as the zombie sniffed the air and then switched its attention back to Jace. *So maybe it was blind*, I thought. *Interesting*. It must be using smell to locate us. From my elevated position, I could also see a shelf holding surgical instruments, some nasty-looking latex gloves, and a couple of aerosol cans.

Aerosol cans. Would that actually work? Only one way to find out. I forced myself to take a deep breath and sprang up with arms outstretched toward the shelf, gripping the thin ledge with my fingertips. Edging along to the far side, my legs kicking against the wall to increase my momentum, I reached the nearest can and grabbed it. I dropped almost silently to the ground, gripping what I hoped was going to be our secret weapon.

I shook the can, thankful to feel a comforting weight and the soft *shhh* sound that told me it was at least half full.

Meanwhile, Jace had kicked Zombie Boy right where it hurt, which was admirably dirty for a guy fighting another guy – even if the opponent *was* a flesh-eating undead . . . thing. It seemed mostly unfazed by the impressive dropkick, but at least Van Helsing Junior was keeping its attention off me.

I pulled Detective Trent's lighter from my pocket and set the flame to maximum height. I gritted my teeth and prepared to get my hands burned. It would definitely be worth it, if only I could take down what remained of Rick before it chewed on any other innocent nurses. Or patients. The thought of leaving it to wander the corridors of a hospital made me feel sick. Weirdly, I felt steadier now. Honestly, I just think my fear had receded in the face of the bizarreness of the situation.

Jace was face down now and struggling to crawl away as the creature grabbed his leg and pulled it toward its mouth. *Ew*, it was looking to try some leg next. Jace yelled a creative combination of obscenities which were tough to make out with his face against the floor, but – 'Get it off me!' – that part I could understand. He kicked out with his other foot and connected with the zombie's chin, a move that looked more like luck than skill.

It didn't matter how he'd done it, but Jace was free and that's what counted. The zombie was out in the open, crouched down and shaking its head in disorientation. Soft red hair glinted under the spotlights and made my stomach twist with pity. This had been a kid – a kid not unlike me or even Jace. A boy whose life was over, no chance of coming back. Not even a chance at a half-life like mine.

I bit down on my pity and focused on Rick's clouded eyes and blood-stained mouth. The remains of Nurse Fox scattered around the floor in glistening piles were all the reminder I needed.

I pressed the aerosol's button and sprayed the hopefully highly flammable contents at the zombie. I flicked the switch on the lighter and watched with grim fascination as the vivid blue flame leaped to a surprising height and ignited the chemical-smelling mist.

The results were pretty spectacular.

It was like having a miniature flamethrower at my fingertips: kind of fun, but also incredibly scary. Not to mention painful. Flames shot out in an arc as I waved the can back and forth, sweeping a long line of fire at the zombie. With a *whoomph* that forced me to take a step back, flames shot up and hit the ceiling as Rick lit up like a torch.

The T-shirt caught fire first, quickly followed by the jeans. Finally the bright orange hair – the most human part that remained – burst into flames. His waxy skin burned and peeled, the smell of rancid meat becoming overwhelming in the restricted space.

The creepiest part of the whole spectacle was the

silence. The zombie didn't make a sound. None of the growls it had emitted earlier; no sign of pain or distress; more like a passive sense of *waiting* for the end. Was it – he – at peace? Death didn't always mean the end of pain and suffering.

For me – for vampires – death wasn't the end at all. I had gone on. I *endured*, whether I wanted to or not.

The thing that used to be a budding artist called Rick fell to its knees and burned.

Water suddenly sprayed onto my face, and I realized that the sprinkler system had kicked in. I tipped back my head and opened my mouth for a moment, closing my eyes against the impromptu shower.

Ouch. My fingers were burning and I'd lost most of the skin on my left hand. Despite the pain, I couldn't help being curious about whether or not my fingerprints would grow back when I healed. Vampires healed pretty fast, even the young ones, so I wasn't worried about burn scars. A lot of the old myths about vampires were true, but not so much where fire was concerned. Sure, I could get burned and it would hurt, but it wouldn't kill me. I'd heal. Maybe if a vampire was set alight the way I'd just burned Zombie Boy, *then* they'd be in trouble.

Whatever. Right now I had to deal with the unfortunate remains of Rick, without getting anybody else killed. And figure out what had actually *happened* to him in the first place. Was his horrific transformation a fluke?

There was nothing left of him – no chance of finding clues that might lead me to his murderer. I'd come here in the hopes of discovering something useful, maybe even something that could improve my standing with Theo's Family and the Elders, but all I had was a pile of dust and an even bigger mystery to solve.

My heightened senses recoiled from the combined stench of blood and ash.

'I gotta hand it to you, that was pretty cool.' Jace used the hem of his T-shirt to dab at the blood that was still trickling from his nose. Sprinkler water stood out on his long eyelashes like fat diamonds. He blinked them away, then shook his head and splashed more water all over me.

'Yeah, I feel so incredibly cool about ending a kid's life.' I tried not to look too hard at the blood on his lips; it was making my stomach hurt.

'I didn't mean it like that—'

The door handle rattled and Jace stopped talking, his jaw actually clicking shut. The color drained from his face as he stared at me and then at the door.

'Oh, shit,' we said in unison.

Chapter Six

'Hey,' a muffled voice said from outside in the corridor. 'There's something wrong with the door.'

Another voice. 'Ah, hell. Foxy must've locked it – we need to get the damn sprinkler system shut off. I told her to leave the door open – the authorities are screaming for that kid's body. The Spook Squad has put in an official request too. Some weirdo in a suit already turned up at Reception.'

'Shut up,' said the first guy. 'You're not supposed to talk about them.'

'Aw, who's listening down here? Stop being so damn paranoid.'

Jace took a visibly deep breath. 'OK. This isn't good.'

'You think?' I swiped angrily at a few tears that had leaked out. Considering the fact that we were both soaked through, I don't know why I even bothered.

'Well, at least one of us *is* thinking. How are we supposed to get out of here? Look what you did to the door.'

I shushed him. 'Wait, I think they might be leaving.'

He rolled his eyes. 'Only to get the *key*. And then they'll figure out it's not even locked – someone *busted* it.' He gave me a meaningful look.

The twisted mess that used to be the door handle mocked me. I bit my lip. 'It seemed like a good idea at the time,' I said in a small voice. 'I was trying to keep Rick *in*.'

Jace ran a hand through his water-darkened hair. 'And what are we going to do about the evidence? Once they come in here and find all this . . .' His voice trailed off. He shook his head, clearly frustrated at the whole new level of crazy his life had achieved. 'There'll be finger-prints all over the place and that's not going to be good.'

'Why do we need to worry about that? It's not like they have us programmed into some sort of top-secret super-villain database.'

Jace's eye slid away from mine.

I put my hands on my hips. 'Why on earth would anyone have *your* fingerprints on record? You're practically still a kid – you're nineteen, right?'

'Depends what ID I use,' he muttered.

I rolled my eyes and concentrated on the door. I had to get it open, and fast. Someone had shut off the water, meaning it wouldn't be long before those guys came back.

I gripped the handle and tried to force the bent metal back into shape – at least so the stupid thing would open. My extra vamp-strength was occasionally useful, but I sometimes wished I wasn't the kind of girl who could pop the top off a beer without breaking a sweat.

With an ominous cracking sound, I wrenched the handle *off* the door. A hole surrounded by tiny, twisted steel teeth seemed to grin at me.

'Oops,' I said.

Jace was by my side in an instant. 'What do you mean, "oops"? I don't like the sound of "oops".'

I tried to hide the door handle behind my back, and then realized it was pointless. He could see exactly what the problem was by looking at the gaping hole in the door. I turned away from the exasperation on his face, wondering if I could catch just one tiny piece of luck today. One stinking break, that's all I asked. *I hardly ask for anything*, I thought. *Is this* really *too much?*

Before Jace could explode, I touched the smooth surface of the door with a tentative hand. Hooking my fingers into the hole where the door handle had been, I tugged gently and was rewarded – *finally!* – when the door simply opened.

'See?' I said, giving my scowling companion a smug look. 'No trouble. I did that on purpose.'

Jace grunted and pushed me to one side. 'Follow me.'

'Hey, *I* got us out of here. I'm going first.' I tried to edge back in front of him, only to find he was already halfway through the door.

'Stop making so much noise,' he hissed as I tried to push him out of the way.

Grumbling under my breath, I followed him out of the basement room, wondering what on earth the authorities were going to make of the mess we were leaving behind. And what was this 'Spook Squad' that those guys had mentioned? They didn't sound like people I wanted to run into anytime soon.

The corridors seemed endless, and I was certain there had been more lights on earlier. Eventually, we saw signs of life and I began to hope that we might actually get away without any further setbacks.

I don't know why I even let myself think such crazy thoughts.

A janitor in gray coveralls and a heavy belt loaded down with tools half-heartedly mopped the floor near a door conveniently marked FIRE ESCAPE – but he didn't seem like anything out of the ordinary.

'Just keep walking,' Jace whispered. 'He doesn't care about us.'

As we passed the 'janitor', the staccato crackle of a walkie-talkie broke the quiet. We froze. The man cursed and grabbed for the black unit hidden among all the other crap in his utility belt. 'Intruders are leaving via exit seventeen!' he shouted into the walkie-talkie.

I didn't hang around to see who he might be talking to, pumping my arms and racing further along the hallway. Jace's footsteps pounded the floor behind me. I heard him panting for breath and forced myself to slow my pace. No way he could keep up with vamp speed, no matter how fit he was.

Slamming through the door at the end, I found myself in yet another corridor, this one lined with floor-to-ceiling storage lockers. It ended in a solid door. Locked. I examined the handle and it looked like one of those fancy hotel mechanisms with a slot for a key-card. I stepped back, preparing to kick it open – or, at least, to *try* – but Jace reached my side and pulled me back.

'Wait,' he said, still breathing heavily. He produced a bright yellow plastic card.

I stared at it for a moment. 'Where'd you get that?'

'That fake janitor's belt,' he replied, flashing me a quick grin. 'Remember, I've been here before – I know a staff pass when I see one.'

I thought: He isn't just a wannabe hunter, now he's a thief. A pick-pocketing, vampire-hunting *thief*. He was even sneakier than me, which was a strange thing to realize. I kind of liked it.

He operated the key-card and the door opened. 'After you,' he said, sweeping me a low bow.

We ended up in a typical industrial basement. It was

huge, badly lit, and smelled of laundry. It was clearly a storage room of some sort, which might mean ... deliveries! I spotted an emergency exit all the way across the cavernous space before Jace did, my eyes adjusting to the darkness almost immediately.

'Over there,' I said, barely able to contain my excitement.

But the very moment I spotted our potential escape route, the door we'd just come through rattled.

'They couldn't have gotten through here,' a male voice declared.

A woman replied, 'I'll be the judge of that. Just get it open.'

I froze, like a rabbit caught in a wolf's gaze, but Jace herded me over to what looked like a utility closet against the wall. He pulled open the door – thankfully, it swung open on well-oiled hinges – and nudged me inside, putting a finger to his lips before following me into the cramped darkness. The closet was empty apart from a long coat and several uniforms hanging from a rail attached to the ceiling. I wondered if I'd find Narnia if I kept walking.

Two sets of footsteps marched into the delivery area, just as Jace pulled the door *almost* shut. He left it cracked open, probably to avoid the noise of closing it fully, but also so he could catch a slivered glimpse of what was happening outside.

I could hear his quiet breathing in the confined space, and for once found myself glad that I didn't have to breathe anymore. I never, ever believed I'd think something like that about my undead status. I leaned against the metal wall of the closet, trying to stay as far away from my companion as I could. At such close quarters, I became horribly aware of his body heat – and of the blood running through his veins. I was tired, hungry and freaked out by everything that had happened in the last couple of hours. Being so close to human warmth was making me twitchy. A faint silver light began to combat the gloom, and I realized that it was coming from me – from my eyes, as they responded to my hunger.

Crap. I quickly closed them and willed them to stop glowing, hoping that Jace hadn't noticed.

I felt, rather than saw, him turn to face me. I opened one eye and almost sank to the floor with relief when I didn't repeat my inconvenient impression of a flashlight. I opened my other eye and we gazed at each other through the gap in the uniforms hanging between us. He didn't look away – surprising, considering how furious he'd been when I'd somehow managed to slip inside his head earlier.

Maybe Jason Murdoch was actually starting to trust me. Saving each other's lives could have that effect, I guess.

The two voices moved further away. Someone cursed

as he – or she – tripped over something, and then the door opened and clicked shut.

Jace nodded at me after waiting another minute. 'Let's get out of here.'

We bolted from the closet and made for the exit. Jace carefully wiped the key-card for prints and threw it across the room as we pushed our way out into daylight.

I blinked, grabbing my sunglasses from an inside jacket pocket as the sudden brightness burned my eyes. I could hardly believe they hadn't been crushed in the fight with Zombie Rick.

We were in some kind of parking lot. A couple of large delivery vans protected us from potential scrutiny, and beyond them I could see the tops of trees hiding where the main road would be.

Jace checked left and right, then ducked back behind the shelter of one of the vehicles. 'So, I guess this is it . . . Moth.'

He held out a business card. I took it and glanced down. A phone number stood out, printed neatly in black ink. Nothing else marked the stark white card. I looked at him, surprised. Confused. Maybe a little pleased but not wanting to show it.

Jace folded his arms and shrugged. 'Just in case you find out what happened to the kid. I have a bad feeling about it – maybe we haven't seen the last of whatever that was. It's probably a good idea to figure out what we can.'

I wanted to make a witty comment, something about how he'd just given a vampire his cell phone number, but for once I was lost for words. Why would he really give me this? *Was* it all about the so-called zombie? What else could he possibly have to gain? I kept my mouth shut and carefully slipped the card into my jeans pocket.

He pulled out his cell phone and raised an eyebrow. The one with the piercing. 'Are you going to give me yours, or what?'

'Oh.' Flustered, I recited my number. *What would Theo say?* I pushed that thought aside. I could make my own decisions.

Jace had an expression of mock-sympathy on his face. 'I can imagine you don't get asked for your number too often.'

I opened my mouth. Closed it again and thought for a moment. 'I do too.' *Genius response, Moth.*

'Riiight,' Jace said. 'Of course.'

I gave him the finger but he just laughed.

'I'm going to do some research,' he continued coolly, as though the whole phone-number thing hadn't happened. 'Dad's books are in our new apartment. Most of them are still packed away in boxes, but I guess this'll give me a reason to sort through them. I'll let you know if I find anything interesting.'

'OK. I'll see you then,' I said, forcing a smile. I took care to keep my fangs hidden. It was so bizarre to actually be having a normal conversation with him – one that didn't involve looking down the business end of a crossbow.

His answering grin was wicked. 'Not if I see you first.'

Chapter Seven

Saturday night I headed over to my Maker's home. This evening had come around far too quickly, but now that it was here I was a bundle of nerves.

The November night was cool and frosted with a light mist that wrapped itself around me, whispering of the hunt. I took an icy breath, shaking off those instincts, burying them somewhere deep.

Theo's house was hidden in the heart of the appropriately affluent Beacon Hill. He owned several places across the country; you don't live for almost two centuries without accumulating wealth and property. But it was no wonder that Theo preferred to stay right here in Boston. You could walk along Beacon Street on a winter's night and truly believe you were in another century. Gas lamps lined the roadside, standing guard over town houses with wrought-iron gates, fancy windows, and even roof gardens. Theo had one of those, of course, even though he could only go out there at night.

Most vampires slept below ground, but Theo preferred to live here, in this house, at all times of day. There were heavy curtains at every window, and he slept in a third-floor room with shutters both inside and out, but he wanted to be in his own home as much as possible.

I waited impatiently for him to finish dressing for the evening's oh-so-joyous activities – my official introduction to the Elders who oversaw Theo's vampire Family in Boston. I was possibly more scared at the prospect of this dubious 'honor' than I had been of my undead encounter with Rick, since by Making me without permission, Theo had apparently broken one of the High Council's most precious rules. Now the Elders had arrived to get an explanation – and to finally meet me, after Theo had kept me damn near hidden for the better part of a year.

My Maker's place had been a surprise to me, back when I'd first seen it. Considering that he purposely cultivated an image of the decadent Gothic vampire, most people probably expected to find his home would reflect that in some way. Lots of velvet, maybe. A four-poster bed and candles on every surface of the room. Black and deepest crimson. On the *outside*, it fitted him perfectly; it was an old, old house, as most were in this part of the city. But it was entirely modern on the inside.

It was kitted out in a contemporary but comfortable style, lots of smooth lines and reflective surfaces. Beautifully cultivated plants filled the entry hall, one of my Maker's unexpected hobbies. And the space . . . space like you wouldn't believe. The first-floor dining room was bigger than the whole of the tiny apartment Holly and I currently called 'home' – owned, of course, by Theo. The fourth floor was the only ornate part of the building, having been converted into a cathedral-style meeting space, all vaulted ceilings and stained-glass windows. I half expected bats to live in the belfry.

Finally Theo sent Kyle down to fetch me. When I walked into the bedroom, Theo was sitting in his favorite chair. It was one of those black leather TV chairs that could swivel and lean back, with a foot rest that flipped out. I never understood why he wanted the stupid thing; Theo didn't watch television, even though he had the biggest plasma screen I'd ever seen fixed to the plain white wall above the open fireplace. Solid silver candle-sticks stood at either end of the marble mantel, a testament to Theo's often bleak sense of humor.

'Moth,' he said. It wasn't a greeting so much as an acknowledgment of my presence.

I nodded. 'Hi, Theo.'

'Come here, let me look at you.'

Theo was what Caitlín would call 'easy on the eye'. He had curly black hair that was a little too long to be clean cut – it swept back from his face now and fell to just below his collar – and sculpted features that never looked pasty or unhealthy. His skin was smooth like the finest porcelain, and his lips were wicked and sensual. The only thing that looked anything less than perfect was the rather hawkish nose, but I always thought it made him look distinguished. And just a little bit dangerous, like a bird of prey ready to swoop down and devour you. Even at somewhere around his mid-twenties (at least to the human eye), Theo looked like a cover model for a romance novel – one that probably involved pirates.

He was slender, toned, no more than five ten, and he moved with a dangerous sort of grace. He was all lean muscle and sharp reflexes. Sharp like a nail. Sharp like a fang.

God, seeing him always brought back memories. Dark, nightmarish images, only half remembered:

'You're not dead,' Theo says softly. 'But . . . you're no longer alive, either. Not exactly.'

I sit in a chair in the corner of one of the many rooms of his house, as far away from the window as I can get. The light hurts my eyes, though Theo tells me that will pass. I clutch a blanket around me.

'I'm cold,' I whisper. 'So cold.' I am numb all through my flesh and bones. My chest hurts so badly I want to cry. It is a constant pain, a pain that devours.

Theo strokes my hair.

I remembered what it was like, waking up and realizing that everything was different. The world smelled different – even I smelled different – and my body was no longer my own. It was a strange, heavy thing. Alien. Nothing worked the way it was supposed to and I was so hungry. So very hungry.

'Let me look at you,' Theo said again, bringing me back to the here and now.

Dutifully, I presented myself and waited for him to say something negative about what I was wearing. Theo hated my clothes, but it was what I'd always worn and I like to feel comfortable. It wasn't anything to do with an 'image' or symbolic of becoming a vampire. It was just *me*.

This time I'd done my best to please him – considering the occasion – while still remaining true to myself. The dress I'd chosen was crimson satin, short and fitted with a Chinese-style collar and long sleeves that practically covered my hands. The black fishnets itched like crazy, but what did that matter when it came to fashion? My huge, almost comically chunky boots made me look like a Manga character, what with my skinny legs, but I didn't care. The bigger the boots the harder you can kick – that's my motto.

I unzipped my leather jacket, trying for the tough-but-vulnerable look. Sort of *Rebel Without a Cause* in a dress.

Theo leaned forward and his light gray eyes began to glow with the ethereal silver light that all vampires' eyes possessed. I knew that my own would mirror his, only ten times brighter. Theo was my Maker – he'd made me what I was – and my body betrayed our connection even if I wanted to deny it.

'Take off that ridiculous jacket,' he said.

I bristled, but did it anyway. I dropped it on the floor just to annoy him.

'You look well, my Moth,' was all Theo said.

I was surprised, but tried not to show it. 'Thanks. So do you.' The words slipped out before I could stop them, but it was true, so what did it matter?

My Maker had been here in the good old US of A since 1847. He had taken a number of aliases over the years, one of which I knew for sure was Theodore Fitzgerald – although I had no idea whether or not that was his true name. Sometimes I fantasized about investigating his origins. The minimal facts I'd managed to gather so far must give me *somewhere* to start. For example, if he arrived in Boston's North End in 1847 as a young man, after the long, slow boat ride from an Ireland being destroyed by the Potato Famine, surely there were records. Wouldn't there be some kind of register of all the new arrivals?

I was pretty certain that Theo hadn't been Made until he'd arrived in North America. It seemed unlikely that he would have survived such a long voyage over water – day and night – had he been a vampire. Unless he was a very new one, I guess. That was possible, but everything I'd managed to glean from him – every titbit that I'd filed away in the hope of learning something about the man I both loved and hated – seemed to indicate he'd become a vampire within a few years of arriving on these shores.

Holly told me that there were rumors of a dead family back in Ireland – a wife, even children – but Theo never spoke of it. I so desperately wanted to know more about him. He was in my heart, my soul – my *blood*. I couldn't go a day without thinking of him, no matter how much that freaked me out and made me feel weak, weak, weak. I told myself that it was the vampire link between Maker and fledgling that did this to me, but sometimes it was more difficult to convince myself of that than others.

'You're staring,' Theo said, his voice radiating warmth. 'Do you like what you see tonight?'

I swallowed. There was no way I wanted to play this game with him – he was a hundred and seventy years too old for me. *That didn't stop you last year*, said a traitorous voice inside my head. I gave myself a stern talking to: I didn't know what he was, then. I didn't know the truth.

'Theo . . .'

He smiled, keeping his fangs hidden. 'To business, then?'

'Business? What do you mean? The meeting isn't due to start yet, is it?'

'I need to be sure you know your role.'

Oh. He was priming me beforehand. Great. 'I wouldn't let you down, Theo. I know how important this is.'

'Do you? Are you quite sure about that?'

I looked at him, realizing that he was being totally serious. 'What do you mean? Of course I do.'

'When I turned you, it was . . .' He shook his head, for once struggling for words. He closed his eyes for a moment. 'I should not have done it. You know this, yes?'

'Yes.' He'd told me enough times. How it was a mistake and I was far too young; how he regretted it, even though there was no way of changing me back. In fact, I heard it so many times in those early days that I'd grown numb to it. I hadn't really given much thought to how other vampires would perceive his 'slip'. Not back then.

Theo nodded. 'You must do everything to convince the Elders that I have you under complete control.'

I gritted my teeth against the suicidal desire to say something snarky. *Under control?*

My phone beeped, saving me. I checked the text message, ignoring Theo's irritated sigh, and raised my eyebrows. It was Jace:

Been researching what we found yesterday. Want to share info? When can we meet?

Well, that was a surprise . . . I honestly hadn't expected to hear from Jason Murdoch again. I glanced up at Theo, guiltily stashing my phone away before he could confiscate it. Seriously, I wouldn't put it past him and I didn't want him to know I was in touch with Thomas Murdoch's son.

'Did you feed before you came?'

Here we go. 'Um . . . no, sorry. I forgot.'

His eyes narrowed. 'You do not "forget" to feed, Moth. All you're doing is proving my point about how I can't rely on you to make sure this goes smoothly.'

'I'll be fine,' I snapped.

He took a step toward me. 'You'd better be. If there was time, I would insist that you feed before we go upstairs.'

'Sorry.' I lowered my eyes, trying to placate him. 'I'm just tired. Maybe I do need to feed.'

'But not from me.'

'No. Not from you.'

There was a brief pause, when I knew my Maker was giving me the opportunity to consider how I insulted him every time I refused to feed from him.

'Perhaps we will rectify the situation later,' he said evenly.

'No,' I said again. 'You *promised*.'

'I promised that I will never take blood from *you*. Not unless you ask me to do so, in no uncertain terms. I also promised that you could feed in any way that you desire, so long as you are discreet. Even drinking from blood bank supplies, for your entire life should you wish it, and not drinking from humans. I do not fight you on this, little one.' He took another step closer. 'But I also said that you may have to feed from me occasionally, *should the need arise.*'

I thought about that for a moment. Had he said that? Maybe he had.

He touched my face. 'Your silence is your answer. I know you remember our conversation.' Now his voice had dropped low, seductive.

When a vampire is first Made, she needs to drink blood pretty much daily – sometimes more than once a day. It's almost as though you come back from death with an unbearable hunger – an eternal thirst for blood that can never be slaked. Theo kept me closely monitored throughout those first weeks and months. He was my nursemaid and jailer all rolled into one beautiful package. He held me tight when I screamed, when I cried, when I attempted to take out a chunk of his throat with my permanently extended fangs that I couldn't tame – no matter how hard I tried.

I was like a savage; my body burning with heat and bloodlust. Savage need and hunger and pain, every inch of me exposed and raw.

Sometimes I wondered why Theo hadn't just killed me, put me out of my misery. If Making me was going to

95

cause him trouble later on – and he must have known that my presence would bring his position within the Family into question – then why didn't he *end* me when he'd had the chance? Even after he'd brought me back, after that night when he'd changed me forever, he could have staked me any time. Cut out my heart and burned it.

I have never asked him, though, because I think maybe I'm afraid of the answer.

I hate it when he tells me that I belong to him; I hate *him*. Hate is so much easier than love, and yet they so often go hand in hand. Sometimes I wonder if he keeps me alive to punish *himself*, but for something far greater than turning me into a vampire. What he did to me was wrong, there's no question about that, but I get the impression that Theo is living under the weight of a guilt I could never even come close to understanding.

'Fine,' I said, swallowing my fear. 'I'll feed from you later.'

'Excellent. Now that we have that arranged, it is time to go upstairs.'

'Right now?'

He inclined his head. 'They're waiting for us.'

Chapter Eight

I was surrounded by vampires.

Every pair of silver eyes was directed my way, as though sizing me up for a snack or trying to figure out what kind of a threat I'd be to the Family. Tension had been slowly rising throughout my entire body, and I wondered if it was genuine adrenaline – if that was even *possible* – or whether it was like the memory of adrenaline. A ghostly presence left over from humanity, like my body was simply having a hard time letting go of human foibles. The anxiety was starting to make my stomach hurt.

Can vampires get ulcers?

I looked around the room and swallowed. A gathering of vampires is called a 'swarm' – bet you didn't know that. A swarm of vampires. It sort of fits, especially if you've seen the vicious activity of a group-feeding. I have, but only once and that was enough. Theo wasn't supposed to know I was watching, but it turned out my so-called genius hiding place wasn't so genius and he'd known I was there all along.

He said it would do me good to see the baser part of vampire nature. I'm not sure it did me *good*, but it certainly made me never want to see anything like that ever again.

This swarm, sitting in Theo's cavernous top floor (which always reminds me of the Bat Cave, except for that fact that it's not underground), was far more civilized. The room was filled with almost twenty vampires, an equal mix of men and women. Apart from Theo, I only knew two of them – Holly and Kyle. Holly, her blue hair in pigtails, winked at me, and I almost ran over and hugged her with gratitude. She must have known how terrified I was and, despite our occasional differences, it was cool of her to give me a small sign of encouragement. Holly was sitting next to an attractive, impressively tattooed brunette who I'd never met. She looked much older than Holly, on the surface, but of course you can never be sure of these things when it comes to the undead. Their shoulders were touching.

I switched my gaze to Theo's Enforcer as he leaned close to his master's ear and whispered something. Theo nodded, seeming pleased, and Kyle glided to his position with his back to the wall and a view of the entire room. If anyone made a move toward Theo, he'd move in faster than a human can blink. That was his job, above all else. Kyle had street smarts that made him a formidable opponent; his cunning had also helped him rise quickly through the ranks of Theo's Family. He was a powerful Enforcer: his fighting skills were impressive enough that he often trained other vampires in hand-to-hand combat – myself included. He was tall and skinny with shoulder-length dirty-blond hair, and he seemed almost to be made of iron. He had that wiry sort of strength that always came as a surprise to his victims.

There was tea and coffee in shiny urns, and dusty bottles of vintage wine alongside super-size carafes of blood. I wondered where the blood had come from – there was no way that the senior vampires in the room would lower themselves to drink bagged blood. They would expect fresh, and Theo would have provided it.

I was sitting as far away from the visiting vamps as possible, but I knew Theo might need to summon me during the meeting. There was an empty chair beside him, which would put me right in the thick of things. I already felt like all eyes were on me – even back here shrouded in convenient shadows. Just imagine what it would be like sitting front and center. I desperately wanted a glass of water. Not really *needing* it, but wanting it all the same. Theo said that human desires, like regular hunger and thirst, would pass as my un-life progressed, but so far I still got terrible dry-mouth whenever I was nervous.

And I had good cause to be nervous. I had cause to be shaking in my steel-toe-capped boots. Solomon, the Elder vampire of the state of Massachusetts, was in the house and, let me tell you, he was pretty damn impressive. And scary.

The vampire hierarchy of the world was complex, but the basics involved different levels of command for each major world territory. Yes, vampires are spread throughout the entire world, everywhere. Organization was imperative in order to maintain secrecy, and that organization started at the city level. Like, Theo is the Master of the Boston Family – he controls any and all vampire activity within the greater metro area and the whole of Boston. Beyond that, there were the Elders who look after a much larger area or state. Vampires call these Enclaves, so the Enclave of Massachusetts is currently overseen by Solomon, and he would report directly to the High Council of Vampires. You normally can't reach this level until you've been 'alive' for a few centuries.

Solomon's presence was like a cold spot in the room. I got gooseflesh just thinking about it, and could hardly bring myself to look at him. Each time his bottomless and surprisingly dark eyes swung in my direction I felt the overwhelming desire to hide under my chair. He was a giant African-American dude, with a huge shaved head that gleamed in the flickering candlelight. The legends about him said that he was a former slave, and now he oversaw vampire activity in the entire state of Massachusetts.

He had the weight of centuries behind his eyes; the wisdom of a man who's been to hell and back, and lived (more or less) to tell the tale.

Solomon caught me looking and his full lips quirked into a tiny smile. 'Come forward, child.'

His voice was soft and deep and filled with something that made me want to get down onto my hands and knees, crawl across the richly carpeted floor, maybe on my belly, just to please him. Just to make him not want to kill me. Or maybe I should offer my throat like a wolf. Show him how submissive I could be, and how he could end my insignificant life with a snap of his jaws if he so desired. His voice filled the room, deep and heavy. I could feel it beating against my heart.

I shook myself. *Shit.* What was happening? I looked at him and realized that he had been inside my head.

The old ones can do that.

'Come,' he rumbled. I couldn't hear exactly what he was saying, almost as though the meaning behind the words were lost. But the sound of his voice was both beautiful and terrible. It crushed me until I felt tiny, each word like a sledgehammer driving me further and further into the ground. Every syllable, a leash tightening around my will.

I stood on shaking legs and stumbled toward him. I was vaguely aware of the gathering swarm, but I only really had eyes for Solomon. I stopped in front of his chair and looked down at him. I realized there was something wrong in the fact that I *was* looking down on him, and quickly lowered myself to my knees to correct that. My head was now below his.

There, that's better.

I saw another smile flicker across Solomon's mouth, realizing – once again – that I wasn't acting under my own power. Crap. I was his puppet. He could pull my strings and make me do anything he chose.

When Solomon spoke, he addressed the whole room. I sat back on my heels but stayed where I was. It seemed safer, somehow, and he seemed satisfied to let me kneel at his feet.

'This child was Made without my permission. What would you have me do with her?'

An unfamiliar female voice spoke up. 'She is innocent. The crime is her Maker's.'

Solomon nodded. 'Thank you, Nicole.'

It sounded like ritualized words to me. As though they were playing their parts for my benefit – or perhaps for Theo's – just to build up the suspense. Solomon would have come here knowing full well what he intended to do. He would have been given his own orders by the High Council, meaning he was as much under someone's control as I was.

It's just that he's much nearer the top of the food chain than I am.

The woman who'd spoken, Nicole, raised her voice again. 'I would like to know what Theo thought he was doing when he Made a *child* into a member of our Family. Turning a girl as young as this . . . What possible reason could he have for doing such a thing?'

For a moment she sounded genuinely upset, and I wondered who she was. Nicole was a beautiful, older-looking vampire, tall and curvy with a glossy mane of black hair that reached almost to her ass. Probably her skin would have been a perfect golden shade during her life, but now she was a little too pale. Nothing that make-up or fake tan wouldn't fix, but right now she was unadorned by anything other than a bright slash of crimson lipstick.

'What is your true name, child?' she asked, turning her calmly superior gaze on me.

I swallowed, suddenly terrified that I wouldn't be able to get any words out. I didn't want to displease this woman. 'Marie.'

'Full name.'

'Marie Katherine O'Neal,' I replied, pleased that my

103

voice didn't shake. I resisted the temptation to call her 'ma'am'.

Nicole blinked her silver eyes once, slowly, like a cat. 'And why are you known as "Moth"? Is this the name you have chosen since joining our Family?'

Vampires sometimes took new names when they were Made. Sometimes it was symbolic, leaving behind their old life and shedding their human selves like a snake shedding its skin. Often it was the name given to them by their Maker, to signify ownership.

For me, it was a little more complicated than that. I didn't know how to answer this beautiful vampire's question without talking about my human family – and without giving too much away about my past relationship with Theo. The name 'Moth' was only really significant in that it was something he had once called me, and it had stuck in my head as who I was now that I was something . . . *other*. I couldn't associate 'Marie' with fangs and blood and shadows. My life had changed forever, and I wanted my name to change with it.

All of this raced through my mind as Nicole watched me. She waved her hand, dismissing me. 'It is of no real importance.'

I felt stupid. Dumb. Why was it so difficult to speak in front of these people?

But I knew the answer to that. They weren't just

people. They were forces of nature, and Nicole was clearly old – older even than Theo.

And just as I thought of my Maker, his voice filled the room and I sank further back on my heels, wishing I could disappear into the floor.

'Thank you for coming today, all of you. We offer welcome and hospitality to Elders such as Nicole and our most esteemed Solomon.'

Ah, I thought. So Nicole also ran an Enclave. I wondered which state belonged to her. I really needed to learn more about our politics but, quite honestly, it was kind of boring. Not all that different from human politics, only with actual blood spilled rather than just metaphorical.

Solomon raised his dome-shaped head. 'Theo, you have questions to answer.'

Theo bowed his head. I had never seen my Maker defer to anyone before. It was a strange thing to witness . . . and a little frightening. 'Of course.'

Nicole leaned forward. 'I have more questions.'

Solomon raised his right hand. 'In time, Nicole.'

But Nicole's face was a cloud of disapproval as she turned on Theo. 'You were lucky things didn't go badly during the turning process.'

Lucky? I remembered the pain. I'm not sure I would call anything about it 'lucky'. The days and days of pain and screaming myself so raw I couldn't speak in anything but a whisper. Even then, when I did force myself to speak, I begged Theo to put an end to my suffering. I didn't understand what was happening to me. I just wanted it to stop.

Each time he found me trying to break my bonds, once even trying to bite my own wrists so I could kill myself – not realizing that it was far too late for so simple a death – he would simply clean me up and restrain me again. All this, kept a secret from the Family. Even, he told me, from Kyle – his most trusted ally in Boston – at least until I was through the worst of it and he knew I would survive. Only then did he let Kyle know what he'd done.

Theo stood, the fluid grace I was so accustomed to seeing still taking my breath away. I sneaked glances at him through my hair. He was like a beautiful predator, a big cat prowling his domain and ready to fight anybody who would dare challenge him as King of this particular Jungle.

'I should never have chosen to tie someone so young to me. Eternity is a long time.'

'So you admit that you had a loss of control.'

'I made a mistake.'

'And do you regret this . . . mistake?'

I swallowed, trying not to watch Theo. I didn't want to see the expression on his face. I didn't want him to regret me.

'No,' he said, surprising me. 'Not now. She is mine, for better or worse.'

If Theo had told his Enforcer about me before I'd become completely Made, Kyle would have tried to convince his master to kill me. I'm sure he would have said things like: *It's for her own good; it's for the good of the Family; it is for your sake.* And maybe all of that was true.

Theo narrowed his eyes. 'And it did not go badly, as you so delicately put it, Nicole. You see the evidence before you. Moth is alive and well.' He gestured at me, and I wanted to sink into the carpet when all those shimmering eyes turned to examine me again.

Nicole tossed her shiny hair. 'I speak of something far worse than death and you know it.'

I frowned. *Worse than death?* What was she talking about? What could be worse than death? Apart from becoming a vampire, I mean.

But before I could think on that any further Solomon cut her off. 'It takes more than blood to Make a vampire, it takes strength of will,' he said. 'Intention. The old myths say that it takes a piece of the Maker's soul to truly turn a vampire. The link forged between the pair is eternal, only ending with the death of one of the vampires.'

And what becomes of the one left behind? I wondered. Perhaps the older you are the more able to stand the loss, but who knows? Maybe when Kyle looked at me the way he did it was because my existence really did make Theo vulnerable. I mean, beyond the damage to his standing within the Family – the evidence of his loss of control – more than that. Because if someone *ends* me, what would that do to Theo? Is it true that I possess a tiny piece of his soul? I tried to imagine it rattling around inside me.

'You will all get your chance to ask questions if you don't hear what you want during these proceedings,' Solomon continued, 'but Theo will first answer to me – his Master.'

'Of course,' Nicole said, lowering her eyes demurely. I didn't believe her false modesty for a second. Something about this whole situation had her ready to rip into Theo. Maybe they'd been lovers. Could she be jealous? Did that even make sense? I mean, look at her, I thought. And then look at *me*.

Nicole glanced my way, turning her head so sharply it made me jump. She smiled, but it wasn't a friendly expression and I wondered if she could read my mind. Some vampires had that gift, although it was rare.

The room was silent, like a church. Which was sort of fitting, considering the way Theo had designed this room. I shivered and my chest suddenly ached. Part of me wished to be far from here, with my birth family – my *first* family – all the O'Neals together on a Sunday. Church, dinner, the Irish Catholic works. Despite my problems with both Dad and Sinéad, that seemed preferable to this. It was, at the very least, way more *normal*.

Solomon fixed Theo with those disturbing dark eyes, so unusual in a vampire. 'All of this is a formality. We have already reached our verdict.'

Theo straightened his shoulders. 'You have not yet deliberated the matter.'

'This order comes from on high.'

He must mean from the Council, I thought. I bit my lip and waited. Why go through all of this . . . charade, if Theo's fate had already been decided? I knew the answer to that the moment I thought it: vampires were all about ritual and performance, in private settings such as this. It was important to meet me, see what Theo had made (literally), and hear what he had to say.

Theo locked eyes with Solomon. 'And what do the High Council have to say?'

Solomon stood in a graceful movement that belied his size. 'A loss of control in the head of a Family the size of Boston's vampire community would, ordinarily, be . . . unforgiveable.' He paused, letting the weight of that word sink in like fangs into virgin flesh. 'However—'

I saw Kyle lean forward, almost imperceptibly. I wondered what he would do if Solomon's punishment for Theo was too great.

'However,' repeated the Elder vampire of Massachusetts, 'it is the finding of this gathering that Theo is too valuable an asset to lose.'

Relief washed over me and I gripped my hands tightly together.

'It is the hope of the High Council, Theo, that one day you will perhaps take a seat at their table. I know it will come as no surprise to you that they have long considered you my natural successor, as Elder of this Enclave, should I be elevated to the High Council. But you also know that your recent actions with the fledgling now known as Moth have put your position in grave danger.'

I wondered if Solomon saw the irony in his choice of words. I suppressed a slightly hysterical giggle, almost clapping my hand over my mouth but just stopping myself in time.

He smiled, displaying terrifyingly long fangs that seemed super-white against his dark skin. 'You have set yourself back some years with a loss of composure more suited to a newly Made vampire.'

Solomon shook his head slowly, playing his role to the fullest. I felt like rolling my eyes, but was scared he'd see me even though he wasn't looking my way. He was tricky, this one.

'In order to prove yourself worthy of your position – and of the faith placed in you by the Council – you will complete a task. A challenge, if you will.' Solomon's gaze hardened.

Theo nodded. 'I can complete any challenge you see fit to set me. Kyle, my Enforcer, can keep watch on my people if the task involves travel, but I am more than capable of taking whatever action is required.'

'*Personally*,' Solomon said.

'Personally,' Theo said.

'Good, then we are all in agreement. Your undertaking is simple: you will find and kill the hunter Thomas Murdoch. And *you must be there at the kill.* Just sending someone else to do your bidding will not be enough. I want his head – and so do the High Council. I want you to bring it to me, *personally*. Do this, and your recent transgression will be overlooked. You will be permitted to keep Moth in your Family and, more importantly, you will retain your position.'

Murdoch! My mind raced and I tried to wipe the expression of shock off my face. My cell phone burned a hole in my pocket as I remembered the text message from Jace. I lowered my head again, nervously running my tongue over my fangs. I peeked at Theo from behind my hair.

He was nodding, his face an unreadable mask. I knew he must be furious. He'd already failed to find Thomas Murdoch, and that was even before he'd been given specific orders by the Council. I wondered if now was the time for me to tell my Maker about my run-in – and unexpected alliance – with Jace. *Yeah, that's a great idea*, I told myself sarcastically.

'How long do I have?' Theo asked. There was always

a time limit on these things; he knew the way the game was played.

'One week.'

Crap. I shifted uncomfortably. That wasn't long, especially considering Jace had told me about his dad's recent disappearing act.

'And if I fail?'

Nicole glared at him. 'You know the answer to that already.'

Theo bared his teeth. 'I am speaking with my own Elder, Nicole.'

Once again, I couldn't help speculating about their relationship.

Solomon shook his head, as though chiding two bickering children. 'Enough. Theo, step forward.'

My Maker did so, ignoring Nicole, who pouted in a dramatic fashion behind him.

'The penalty is simple: the source of your weakness will be destroyed,' Solomon said. He reached out and lifted my chin with surprisingly warm fingers. His hands were huge. He could swat me like the insect he probably thought I was.

'If you fail, this one will die – taking a piece of your soul with her.'

Chapter Nine

Dawn was approaching. Another hour or so, but we could all feel it.

Almost as soon as the last vampire had ventured out into the cold, Theo and I faced each other across his ridiculously huge bedroom. He'd dragged me in here once the other vamps had slipped quietly away, heading to the basement at Subterranean to sleep out the day before making their journeys to wherever they belonged. Subterranean had opened more than five years ago and was a popular hangout for the young and beautiful. It was frequented by Goth/wannabe vampires, and was also a front for Theo's business interests. He operated all kinds of businesses from the lower levels, and in the sub-basement there was a giant crypt filled with coffins where the city's older vampires – and any visitors

– could sleep in perfect safety during the day.

I tried to clamp down on a sense of rising panic. What should I do? I had to tell Theo everything that had happened now, surely? About Rick and what he'd become. More importantly, I needed to tell him I was in contact with Murdoch's son. I couldn't let a brief connection with Jace get in the way of my Maker's task – a task that both our lives could depend on.

And yet . . .

I tried to think clearly, but still found myself hesitating, making excuses. Like: surely I didn't have to tell about Jace, not when his father had already been missing for weeks, anyway. *Skipped town*, he'd said, hadn't he?

'What's done is done,' Theo said, pacing back and forth in an uncharacteristic show of tension. 'I will find Murdoch and I will *kill* him. Nothing has to change.'

'Just let me go,' I said. 'If you let me leave, forever, they can't use me to get at you.'

Theo's beautiful pirate's face was impassive. 'You can never leave me.'

I continued as though he hadn't spoken. 'I'll run away and hide – far away. Nobody will find me. I swear!' I swallowed. 'I'll even promise never to contact my . . . my true family.'

'That will make no difference to what I did – or to the challenge I've been set.'

'I'll be just like a ghost,' I said. '*Theo.*'

He moved so fast that he blurred across the room. His hands gripped my shoulders and he turned me to face him. 'Stop asking for what cannot be. Ever.'

I shook myself free of his grasp, knowing, even as I did so, that I could only manage it because he let me. My voice was thick with unshed tears as I replied. 'Why? Because it's "forbidden"? Why can't you fight the system, Theo? I thought you wanted to join the Elders. Don't they *make* these stupid rules?'

'I am not an Elder yet.'

I ignored him. 'You could start fighting them now. Start over me.'

'You don't know what you're asking.'

'No, it's just that *you* don't give a *shit* about me. You never have.' I gritted my teeth to stop my jaw from wobbling.

His hand shot out, so fast even I didn't see it. He gripped the front of my dress and lifted me straight up. My feet dangled inches above the ground and I felt the collar begin to tear.

I tried to kick him, but he just held me out to one side so I couldn't reach. 'Put me down!'

He shook his head, granite-faced, a vengeful god woken before his time. I knew I'd pushed him too far, but I really didn't care.

'Theo, let go of me!' I struggled more violently,

grabbing his wrist with both hands and trying to wrench myself free.

He shook me pitilessly. 'Be still.'

'Get off me,' I said, hating that I'd begun to cry and couldn't stop the tears from rolling down my face.

Theo watched me without expression.

'Please,' I said, not caring in that moment that I'd done the one thing I had promised myself I'd never do: beg.

He released me without warning and I hit the floor – hard. I couldn't get my feet under me in time, despite my superhuman reflexes, and I sat where he dropped me.

Wow. Could my life *suck* any more?

'Get up,' he said.

I didn't move. There was an empty space inside me that even blood couldn't fill.

'Get. Up.'

I raised my chin and met his eyes. 'I hate you.' He could kill me for that, but so what? How could things get any worse?

He took a step toward me and I flinched. Theo saw me do it and his eyes widened in something close to shock.

'Moth . . .'

'Leave me alone.' I hardly recognized my own voice.

'Marie, I am s—'

116

'I said, *leave me alone*. Didn't you hear me? Leave me with some dignity, for God's sake.'

He laughed, an awful sound filled with bitterness. 'God? Your so-called *god* doesn't want you anymore, little one. Better to stay close to those who do want you.'

'Don't say that,' I whispered.

'You have a new Family now,' he said. 'Get used to it.'

I pulled my knees up against my chest and wrapped my arms around them. I couldn't bear to look at him anymore.

And then he did something that I would never have expected. He had that about him – the ability to take me by surprise just when I was getting good at hating him. He knelt down in front of me, unclasped my cold hands from around my legs and held them in his own. He could have continued to play the scary vampire. He could have punished me for my behavior, like he would do with any other member of his Family. Instead, he offered me one last drop of kindness.

He took both my hands in one of his, placing the other beneath my chin and forcing me to look at him.

'Surely you understand why I can't let you go. Surely you are not so naïve.'

I licked my suddenly dry lips, not wanting to meet his eyes but unable to look away. 'You can't be seen as weak. I know that.'

He shook his head slowly. 'More than that, my little

117

Moth. If I cannot keep you by my side, then you will be considered a risk to the entire Family.'

'I would never tell!' I glared at him. 'Never. I can keep secrets, Theo. You know I can.'

The mask finally dropped and I caught a glimpse of the exhaustion on his face. 'If I can't control you, they will force me to end you. Do you understand?'

He looked old for the first time since I'd known him. It scared the crap out of me.

I shivered. 'You mean . . . kill me.'

'The Elders believe that is what I should have done already. It was a weakness to turn you in the first place, when what I should have done was to let you die and simply covered up any evidence of vampire involvement.'

I felt numb. 'What don't they like about me?'

His hand caressed my cheek, but I could hardly feel it. 'It isn't personal.'

'Not *personal*? They want me dead!'

'This is not about you. It's about me and my loss of control. About what message that sends to the Family – and the Elders.'

I knew what he was saying was the truth. Vampire Families are important for a number of reasons: they offer protection and control. The Master of a Family is responsible for ensuring his or her vampires don't go on a rampage among humanity. Being a member of a Family ensures that everyone is accounted for. We needed to stay hidden to survive – avoiding mobs with torches and pitchforks was imperative. We had to police *ourselves*. But when the Master vamp's ability to protect his or her Family falters, that's when problems begin. If the system falls apart, it could lead to anarchy.

I listened to the ticking of the clock, trying to imagine it was my heart. 'I suppose, if it comes to it, the Council would make *you* the one to kill me.'

'Of course.' His mouth quirked into the ghost of a smile. 'What else would they do?'

I pushed up onto my knees, rested my hands on his shoulders and looked into his endless silver eyes. 'Could you do it?'

He didn't reply, but neither did he look away.

I cupped his face in my hands. 'Could you end me?'

Theo covered my hands with his own. 'Let's not find out.'

I shivered as he pulled me into his arms and pressed my head to his chest. He stroked my hair and I endured it because I knew it was what he would want. But my mind had gone elsewhere – or else*when*. Same place, different time. A year ago in this very house:

On the first day, I wasn't even conscious. That time is a long, dark space of nothingness.

On the second, I drift in and out of consciousness. Toward the end of Day Two, I become more aware of my surroundings. I remember bits and pieces of what happened to me, confused images, but nothing I can really grab hold of. I remember sleeping with Theo, that much becomes clear. I remember how beautiful it had been, how kind he was.

And then I remember the pain as he ripped into my throat afterward.

On the third day, I am racked by convulsions so violent that Theo has to hold me down so that I don't hurt myself. He ends up sitting behind me on the sweat-soaked bed, arms wrapped around me as I have some kind of seizure, coughing up blood — the blood he'd forced me to drink — and whispering, 'Kill me, please kill me' over and over again.

He tells me that he cannot kill me, and I don't understand why.

I threaten to kill myself and he laughs when I tell him I will find pills and swallow them all.

The one time he leaves the room, I rip a bedside lamp to pieces and use the jagged metal base to slice open my wrists. Theo returns to the room to find me screaming as I watch my flesh knit itself back together, slowly but surely.

He doesn't kill me, and I don't know whether I am grateful for that. I only know that I have never felt such pain in my life. I want to scratch out my eyes as they burn and itch. Theo ties my hands to the bed, but I break the bonds each time. He cannot leave me, even for a moment.

Until finally, just when I think I can't take any more, I awake one morning and the world looks different.

120

Everything has changed. I burst into tears because there is no way out of this, no denying how different I am. It isn't just a surface thing – I have been remade, right down to the bone. No, beyond that: my cells have been completely trans-formed. Reshaped and energized in ways I can't even begin to comprehend. All I can think about is how much I want blood and that the sun hurts my eyes, and I know that there is no going back.

Not ever.

Theo gently pushed me away, breaking the delicate thread of memory. 'Are you ready to feed now?'

I closed my eyes. There was no point in resisting; not when I'd already agreed to this earlier. I tried to say some-thing – Theo was waiting for my reply – but my throat had gone dry and no words would come.

'Let me offer you my hospitality, Moth. It is im-portant that the Family see you as part of me – if you still won't permit me to feed from *you*, then you must at least do this.' His eyes glittered. 'I insist.'

'What are you offering?' I tried to keep the dull resentment out of my voice.

'I know you won't drink directly from a human, and I don't push you on this,' Theo said. His voice was hard, letting me know that this was a concession he made especially for me. He smiled, flashing fang. 'But I fed from a beautiful girl this evening, before the meeting.'

I closed my eyes. 'How old?'

'What do you take me for?' His lips pulled tight so I could see his fangs. 'She was a willing donor.'

'I'm sorry, Theo.' My words tumbled out too quickly, making me feel immediately ashamed of how much I still wanted to please him. *Willing donor?* Please . . .

'The girl's blood nurtures me, even as we stand here talking about it.' He tilted his head, watching me carefully. Oh, so carefully. 'Drink from me, little Moth, and take this gift I offer you. You did well tonight. Let me give this to you.'

He was turning this into *a reward.* I wanted to cry, but it would do me no good. Sure, I drank human blood – vampires needed it in order to survive – but I drank from blood banks and hospitals. And no more than once a week if I could get away with it.

Theo was still watching, waiting to hear my response. Waiting for my refusal so he could force me. I gritted my teeth together and allowed myself the luxury of imagining myself defying him. Saying 'no' and leaving the apartment in a righteous cloud of anger. Leaving the whole Family – including the Elder of Massachusetts. The Council. All of it. Letting Theo explain it to them.

Yeah, right. If I did that, I'd be signing my own death warrant. And not even *I* could be 'lucky' enough to get a third chance at life.

'OK,' I sighed, allowing my hunger to show in my

brightly glowing eyes. I tried to keep the anger out of my voice. 'I accept your *gift*. Thank you.'

Theo's eyebrows raised, but other than that he didn't betray his surprise. He removed his shirt, allowing it to slip from his marble-white shoulders and slide to the ground.

I swallowed and focused on his chest, where his heart would be beating with anticipation – if he were still human. Vampire hearts didn't beat, of course, although newer vamps like me could still feel the echoes of our humanity.

And I did need to feed, now more than ever. I just wished it didn't have to involve sticking my fangs into Theo. In the end, though, it didn't really matter how I did it. The hunger was always there, whether I was awake or asleep: jagged, carnivorous, almost a living thing in itself. Whether I fought it or not, that was a fact of my life now. Like having a terminal disease you're always aware of. *Owned* by it.

As I placed my hands against his chest and raised myself on tiptoe, Theo wrapped his arms around me and pulled me against him, lifting me off the ground. My lips found the delicious spot just over his carotid artery, and I waited for him to give me permission to drink. He smelled of blood and moonlight.

Almost every other vampire I knew would gladly die (for real) to be in this position, but all I felt was a feral urge – like an itch that needed to be scratched. And underlying that a deep and bitter resentment, mixed up with the painful desire to be human again.

As my fangs extended, making my gums throb and my head tingle, I trembled in my Maker's arms. I ran my tongue across his skin, shivering with anticipation.

He tasted like home.

Theo's voice sounded more like a growl in my ear. 'Now,' he said.

I wrapped my legs around his waist and plunged my fangs into his throat.

Chapter Ten

Feeding from Theo had a side-effect that I hadn't immediately remembered: it left me completely open to him. My mind, my heart. He only had to take a quick look inside to see that I was hiding something from him. Luckily, I managed to hold back something for myself, but the damage was done: Detectives Trent and Smith, my unsanctioned 'mission' through the tunnels to the hospital, fighting Rick . . . Theo saw flashes of all those things as I drank from him. Although vampires can't compel other vampires with their gaze unless they are *very* old, your Maker does have some power over you. Enough to make it difficult to keep secrets.

Events moved quickly after that – too quickly. I tried to get him to listen, tried to explain, but he was having none of it. He called his Enforcer to the room, once we'd cleaned up, and demanded that I tell him about what had happened to Rick.

Kyle glided in on silent feet, ninja-style and creepy as hell.

I nodded at him. 'Kyle.'

His too-red lips spread into a nasty grin. 'Moth. How nice to see you back where you belong, at your Master's side.'

I didn't reply, deliberately turning away from him. Until now, he and Holly had been the only other vampires to know about my existence – a fact that had irrevocably changed tonight. Kyle didn't like me, seeing me as proof of Theo's massive slip in . . . *discipline*. And judgment. He certainly hadn't made a secret of his disapproval, and I couldn't help but wonder why Theo let his Enforcer get away with such an attitude problem. They'd known each other for decades, but Theo was still the older and more powerful.

Kyle had taught me a little self-defense. Nothing specific – more like he took parts of a whole host of martial arts and mixed them all together. The real purpose of the lessons was to help me to control my strength after I'd adjusted to being turned. There was an element of discipline in the blocks and falls and punches that I appreciated. I fell down a lot more than I wanted, and we didn't use mats or anything like that. The floor was hard and I was constantly picking myself up, always trying to prove that I could take whatever Kyle dished out. Which of course I couldn't. The only reason I was still in one piece was because Theo would kill him if he really hurt me.

I suspected that Kyle hated that more than anything else.

I ignored him and instead focused on Theo. I wanted to get this little session of show and tell over with so I could go home. I wanted to sleep, and I knew that the two older vampires must be feeling the approach of the day.

'Now,' Theo said. 'Tell us.' He stretched his arms above his head and watched me as I tried not to notice the white flesh peeking out from beneath the raised edge of his black shirt. His black pants sat perfectly on his slender hips.

I swallowed and looked away. Why did I let him do this to me? It was so seriously screwed up and we both knew it. But there was a lot more going on here than simple attraction to an older guy. A *much* older guy. His vampire abilities were an integral part of his existence. They helped him catch his prey; they intoxicated his people and enabled him to keep control of such a large group of vamps; and they transformed his bite from something to be feared into something we all craved.

I forced myself to focus on where we were and what I was supposed to be doing, filling them in on everything that had happened at the hospital. Well, OK . . . not *quite* everything. I managed to tell the whole story without a single mention of a certain vampire hunter's son. Don't ask me why – I just didn't want to effectively hand him over to Theo. At least, not yet. Maybe I could find out Murdoch Senior's location without my Maker hurting Jace. I wanted to give myself the chance to try.

Theo's face registered a dark flash of fury as he heard what I had done without permission, but it creased into a thoughtful frown as I got to the part about Zombie Rick. 'This is worse than I imagined.' He began to pace, stopped and gazed at me. 'You're unharmed, though? I am still angry with you, Moth, but that was excellent thinking to use fire against it.'

I ignored the swell of pride in my chest. I hated it when his praise made me feel like a little kid looking for Daddy's approval. Instead, I shrugged. 'I've watched a lot of TV. But I never expected to actually face a zombie. Not in real life.' I glanced at him, almost shyly. 'I wasn't even sure I believed in them. Until today.'

Theo chuckled, a sound that gave me goosebumps. 'Like humans don't believe in vampires? Ah, my little Moth. There are things out there that I used to find difficult to believe.' He shrugged flamboyantly. 'If I hadn't seen them with my own eyes, I would probably have dismissed them as legends – fairy tales to scare children into good behavior. Although I despise the term *zombies* – it's nothing more than a pointless link to popular culture.'

I frowned. 'What do you mean?'

'Simply that the correct term for the boy you en-countered is *Unmade*. Zombies aren't connected to the . . . mythology of our world. You would do better to look at Haitian and African folklore.'

'Like . . . voodoo?'

Theo nodded. '*Vodoun* is the correct term. But yes, that kind of magic is not something that's common in Massachusetts.'

I was getting a little bored with the history lesson, but Theo was on a roll and this might be important. 'What about down South? New Orleans is famous for black magic.'

'I can assure you, that boy you encountered has nothing to do with places such as New Orleans. Creating a true *zombi* is an art that very few practitioners have the power for; it is a complex procedure. Now, the Unmade are much easier to understand. They are far more similar in nature to vampires – more similar than many of the Elders would like to admit.' He curled his lip in distaste and exchanged a knowing look with Kyle.

I was getting confused. 'But what's the difference?'

'The Unmade are not the result of magical ritual. They are the result of a vampire attack gone very, very wrong. The victim returns as nothing more than a shell – a *revenant* of sorts. Only survival instinct keeps it going until it runs out of energy. Like a wind-up toy at the end of its life.'

I shifted from one foot to the other, trying not to picture Rick's face. 'So he really wasn't brought back by a voodoo priest or something?'

Theo smiled. 'A *bokor*? In Boston? You really have watched too many horror movies, child.'

I used to love horror movies, but it's something my Maker finds amusing. After what I'd witnessed just the previous day, I didn't think I'd find it so easy to watch fictional zombies going about their zombie business.

I shivered. 'But why did he . . . it . . . eat human flesh?'

'The flesh isn't so important as the life force that it contains. Eating something living – and it wouldn't necessarily have to be human – will keep it going for two or three days. Revenants, the *Unmade* . . . these creatures need more than just blood to survive. A more dense meal would provide a greater charge of energy.'

'Sort of like keeping a dying battery running?' I tried not to think of the 'dense meal' that Nurse Fox's arm must've provided.

He narrowed his eyes. 'A little. Now, enough of this.' He gestured to Kyle. 'Look into this matter for me – begin as soon as you wake tonight. I'm sure we would have heard if there had been similar . . . incidents. But it can't hurt to be certain.'

'Done,' Kyle replied. He turned to leave but then spun back to face me, taking me by surprise. 'You did well to defeat the revenant, Moth. It looks like you remembered more of our training than I would have thought.' His tone was grudging but seemed genuine.

I raised my eyebrows, not quite knowing how to reply. There was a tiny part of me that was pleased with his veiled compliment – Kyle did not give praise lightly.

'Um . . . thanks,' I said.

He nodded and fixed me with a look that I couldn't even begin to decode.

Theo held up his hand, commanding his Enforcer to wait another moment. 'Keep this quiet, you understand? Do not let anyone else know what you're doing. At least for now. We do not want any . . . rumors.'

Kyle inclined his head, flicking an amused glance my way, then left the room as swiftly and silently as he'd arrived.

I returned home as an appropriately bloody dawn splashed the sky. I stopped in my tracks on the street, mouth hanging open.

Jason Murdoch was waiting outside my apartment building. He slouched against the wall beside the main entrance, as though he had all the time in the world. His hands were in the pockets of his army jacket. Pale moonlight glinted off his hair and brow-piercing, and his eyes were lost in shadow.

We stared at each other for a good thirty seconds.

'How did you know where I live?' It was all I could think of to say.

He raised his eyebrows. 'You're way too easy to find.'

Oh. My. God. If I could still hyperventilate, that's exactly what I would be doing. As it was, I had to lean against the wall next to him and force out a couple breaths. It made me feel better.

'Is there a problem?'

Bastard. 'Now I have to move apartments.'

'Why?' He made a big show of examining the place. 'Nice neighborhood. Lots of Italian food practically on your doorstep.'

Bastard! I couldn't speak. I just stared at him some more.

He winked. 'No, it's cool. I won't tell anyone where you keep your coffin.'

I felt an illogical stab of guilt. He and his father had been forced to move after my first encounter with the younger Murdoch at Thomas Murdoch's Boston apartment.

Jace broke into my thoughts. 'You didn't reply to my text.'

'Oh!' I remembered getting the message before the Family meeting. Unsurprisingly, it had slipped my mind.

He looked amused. 'I take it, from your deeply intelligent response, that you at least got it?'

'Yeah. Sorry. Wasn't exactly a priority at the time.' I crossed my arms across my chest. 'What did you mean about "sharing info"?'

'Exactly what I said. I've been doing some research into our friend, Rick. I'm assuming you've spoken to your Maker about it by now?'

I nodded. 'But can this wait? I'm really tired, I need to sleep.' And I couldn't exactly invite him in because then Holly really *would* kill me. Although she wasn't actually here, that much was true. She was staying with her friend – the brunette vampire, who I found out was called Alanya – at Subterranean.

'Cool. Why don't you come over to my place tomorrow night? Well, I guess that's this evening, really.'

'OK,' I said carefully. I was sort of waiting for the catch. Couldn't really help it when Jace was around. Was it a trap? But I should go, right? I might find some clue as to where Murdoch Senior had gone. Theo didn't know where the hunter was currently based, and now I had to think about the task set him by the Elders. And about how our survival rested on his ability to find and kill Jace's father.

I swallowed, feeling like a traitor. Then I mentally kicked myself for being such a wuss. It wasn't like Jason Murdoch and I were BFFs.

'OK?' he repeated. 'That's all you have to say?'

'No, I have plenty to say.' I pouted, trying to think of something to say.

'Who knows,' he said, with a half-smile, 'maybe we'll make a good team.'

'And what will *you* be bringing to this so-called team?'

'My superior knowledge of how to kill vampires.' His face was totally deadpan. I honestly couldn't tell whether or not he was joking.

'And that's supposed to make me feel better about partnering up with you?'

He flashed me a grin that was all teeth. If anything, it made me feel worse.

Chapter Eleven

I drifted up from the dreamless dark, staring at the ceiling of my bedroom and trying to remember everything that had happened last night. My head ached, almost as though I was hung-over. Gray light filled the corners of the room like fog.

I pushed my hair away from my face, shivering as I recalled the sensation as my fangs slid into Theo's throat, the feel of his body against mine.

Rolling over, I buried my head under the duvet and tried to forget the taste of Theo's skin and the fresh blood that I'd taken from him. *His* blood, but not quite his blood. The mixture of almost-two-hundred-year-old vampire blood and that of the human girl he'd compelled into being his snack for the night was difficult to forget. Human blood alone still bothered me, but my Maker's was something else entirely. Theo was like a drug that would be impossible to give up.

And now Jace wanted to 'share information' and work together in some way. What was *that* all about? I wasn't dumb enough to think he didn't have some kind of ulterior motive, but I was too curious to pass on the opportunity. Jace . . . interested me. I couldn't help that. He was the son of a hated vampire hunter, and he clearly had more than his fair share of damage, but he also seemed almost reasonable. At times. And it couldn't hurt to use him to figure out more about Rick. Perhaps if I showed Theo's Family that I could be useful, that I had resources, they wouldn't want me dead.

I showered and dressed before midday, then spent five minutes looking for my cell phone. Finally found it back where I started, underneath my bed. Frowning, I checked it and realized I had three missed calls, all from Caitlín. Now what? Was she calling to make me feel guilty for not going to dinner? I'd already told her I couldn't make it. Irritated, I tossed my phone onto the kitchen table, next to the television remote, and set about making coffee. I'd call Caitlín back later.

The apartment's buzzer echoed down the hallway the moment I got settled with my coffee. I rolled my eyes and wondered if I could get away with ignoring that as well. It was probably only another delivery of crafting materials for Holly's business.

The insistent buzzing of the intercom ruined my first sip of coffee. 'All right, I'm coming!' I muttered under my breath as I muted the TV and shuffled to the door in black fluffy slippers shaped like bats. They were Holly's, but she didn't have to know I was making use of them while she was staying away from home. 'What?' I stabbed at the intercom's button so hard the cheap plastic coating cracked.

The crackle of static interspersed with silence greeted me and I cursed, stomping back into the kitchen. Probably just kids screwing around.

I'd just sat down again, resting my feet on the shiny wooden table and getting myself comfortable, when someone knocked on the apartment door. OK, now I was seriously pissed. I slammed down my favorite Catwoman mug, watching sadly as coffee sloshed over the sides and onto the table.

I flung open the door, mentally preparing myself to tell whoever it was to go to hell.

Which worked out perfectly, because it was my big sister.

'Hello, Marie,' Sinéad said. 'Aren't you going to invite me in?'

Sinéad had refused coffee and opted for water. She sat on one of the kitchen chairs and looked every inch the ambitious young lawyer-in-training. Today she was dressed casually, but she still managed to look perfectly groomed in an emerald-green blouse, very properly buttoned up, with black jeans and black patent ballet flats. I wished my big sister didn't always look like she had a particularly long stick shoved up her ass. To be fair to her, Sinéad had the unfortunate role of being the oldest of the O'Neal sisters and therefore the one that our unpredictable father had turned to for support when Mom was sick. After she'd passed away, Sinéad had opted to stay at home with Dad and help him get back on his feet.

I couldn't help the sharp stab of resentment toward him, though, for the fact that *his* grief always took over. What about Caitlín? Our father hadn't been there for her at all – he couldn't see beyond his own pain and bitterness.

Sinéad stopped fiddling with the tall glass I'd given her and pushed it away. 'I know this is a good area, but isn't this place a little small for two people?'

'It's fine, Sinéad.' She'd never bothered to come here before, which I was glad about. Holly would have even more reason to complain if my human family made regular visits. And she'd rat me out to Theo. 'Just tell me what's wrong. You wouldn't come if it wasn't something important.'

My sister looked away and twisted a strand of her thick, red hair. She seemed genuinely distressed, and I began to get that horrible sense of dread in the pit of my stomach.

I pulled my feet up onto the chair and rested my chin on my knees. 'Sinéad?'

'It's Caitlín,' Sinéad blurted out. 'She's gone.'

My feet hit the floor and I was standing before I could stop myself. 'Gone? What do you mean? Where did she go?'

'Marie, calm down.' Sinéad's voice was tight and controlled, something that drove me crazy and made me want to shake my sister's composure all over again. 'We've already heard from her – she sent me a text message and then called Dad last night – but she wouldn't say where she was. She said she needed some time alone and that she's staying with a friend. Honestly, I thought she meant here with you, but I can see that's not the case.'

I frowned, sliding back into my seat. 'You mean . . . she ran away?' That didn't make sense. Cait could be impetuous at times, but she also handled problems head on, no running away – she *dealt*. Didn't she?

And anyway, I thought that I had the market cornered on rebellion.

I scowled at Sinéad. 'OK, so you thought she might be here. I get that. But she's not, so where does that leave us?'

'Do you know which friend she's talking about?' Sinéad asked. 'Who she might be staying with?'

'I don't even know who her friends *are* anymore.' Just

139

saying it brought the truth home to me. No wonder Cait was always chasing after me, trying to track me down and get me to go visit. Maybe she was lonely. As much as I loved my little sister, it was becoming more and more obvious that a decision had to be made. Could I tell Caitlín the truth about my existence? What would I do when I still looked eighteen ten years from now? Twenty? What then? Would I have to disappear from my family's life forever? Life without my baby sister was something I didn't want to contemplate.

My older sister sighed. She looked tired and I felt vaguely guilty for always giving her such a hard time. 'When was the last time you spoke to her?'

'She called me on Friday morning.' I glanced at my phone. 'And I had missed calls from her this morning. No messages.' I fiddled with my coffee mug, tracing the faint lines that spider-webbed its crimson surface. I'd slammed the cup down one too many times in a fit of temper. I sighed. I knew I couldn't have Sinéad come here again. 'I'll call you if I hear from her, OK? I promise. And I'll keep calling her.'

Sinéad's perfectly plucked eyebrows rose. 'You don't sound very worried. A minute ago you were leaping up and looked ready to go walking the streets until you found her.'

'Of course I'm worried. I'm freaking out, OK? But you already said you've heard from her. Maybe she really *is* just visiting a friend. She's not a child anymore.' A statement that I still found hard to accept.

'She's sixteen. I want her back home and she should be in school. They told me that she cut classes on Friday, and now this.'

'Did something happen? Did she have a fight with Dad? Or with you?'

Anger splotched her cheeks. 'Dad wouldn't upset Caitlín and you know it. He adores her.'

'But that doesn't stop him from ignoring her and drinking too much,' I muttered.

'Don't speak about our father like that.' Sinéad's tone was sharp.

'"Father"? What kind of a father has he been during the past year? He's hardly ever present, unless he's had enough booze to deal with the fact that he actually has a family! He may have drunk away his job, but he still has kids.'

The color drained from my sister's face almost as quickly as it had appeared. I could hear her heart beat. 'And I could say the same about you! You left us when Mom died. You dropped out of college, live with a stranger, and spend your time running around the city doing God only knows what. Mom would be ashamed of you!'

I took a step back. If my sister had hit me it probably would have been better than this. I sometimes wondered if Sinéad hated me for being Mom's favorite – even though our mother had done everything in her power to hide it – or whether she just didn't like me. After Mom died, I'd fallen apart. Fallen into Theo's arms.

It wasn't my fault that I'd dropped out of sight. Was it?

Sinéad pushed past me and headed for the door. 'I'll let you know if we hear from her,' she said, not even bothering to turn around as she stalked down the tiny entrance hallway.

'Wait,' I said, immediately regretting the pleading note in my voice. Why did I always get this way around my family?

'There's nothing else to say, Marie. If you could tell me the minute Caitlín gets in touch with you, that's the best thing you can do for all of us.' Sinéad had her hand on the door latch, but she wasn't actually leaving, which I took as a hopeful sign.

'Sinéad, look at me for a moment.' I cleared my throat. 'Please?'

My sister's hand fell back to her side and she turned around, surprise evident on her face. 'What?'

I wanted to say so much. The words were all there, crushed into the tight space of my throat. Words that meant reaching out, making myself vulnerable. Revealing secrets that could get everybody I loved killed.

I dropped my eyes to the worn gray carpet. 'I only

wanted to say that I'll go out and look for Caitlín. There are places we've had coffee before. I'll try those.' My voice was husky and I felt on the verge of tears.

Sinéad's lips tightened for a moment, but then she nodded. 'OK, that's a good idea.' Her hand went back to the door and she turned away. 'Thank you.'

I watched my sister walk into the spacious public corridor.

I headed back inside and steadied myself against the kitchen counter. I had to look for Caitlín. She *was* still only a kid, Sinéad was right. She shouldn't be out there alone, no matter how grown up she thought she was.

Grabbing my boots, I started lacing them up, my mind racing. I glanced up at the silent television screen and realized that the local news was on. Something about Boston Common . . . Maybe there was some kind of festival happening today. Something Caitlín might want to go to? But I didn't want to risk getting caught up with crowds of tourists either. I snatched the remote from the table and punched up the volume so I could catch the end of the broadcast.

The perfectly groomed newscaster flashed into view, adjusting his pastel tie. His face presented a melodramatic picture of concern, slightly marred by his glaring white teeth and fake tan. '. . . and the police have no comment at this time. They advise avoiding the Common and surrounding roads for the foreseeable future.'

Another image appeared, this one taken with what appeared to be a shaky handheld camera – perhaps from a cell phone. I couldn't make anything out clearly, but it looked like someone was lying down in a pile of fallen leaves. I was pretty certain it *was* a human figure, but the lighting was terrible and there was no way of seeing details. The one thing that stood out, though, was a quick glimpse of long red hair. *Caitlín?*

My throat burned and I squeezed the remote so tightly that it shattered. 'Crap!' I brushed plastic shards off my lap and ran to the TV, manually adjusting the sound so I could hear properly.

The newscaster continued: 'This footage was taken by two teenagers this morning, and an inside source reports that the victim could have been mauled by an animal. The area has been cordoned off in the last half-hour, but speculation is growing that this girl could be the third in a series of deaths that began on Friday. The Commissioner urges calm, and will make a full statement this afternoon at . . .'

My ears were buzzing so badly I couldn't listen to any more. Long red hair on that 'victim' couldn't possibly mean Caitlín, could it? It was a ridiculous, crazy coincidence. Nausea hit me like a punch to the gut, and I had to force myself to take a deep breath.

It didn't help.

And what did the newscaster mean by this being the

third victim? Was there someone else, someone other than Rick who'd already been killed? Or were they talking about Nurse Fox? What if this new victim – *who couldn't be my sister* – went the same way as Rick? I didn't know what I could do at a major crime scene surrounded by the police and media, but I needed to at least *try*.

And then I wondered if maybe I could get some back-up. Hadn't Jace told me, just last night, that he wanted to share information? Well, fine. I'd give him some information.

The phone rang several times before somebody picked up. If it was Jace, he was waiting for me to speak first.

'Hello?'

Silence.

I frowned. 'Um . . . Jace? Are you there?'

'Moth?'

'Yes,' I replied. What was *up* with him?

I heard a rustling sound, then his voice returned, muffled. 'Sorry, I didn't recognize the number. Haven't programmed you in properly yet. What do you want?'

'Switch on the TV – there's been another attack. Maybe it's the same as before.'

'And?'

I huffed a little. 'You said to let you know if anything happened! Well, something happened. Something big.'

'OK, I'll try to meet you there.'

I frowned, annoyed that he wasn't committing to it. 'Do you have better things to do?'

He hesitated. 'I'm looking for my dad.'

'Oh. Listen, my sister's gone missing too, you know. I want to look for her – I *need* to find her – but someone died. Badly, by the sounds of things. We should check it out.' And that person might even *be* my sister, a nasty voice whispered in my head.

I didn't believe it. Not really. I *couldn't*.

Jace lowered his voice, like he didn't want someone else who might be there to hear him. 'I can't talk now, but I *will* try to get over there.'

'Fine.' I wondered what he was hiding.

'Be careful.'

'Really? Aw, shucks. I might start thinking you care—'

He disconnected.

I rolled my eyes at the phone and pushed Jason Murdoch out of my mind. There were far more important things happening in the world.

I raced down and out of the building and hailed a cab.

Chapter Twelve

The sky was brittle-blue and the sun was so bright and jagged that it hurt my eyes, even though I was wearing shades. Was this winter brighter than usual? *Maybe it's always been like this*, that nasty little voice whispered at the back of my mind. *You're getting more and more sensitive. Soon you won't even be able to go outside at all in daylight, and you'll have to live in shadows for the rest of your very long life.*

I shivered, resting my back against the cool stone of a tall building across from the Common. I'd never been at a crime scene before. Not an authentic one, I mean; a murder scene. It seemed a lot like on those *CSI* TV shows, but there was a truly unnerving quality to the stark reality of it. It was as though we'd walked onto a movie set only to discover this was the real deal after all, and there was no switching channels to something more comforting. The whole corner of Boston Common, on the Boylston Street side near the Central Burying Ground, was cordoned off by police cars and fluttering yellow tape. An ambulance was parked there too, and people wearing uniforms and plastic gloves surrounded the area. Everybody looked focused and busy. There were also news vans parked as close as they could get to the crime scene. Uniformed officers held them at bay, but that didn't stop cameramen trying to get video footage from a distance.

A small crowd of onlookers had gathered closest to the barrier. Everyone had thick winter coats on, aside from Detective Alison Trent, who stood a little apart from the center of the action. She was sipping from a steaming paper cup of what I assumed was coffee. That was what cops drank, right? Like my dad. It ran through their veins. Smith was on the other side of the police tape, crouched down by what I guessed must be the victim.

I hadn't even thought about my friendly neighborhood detectives being around. What an idiot! I'd been so keen to get here, I just dived into a cab and headed straight across town. Now I had to worry about being spotted by Trent and Smith – they wouldn't have lost interest in me, and seeing me at the latest crime scene was only going to stir their suspicions.

Checking my sunglasses were in place, I pulled up the

collar of my jacket and approached the crowd of vultures, who were all hoping for a glimpse of a dead body to tell their friends about back at work. Human beings never failed to amaze me, but then I guess it's hard to blame them. Life must seem unbearably dull; a murder in such a public area of the city was something to talk about.

I edged closer to the barrier, focusing on the events unfolding around the crime scene in the distance. The group of men and women in nasty shiny jumpsuits were moving away from their huddle beneath the skeletal trees. Surely, surely, it couldn't be Cait . . . A gap opened, just for a moment, and I was, for once, grateful for my increased vampire senses, especially my enhanced eyesight. I craned my neck, pushing a tall man to one side in my rush to get to the front of the barrier. I caught a fleeting glimpse of the victim –

– and almost cried with relief. It wasn't Cait. Thank God! That horror and doubt back at the apartment had shaken me to the core. And then guilt crept up on me, because it was awful to feel grateful for the death of another. This girl had been someone's daughter, maybe someone's sister. I swallowed and closed my eyes, that brief image imprinted on my memory.

Her eyes were open, which somehow made it worse. They were wide and shining under the cloudy sky. Her wavy red hair was crusted with blood – you almost couldn't tell, at first, but I could smell it on her. The girl's throat was gone – and so was she. No spark of life left inside, just cold death, her body splayed out like a discarded doll at the edge of Boston Common at the beginning of a new day.

And then I realized that I *did* know her.

Her name was Erin Doyle, and she was gone. Just like her twin brother, Rick. Holy crap, there was *no way* that was a coincidence.

Erin's body lay spread-eagled in a shallow ditch on the very edge of the Common. The hard ground, still frozen from last night's low temperatures, looked half dug, as though someone had attempted to cover the girl's body with dirt but given up halfway. I suspected that whoever had dumped her hadn't exactly made a serious attempt to hide the evidence. Maybe they really *had* been scared off partway through digging, or maybe the ground was just too winter-hard. Dead leaves scattered the area and crunched under the feet of the various technicians who attended the scene.

I couldn't see all of her injuries, but I could smell the blood – even from here. Her body was zipped into a body bag and hoisted onto a stretcher. More police came to move the crowd further back. Somewhere nearby, I could hear a child crying and wondered why the kid's parent wasn't taking it away from this ghoulish spectacle.

I turned, trying to ignore the sick feeling in my stomach, and found myself way too close to Detective

Trent. I caught a whiff of her menthol cigarettes, a scent that made me think of her lighter and what had become of it back in the basement of Mass General. Trent was talking to a tall Goth boy who stood hunched into a long black coat, his arms wrapped around himself as though he were trying to hold himself together. I narrowed my eyes, taking in his long face, spiky black hair, and Prometheus band T-shirt. I realized that here was another familiar face, and something went cold inside me. Why were all these victims and their friends people I'd known – well, at least met – in my previous life?

This guy had the unfortunate luck to be named Byron Castle Jr, after his father, who was the guitarist in a rock band called Prometheus. They weren't huge, but they were a Boston band with a cult following of kids – despite the fact that most of the band members were over forty. I wondered what Byron was doing here, trying desperately to remember the couple of brief times we'd met at college. We weren't in the same classes, but I'd seen him with Rick and Erin, I was *sure* of it. Was he Erin's boyfriend?

I wanted to hear their conversation, perhaps learn something important, but at the same time Erin's body was being dumped onto a gurney and rolled past the still gathering crowd toward a nearby ambulance.

Dammit, I needed to get closer – especially after what happened to Rick. Any evidence that might've remained

151

on his body had, quite literally, gone up in flames. I couldn't afford to lose what might be my one opportunity to check out Erin's body and see if I could pick up the scent of her killer. That had been the plan with Rick, until he went all *Dawn of the Dead* on our asses.

I swallowed and gazed at the watery sun high above in the blue-white sky. If a vampire was responsible for this attack – which was almost certain – then it must have happened during the night when the undead hunted. Saturday night, when so many of us had been at Theo's. There had been a lot of non-Boston vamps in the city last night. But her body had been dumped in the morning, after the sun had risen. I'd already overheard Trent say this.

Which meant one of two things: either someone was trying to make the death look like a vampire killing, or there were two killers. A vampire and a human, working together.

I shivered, trying to wrap my head around that.

'Move aside please, miss,' a neutral male voice instructed as I was nudged out of the way of the passing gurney.

I tensed as Erin's covered body was wheeled right past me. It was now or never. What was the worst that could happen? A telling off from a cop or paramedic? I could live with that.

I grabbed a corner of the body bag and walked into

the gurney. I cried out as though in pain when the metal trolley made contact with my legs, and fell to my knees, dragging the slick blue-black material with me as I went down. I'd been pretty good at drama, back in the day. Here was an opportunity to relive my school theater memories. My enhanced strength came in useful sometimes, and I pulled Erin's concealed body halfway off the gurney. Somehow, I made it all look like a crazy accident and shrieked as I landed on the hard earth.

One of the paramedics cursed and tried to pick me up, and I quickly jammed my foot against the nearest wheel so the other guy couldn't get the body away from the crowd.

'You've got it stuck on something,' muttered one of the cops standing guard. The tall, skinny paramedic who'd been trying to help me to my feet began looking at the ground for stray stones or gaps in the hard, cracked earth.

Meanwhile, I took advantage of the confusion and pulled the body bag's zip down a few inches. I crawled forward and leaned over Erin's cold body and put my face as close to the livid gash in her neck as I dared, taking a long slow breath and pushing out with my senses. Searching for any clue, no matter how slight, of who or what might have done this. Rick's transformation had erased any scent other than that of dead meat. Here was my chance with a fresh corpse.

I shuddered as I caught myself with that thought. What had my life become? What had I become? Was I really all Erin had to help her find true justice?

Poor kid.

I looked at this girl – her face, what was left of her throat – and remembered the way Theo had torn into *my* throat and could have left me for dead. This girl could just as well be me.

And then police officers converged on the scene, helping the paramedics to pull the body back onto the gurney and wheel it away – over my foot, I might add – and into the waiting ambulance. It all happened so suddenly, I was left standing on the common with all of my senses focused on the faint aroma of vampire that I'd managed to detect through the slight opening in Erin's body bag.

The sudden pain that gripped my chest was overwhelming. Like a panic attack, only worse. I curled my fingers into fists, trying to calm the crazy thoughts and feelings that threatened to crush me. There had to be a mistake, it was as simple as that.

I stumbled as a tall man in a dark uniform pushed past me on his way toward the line of emergency vehicles spilling out of the common. For once, I couldn't be bothered to react to being rudely shoved aside. Numbness began to settle in – a welcome white noise that helped to mask the confused sensations swirling in my gut.

I felt guilty by association – which was weird and totally twisted, but I couldn't help it. And maybe I *was* partly responsible. I shook my head and forced myself to take a deep breath of the cold air.

My Maker's scent had been all over that poor girl's body.

If the Elders found out what Theo had done – what it *seemed* he'd done – their response would be swift and without mercy. No head of a Family would be allowed to go around murdering innocents. If Theo had been a low-level vamp, somebody who wasn't planning on a diplomatic career within the highest ranks of vampire politics, he might have gotten away with it.

And if anything happened to Theo, what would that mean for *me*?

Or maybe he thought he *would* get away with it – why wouldn't he? Theo was powerful enough to cover his tracks, and he was very far from stupid.

Cold fingers of doubt poked at my terrified brain but I did my best to ignore them. *No way*, I told myself firmly. Theo was the one who was concerned the murders would draw attention to the real monsters hiding in Boston. He was the head of our Family – a master vampire who knew better. He had *control*. He could certainly feed without killing. I tried to focus.

Why had he made me drink from him last night? The girl's scent was so familiar to me now because it was *her* blood that had fortified Theo last night and that I had tasted during our feeding. Surely he hadn't killed Erin? Even if he had, surely he wouldn't have left her body right out here on the common? Unless he just figured that the authorities would be called and nobody would suspect anything other than a violent murder. His DNA and fingerprints couldn't be traced, for one thing. As long as there were no witnesses, he'd be free and clear.

Theo was ambitious. If he'd been tempted last night, or had been overcome by instinct in the heat of the moment as he fed, surely his intelligence would've stopped him from making such a fatal error.

Like he stopped himself when he lost control with me?

I shook that treacherous thought off and tried to pull my face into an expression that might look halfway human. What should I do? Should I go to Theo and confront him? What if he really *had* done this and wanted to keep it hidden from everyone – *including me.*

I walked slowly across the common, my head buzzing with possibilities – none of them good. The world seemed to be turning too quickly and my thoughts were spinning to match it. Did I believe that Theo was capable of killing Erin? Capable? Yes. But would he do it? Would he risk everything in a moment of bloodlust?

I didn't know the answer to that. Just because you don't want something to be true doesn't make it *not* true.

Of course, me being me, there was no way I would let

this new – potentially shattering – development stop me from finding out what was going on. One, I'm nosy. Two, I'm determined. Three, I'm nosy.

I grabbed my cell phone and called Jace. I needed to talk to someone and, once again, it was the hunter I turned to. I tried to tell myself that by staying in touch with him I might find out more about Thomas Murdoch's whereabouts – something that could help Theo – but I didn't know if I was convincing myself anymore.

He answered quickly, sounding out of breath. 'What?'

'Sorry, am I *interrupting* something?' I put lots of innuendo into my tone.

I could almost see him rolling his eyes. 'What's up?'

I told him everything I'd just seen. I even swallowed my doubts, convinced myself that I wasn't betraying Theo but *helping* him, and told Jace what I'd smelled.

'So,' he said, after listening for a few minutes, 'you need to at least accept the possibility – the *possibility*, that's all I'm saying – that your Maker is responsible for this.'

'No.' I could think it, in the privacy of my own head, but Jace wasn't allowed to say it. I know that's not even remotely logical, but there it is.

'You told me yourself that you scented your Maker on Erin's body! Who is he, Moth? Who *is* your Maker? Who turned you?'

I ignored that. 'Just because your father is a killer doesn't mean that my Maker is one too.'

'Oh, don't start this crap again. What my dad does . . . that's totally different.'

'Why? Because we're monsters? Because we're not even human?'

'Listen, I don't want to have this argument with you. I understand why you want to defend him, but all I'm asking is that you consider it. I don't think that's un-reasonable.'

'Stop it.'

'What?' He sounded genuinely confused.

'Being so reasonable!' I couldn't argue with him, then.

'There's nothing wrong with wanting to think the best of people,' he said. 'It's a good character trait.'

'Then why do I feel like crap?'

'Maybe because it could get you killed?'

I shook my head. 'I just know I'm right on this.'

'Which part? The part where your bizarre optimism gets you killed?'

I sighed. 'No. About my Maker.'

'What's your reasoning? There's gotta be something concrete you can point to.'

'It wouldn't have been him who planted my address on Rick's body,' I insisted. 'And it wasn't my Maker who killed him in the first place. Or turned him into a revenant.'

As soon as I said it aloud, I realized that I *believed*. I really did. It didn't matter what the circumstances were, or could possibly be – Theo wouldn't lose control like that again. Not after what he'd done to me. He'd rather die.

Jace sighed. 'So, were you still coming over this evening? Why not come now?'

'OK, I'm on my way.'

'You'll need the address first.'

'Oh. Yeah, I knew that.' I blushed, for all the good it would do me.

'You're not exactly Nancy Drew, are you?' He sounded like he was smiling, but he gave me the address and directions before we hung up.

I stuck my phone in my jacket pocket, tapping my foot as I waited for the next set of lights to change. As if vampire-related murders and sort-of-zombies weren't enough, Sinéad had blindsided me by showing up at the apartment. It was the last thing I'd expected, and now I also had Caitlín to worry about. I called her again, but her phone rolled straight over to voice mail. I tried not to think about what that might mean.

I glanced over my shoulder, more out of instinct than anything else. You know that feeling? The one you get when you're sure someone is standing right behind you – or, at the very least, watching you? Yeah, I had that feeling right now. I scanned the area, my gaze drifting over pedestrians and traffic, trying to find whatever had made my flesh crawl in the increasing gloom of the afternoon.

There was nothing to see. Now, on top of everything else, I was imagining things.

Of course, then the rain started. I shivered and pulled up the collar of my leather jacket. One of the advantages of being a vampire was that I didn't really feel the cold. Although I still *noticed* things like heat and cold, extremes didn't bother me in the regular human way. Weather was just something that happened around me. But the rain was making my bones feel sort of damp.

I took a quick short cut over a nearby wall, landing softly on the sidewalk on the other side. A middle-aged man sheltering under a newspaper was walking past as I landed, and he caught my eye as he squinted through the drizzle. Instinctively, I gritted my teeth and shook soaking strands of hair out of my face. The guy did a double take and almost dropped his newspaper.

Oops, fang-alert. I lowered my head, quickened my pace and began running. Running to Jace.

Chapter Thirteen

'What a pleasure it is to see you again,' Jace said, all faux manners. 'Please, won't you come in?' He swept me an impressive bow and almost fell over.

'Have you been drinking?' I asked, wondering what else could've possible gotten into him.

'Only a little,' he said, waving a bottle of beer in my face.

Great, and it was still only the afternoon. I was visiting a drunk wannabe vampire hunter. My life was perfect.

Jace suddenly realized how soaked through I was. 'Hey, get over here – you're dripping all over Dad's rug.'

I couldn't resist an internal chuckle at that: big strong vampire hunter, scared of what Daddy might say if he wrecked the apartment while he was away.

Jace led me into a bathroom and handed me a huge navy blue towel. As I rubbed the soft material over my sopping hair and tried to squeeze out some of the water into the bathtub, I couldn't help noticing something different about him. I mean, about the way he was acting around me. Sure, he was drinking a beer, but I didn't really think the alcohol was affecting him as much as he pretended.

That annoying little voice that bugged me whenever I was feeling tired or depressed began to pipe up: *Look at you, thinking about Jace Murdoch again. You so have a crush on him.*

'Do not,' I growled.

Jace raised his eyebrows. 'What?'

'Nothing.' Blushing furiously, and then furious that I was blushing at all, I buried my head in the towel and ignored him.

Or at least, I tried to ignore him. It was pretty tough not to notice how good he looked in those black cargo pants and the casual sludgy green shirt that made his eyes look more hazel than brown. His arms were well-defined with muscle, and I could see his tattoos peeking out from beneath the arms of his shirt. A black Celtic band circled his right bicep and there was a phoenix inked with red accents on the outside of his left arm.

'What are you thinking about?' Jace asked.

'Why?'

'Because your eyes have gone bright silver.'

Crap. 'I can put my sunglasses on if it bothers you,' I said, aware that my voice sounded incredibly stiff.

He looked at me for a long moment. 'Don't be stupid,' was all he said.

I wanted to say: *Don't call me stupid, you don't know anything about me.* But I held it in, along with all the other things I wanted to say to people – my father, for example – who treated me as something *other* because I looked a little different or liked to dress in Goth-style clothes. Just because I'd had dreams – dreams that were now nothing more than ash, like the urns filled with vampire remains I knew Jace's father would have hidden in this apartment, just like he had before.

I handed back the towel. 'Thanks.'

'Sure.' Jace touched the sleeve of my shirt, as though touching me had suddenly become the most normal thing in the world. 'You should get changed out of those things. You really are soaked.'

I looked down at the floor, watching in quiet fascination as the puddle of water at my feet slowly extended outward. In the dim lighting and against the midnight blue tile, it looked like it could be blood flowing in an ever-widening pool of darkness. I thought about Erin and the dried blood in her hair, and about the blood surrounding Nurse Fox's body. I shivered and looked away, my eyes finding Jace's.

'Moth—' he began.

It was his using my name that did it. Not 'freak'. Not even 'Marie'. He had simply said 'Moth', the name I'd taken for myself and made my own – a shield against the human world that might harm me if I only let it in.

A tear ran down my cheek, totally taking me by surprise. I quickly wiped it away with the back of my hand. 'Shit.' Another treacherous tear leaked out. Jesus, it was so humiliating. I totally would've died if I wasn't already . . . you know . . . dead.

Jace watched me with a strange expression on his face. I half expected him to be embarrassed, unable to handle a sudden display of emotion. But instead, he had a sort of blank look, like an untouched canvas waiting to be filled. I tried to find pity in his eyes, but if it was there I certainly couldn't see it. There was just a weary acceptance of what was happening in front of him – he was right there with me, not turning away from my pain but simply acknowledging it.

He didn't try to touch me, just waited it out until my tears stopped. What was I even crying for? Relief that I hadn't found Caitlín in Erin's place? Worry about Theo, and what all of this meant? His task, and how Murdoch's death would affect Jace? There was so much happening, I was bound to crack eventually. I just hated that it had to happen here and now, in front of Jason Murdoch.

'Jace, I'm sorry, I couldn't help it.' *What was I even apologizing for?* 'I really am sorry—'

'It's OK,' he said. He held up a hand as though to stop another outpouring of apologies. 'Really. Forget it. Wait here – I'll get you a dry shirt.'

And that was that. He left the bathroom and returned seconds later with a long-sleeved baggy T-shirt. It was soft and worn at the seams, something that looked like it had seen a lot of wear. It was also black, and had a splashy crimson logo that read: *CREATURE OF THE NIGHT!*

Nice to know Van Helsing Junior had a sense of humor hidden underneath all that macho angst. This shirt must be merchandise from a cheesy creature flick I'd never even heard of. It came almost to my freaking knees. My jeans were damp, but there was no way I was taking *those* off.

I padded into the main room and tried not to think too much about my experience in a similar apartment with Jace, six months ago. This was different. *Jace* was somehow different. He wasn't going to drug me, chain me up with silver and try to end what was left of my life. I wondered if he was sorry for what he'd done back then. He seemed much nicer to me now, that's for sure. Maybe we were coming to some kind of . . . understanding.

His mouth quirked up in that rare half-smile I'd seen only a couple times before. 'I knew that was perfect for you.'

I grinned. Couldn't help myself, and anyway, I needed the release.

Jace gave me one of those strange looks, the ones I found impossible to decipher. 'I can see your fangs,' he said. But he said it in that singsong tone a kid might use to proclaim: 'I can see your panties.' Yeah, he was definitely drunk.

He busied himself closing the long floor-length drapes, the heavy-looking velvet making the large room seem cozier. He threw some cushions down on the floor and then gathered a pile of books from the table by one of the armchairs. 'You OK sitting down here?' He didn't wait for a reply and sat cross-legged on one of the cushions. He was graceful for such a tall guy, especially considering how much muscle he seemed to have gained.

Feeling faintly ridiculous in the oversized T-shirt, I curled up on the cushion furthest from him. My hair hadn't even *begun* to dry. It was a sodden mass on top of my head, doing that annoying thing it does, thanks to the crazy corkscrew curls that hadn't become any easier to tame since I'd died. Who knew that being a vampire still involved hair disasters?

'So, what are we dealing with here?' I asked. 'You said you had answers.'

Maybe if I pretended that I hadn't just had a minor breakdown in the bathroom, we could forget it ever happened.

He pulled an ancient-looking book onto his lap. It was bound in cracked brown leather and the pages were gilt-edged with crumbling gold. 'This is the book my father spent most time with. He'd start here, at least, any time he had the trail of something unusual.'

I tried to read the name of the book, but he'd already flipped it open. I sat back and pulled my legs up to my chin, pulling the shirt down over my knees. 'What about the internet? Had your dad heard of that, by any chance?'

Jace glanced up from the yellowing pages. 'Stop talking about him in the past tense. He's coming back, OK?' He took a deep breath and gazed back down at the book. 'And yes, of course he'd heard of the internet. I even did most of our research online, but you have to wade through a ton of bullshit just to find one useful piece of information.'

'And what's so special about these books?' I waved at the pile resting by his right knee.

'I don't know where Dad got them from,' Jace said, 'but they're old. Really old. And he always seemed to find *something* that he needed in them.'

'OK then, amaze me,' I said. 'What have you found out about these revenants so far?'

Jace raised an eyebrow in that super-cool way few guys could master. 'Revenant?'

'Oh, that's what my Maker said it might be. He said that there's no such thing as zombies – at least, not so far as vamps are concerned. Maybe in places like Africa. Or in the movies. Revenants are like . . . vampires gone wrong. We call them "Unmade", apparently.'

Jace frowned. 'You didn't say anything about finding me there, did you?'

'Of course not,' I snapped, immediately regretting how defensive I sounded. 'He'd only want to kill you.'

'Why? Because I'm Thomas Murdoch's son?'

Anger flooded my chest and I swallowed hard against the sudden heat. 'No, you moron, because of what you did to me the first time we met.'

I held out both my arms until he looked at them, watching him with a tangled knot of emotions in my stomach. The scars had faded significantly, but even Theo wasn't sure whether they would disappear entirely. As long as nobody staked me, I was probably going to be around for a long time – maybe I'd find out if vampires really *could* heal from severe silver burns.

His cheeks flushed. 'Did I do that to you?'

I nodded slowly. 'Unless I'm a vampire who self-harms with silver.'

At least he seemed genuinely . . . *something* about it. I wasn't sure quite what. I could smell anger for sure, but other than that the young hunter was sending out all sorts of conflicting messages. But then, that seemed to sum him up most of the freaking time.

Jace reached out toward me, but pulled back when

the lamp over his shoulder flashed on a ring he was wearing. The silver ring. It was a heavy Celtic band, similar to one of his tats. I watched his throat move as he swallowed, and tried not to wonder what it would feel like to press my face against his carotid artery and listen to the blood pulsing through it. *Ew, why did I have to be so gross?*

'Shit,' he said. He tugged the ring off his pinky and flung it away like it might burn him. As though it was *him* who was the vampire and not me.

I watched all of this in silence, something older and wiser in me knowing when to keep my big mouth shut. Although I still couldn't help gasping when he grabbed my left wrist in his warm right hand and tugged me toward him. We were just inches apart, my legs still curled beneath me as I knelt in front of where he sat coiled with a dark sort of energy I didn't understand.

OK, I'm not dumb. Maybe I understood what was going on here, but that didn't mean it made *sense*.

Jace ran his fingers over my scars, head bowed so that all I could see was the top of his blond spikes. I didn't know what I was supposed to do. Should I stop him? Pull my arms out of reach? Say something? My arms tingled wherever his flesh touched mine and I tried not to gaze at his slightly too thin lips.

And then his eyes met mine and there wasn't any need for anything as lame as words. His eyes told me

169

everything I needed to know about his regret. The expression on his face dared me to challenge him, and for a moment I was tempted to do exactly that. But the moment passed and I moved back to my own pile of cushions, rubbing my arms as though I was cold and wondering what I was even doing here.

Jace ran a nervous hand through his hair, making it stand up more than ever. 'Let's get back to the research. That's what you came here for.'

I bit my lip, then realized I was giving him another good look at my fangs. I looked away.

'Moth?' he said.

'Sure, research is good.' *Safe*. 'That was getting way too touchy-feely for my liking.'

He scowled at me and carried on talking. 'What was it you were telling me about – the "Unmade"? I've never seen that term in any of these books.'

It was my turn to raise my eyebrows. 'I thought these books always held the answer.' I pushed wild strands of hair out of my eyes. 'You spent all this time telling me how great they are, and how your dad always finds the right information at the right time. But now you're pretty much saying: *Dude, I got nuthin'*.'

Jace half smiled and went back to scanning pages. If I didn't know any better, I would say his expression looked sort of indulgent. It reminded me of the way Theo regarded me when he was in one of his better moods.

I grabbed one of the smaller books and read the title stamped on the cover in intricate gold lettering: '*How the Undead Almost Ruled the World.*' I shook my head. What was this crap?

Jace made a triumphant sound and thrust the heavy book into my hands. 'Oh ye of little faith. Told you so.'

A line-drawing of an ugly creature took up most of the page he was pointing at. The pen strokes were crude, a simple black ink sketch, but the revenant still seemed to come alive on the page. Which was ironic, I thought, considering how truly dead it was.

This picture certainly had the eyes right; they were blank and milk-white, the iris and pupil hidden behind an opaque film. How could such a two-dimensional drawing look so realistic? I shivered and forced myself to stop staring at it. It seemed almost as if somebody had sketched it while actually looking at the subject – which was obviously crazy, because if anyone tried to do that they'd end up with their arms ripped out of their sockets. Like poor Nurse Fox.

Underneath the drawing was a dense paragraph of text in a spidery, hard-to-read font. I squinted at the page and slowly read the words: *The Revenant is an empty shell of humanity, created by the bite of an over-zealous Vampyr.* I looked at Jace. 'What does that even mean? *Over-zealous?*' I had a horrible feeling that it was pretty obvious, but was hoping to hear his take on it before I completely freaked out.

Jace stabbed his finger at the book. 'What do you *think* it means? It must be when a vampire feeds too much; maybe it takes the victim—'

'Oh,' I cut in. 'Right, it says here in the book: *For when the Vampyr feeds until the heart stops beating and all signs of life have faded from the human eye, then the Unmade will rise.*' I shoved the book back into Jace's hands. 'Great. So, is this something that happens all the time? Like when *vampyrs* feed from someone for too long?'

I didn't want to touch the stupid book anymore; it weirded me out that it seemed to know more about what I'd become than I did. And I sure could've done with some of Murdoch's books when I'd first woken after Theo turned me. Everything I'd found out by myself seemed tame, controlled . . . incomplete.

I thought about it for a moment. 'Surely if it was that easy to create revenants by accident, there'd be hundreds or *thousands* of them wandering around in search of *braaains.*'

Jace rolled his eyes. 'No – listen to this: *The Vampyr must be young, having walked the Earth for less than two centuries. It feeds on blood past the point of possible return, so that the victim travels* beyond death. *Any attempt to make a new Vampyr will end in failure,*

Unmaking the human and leaving a Revenant in its place.'

He looked more animated than I could remember seeing him. Apart from whenever he'd been trying to kill me. 'So these revenants are made by vamps who try to turn a human, only they're too inexperienced and it goes wrong. That's where your Maker got the term "Unmade" from.'

Something in his tone irritated me. 'You don't even know what you're talking about; stop making out you're this big authority on the undead. You haven't got a clue, Jace.'

His eyebrows shot up. 'I'm not trying to pretend anything. And just because you've been a vamp for all of . . . what? A year? . . . that doesn't make you an expert either. And you certainly don't know anything about the *Unmade*. Or revenants, or whatever they're called.'

I frowned, trying to stay open-minded despite the doubts that were crowding me. 'I knew more than you did, back at the hospital, while I was busy saving our lives. It's thanks to me we're even having this conversation.'

'If you say so,' he muttered, as he continued flipping through the book.

'Seriously, though. I don't think it can be that simple. I wouldn't be able to turn you into a vampire – Unmade or otherwise – if I bit you. And I'm less than two hundred years old.'

His lips quirked into a smile that was more of a challenge. 'I guess we'll never find out, because you're never going to bite me.'

I rolled my eyes. 'I wasn't thinking of testing my oh-so-scientific theory.'

'Good, because I'm sort of getting used to you. It'd be a shame to have to stake you when things are going so well, right?'

'You could try,' I muttered.

Jace put the book aside and watched me, his gaze steady. 'Don't you ever wonder about it, though?'

'About what?'

'About how powerful vampires are. The things you could do if you really cut loose.'

'I wonder about a lot of things,' I said. 'But mostly I just wonder how I'm going to get through the next day, and then the one after that.'

He continued as though I hadn't spoken. 'You're stronger than humans. What's to stop you from rising up and attacking us? Or even just going on a crime spree?'

I shook my head. 'A vampire Bonnie and Clyde, you mean? That's ridiculous.'

'Why? Vampires are predators, pure and simple. What's to stop them taking whatever they want?'

'Humanity,' I said. 'You want to forget that part, I know. But it's way too convenient. Vampires aren't born, they're made. *I* was made. I used to be human – just a year ago, I was as human as you. Don't you think I remember what that was like? Don't you think I still feel human?'

'But you're not. Human, I mean. Not entirely.'

'Listen,' I said, getting annoyed. 'If vampires choose to live in the human world, that means they should live by human laws. That's the rule.'

He raised his eyebrows. 'There are rules?'

I'd said too much. Me and my big mouth. Oh, well. Why stop now? 'If you're part of a Family, yes.'

'Which you are? Part of a Family, I mean.'

'Yes,' I muttered. 'Can we change the subject?'

'Fine, how about *this* subject?' He shifted position, leaning forward almost eagerly. 'Could your Maker have done something like this? Created revenants, I mean. Now that we know a little more about it, could he be the one who *Un*made Rick?'

'I don't know,' I lied, examining the deep red satin cushion that Jace was sitting on. It was easier than looking at him.

He fixed me with those intense brown eyes. 'Really? After what you told me you scented on Erin's body?'

I wished I'd kept my big mouth shut about that now. But I'd been scared and alone; confused. 'I just don't want to talk about it with you right now.' I didn't really want to *think* about it.

'What are you protecting him for? Do you still have a

thing for him?' His voice was mocking, but there was something else in his voice. An edge that I tried to ignore. 'Has he bitten you lately?'

'No, he hasn't bitten me since he turned me. *Actually.*' I licked my lips. 'I've bitten him . . .' My voice trailed off as I felt my cheeks burn. What did I have to tell him *that* for?

'Well, then.' He looked angry, and I wasn't entirely sure I liked this sudden change in his attitude toward me.

We sat in silence for what felt like hours.

'Jace?' My voice was small in the sudden quiet of the room. 'How did you learn about vampires, and all of this stuff? I mean, obviously from your dad. But did he wait to tell you the truth until you were a certain age or something?'

'I've always known about the monsters.' He winced. 'Sorry. You know what I mean.'

I shrugged, looked down. It pissed me off, hearing him talk like that, but I still wanted to hear what he had to say.

'My family are a family of hunters. It's not just my dad.'

I waited for him to go on.

'There's an uncle and a couple of cousins. My grandfather. And my mom. She used to hunt too.'

'Your *mom*?'

'Sure. It's not just a male occupation, you know.'

'I'm just surprised,' I said. 'I don't even know why.'

'She died.' His voice was quiet and I remembered the glimpse I'd had inside his head. I wanted him to say more, but at the same time I suddenly felt afraid. This was too much, too soon. The intensity made the air in the room feel like static electricity.

'Mine too,' I replied.

We stared at each other for a moment that stretched out and out . . . Until Jace looked down and began sorting books into piles again.

The moment, as moments like that have a habit of doing, passed.

I jumped to my feet, unable to sit still any longer. 'My shirt must be dry by now.'

Jace looked up at me with lazy eyes. 'You can just have that one.'

The desire to keep his T-shirt was so visceral that for a moment I was overwhelmed. I stomped down on it as hard as I could. 'No, it's cool. Thanks, though.'

I fled to the bathroom to see if my clothes were dry. Sadly, my shirt and sweater were still damp, but at least my trusty leather jacket was dry. As I finished pulling the sweater back over my head, a knock at the bathroom door made me jump. Then I got distracted by how freaking uncomfortable I felt. Was it my imagination, or had the stupid thing shrunk already?

Another knock at the door made me squeal. *Ugh*. I

was turning into such a *girl*. 'What?' I shouted.

'Can I come in?' Jace's voice was muffled through the door, but I could hear the note of uncertainty running through it just fine. I couldn't get used to this all-new 'nicer' version of the young hunter.

'Sure.' I opened the door and we stood looking at each other for an uncomfortable few seconds.

Jace fixed me with a serious expression. 'So call me if you find out anything, OK? Or if something else happens.'

'Right.' Of course, what else did I think he wanted to talk to me about? It was all business, all the time, with Jace. But he was still giving me that weird look.

'I'll let you out when you're ready,' he said, turning quickly and leaving the room.

I let out the breath I hadn't even realized I'd been holding. What was *that* all about? I suddenly wished that Caitlín was here, right now. This is just the sort of thing she'd love to hear about.

My little sister was out there somewhere, and the urge to find her and see that she was safe hit me in the stomach like a punch. The primeval sensation even overcame my creeping doubts about Theo; she was my family, after all. My *blood* family. (That irony made me smile.)

Now that I had more information about what might have happened to Rick – and what I feared might yet happen to Erin – I felt more confident about confronting

Theo. OK, maybe just a tiny bit more confident. I checked the time on my phone and figured that Theo would be long awake now. Perhaps he'd be at Subterranean.

But first, before *anything* else, I wanted to spend some time searching for Caitlín before it got too late. I looked down at my damp clothes. I really need to get home and change.

There was a bang on the door and I almost leaped out of my skin.

'Moth, what's taking so long?'

'Sorry,' I muttered. 'Coming.'

I joined Jace in the narrow hallway and watched him as he put one hand on the apartment door handle, ready to let me out. He turned to me, obviously preparing for another one of his oh-so-eloquent speeches.

That was when I heard . . . something.

'Wait.' I put my hand over his, trying not to think about how warm his flesh was. I could feel every scar across his knuckles.

'What?'

'Someone's coming,' I said.

Jace frowned. 'You're sure?'

I pointed at one of my ears. 'Hello? Vampire hearing.'

And then there was no doubt that someone was very definitely coming, because footsteps marched clearly up to the door. Whoever it was, he – or she – wasn't trying to make a secret of their approach.

Jace slipped into the living room and returned with a gun. I raised my eyebrows at it and he shrugged. He nodded at me to go back inside the bathroom.

Screw that. I shook my head and took up a position on the other side of the door from him. It felt unbelievably weird to be 'working' with Jace again. I wondered if our fragile connection could last.

But all these thoughts disappeared when the door burst open with a *crack*, as someone kicked it so hard that the lock and catch flew off and screws showered the air like dangerous confetti.

I ducked a piece of shrapnel, and when I lifted my head I saw Jace facing off with a mountain of a man holding a crossbow cradled lovingly in his arms.

'Hello, son,' the man said. 'I see you've been busy while I was away.'

Shit. Like father, like freaking son.

Chapter Fourteen

Thomas Murdoch was tall, even taller than Jace. He must've been at least six-foot-three, maybe six-four. He was wearing a long duster that made him look like an ageing cowboy. His hair was a slightly darker blond than his son's and it was cut short – military short – so I could almost see the pale flesh of his scalp. Silver was generously scattered throughout the golden bristle. He can't have been all that old, but he looked totally haggard to me.

Vampire hunting can't have very good health benefits.

We stood in front of him like two kids caught out after curfew. Something about the man's dark eyes reminded me of Theo when he was controlling his anger, but the rest of him was all Jace – Jace in thirty years from now, after a lifetime of violence.

Jace's father was looking at me like I was something nasty on the bottom of one of his huge army boots. And all I could think was, *He's back. Now Theo can kill him – and I'll be safe . . . We both will be.*

'Dammit, son. You're not *banging* her, are you?' Murdoch shuddered and his mouth pulled down into a grimace. 'It's as bad as . . . necrophilia.'

Jace's face tightened with something like anger, only much, much worse. It was like watching storm clouds gather in his eyes until they turned black with murderous rage. If I had been in the position to applaud, I would've done. He didn't say anything, but he was definitely poised for action – and he was still holding the gun.

Murdoch Senior continued to glare at me. 'I should kill you right now.'

'You could try,' I growled, showing him my fangs. They'd fully extended and my gums ached.

'Dad, let her go,' Jace said. 'Just . . . let her go.'

'Don't defend it,' his father snapped. 'What do you think you're doing?'

'Where have you been, Dad? It's been six *weeks*.' Jace's voice was stretched tight. He sounded like he was waiting to explode.

'On a job, where the hell do you think?' Murdoch's body language was relaxed, as though it was absolutely fine that he'd upped and left his son without a word of explanation. 'You're not a child anymore. I thought you told me you could take care of yourself.'

'Of course I can take care of myself. I just didn't expect you to disappear without even leaving a message to let me know you were OK. What am I supposed to think, knowing the kind of life you lead?'

Murdoch waved his hand dismissively. 'We don't have time for this, Jace. I was on a job – deep cover. I couldn't talk to you about it.'

'You didn't even leave me a sign! Just something to let me know you were still alive.'

'Jason, since when have you ever known the monsters to get the better of me? What happened to your faith?' The hunter shook his head, as though genuinely disappointed.

Jace flushed. 'I was worried about you, Dad. Don't you get that?'

'Worrying is for the weak,' Murdoch said darkly. 'I taught you better than this.'

'So you can't tell me *anything*?'

Murdoch Senior turned his attention back to me. 'I sure as shit don't want this conversation in front of that.'

Jace scowled. 'Don't talk about her like that.'

'You'd better not be going soft on me, kid. Especially not when it comes to the vamps.'

I took a step back from the hatred in the man's eyes.

I growled, baring my fangs. Jace was watching me with something like panic in his eyes.

Murdoch Senior grinned. 'Or maybe she should stick around – find out why her boss hasn't managed to stop me from taking down more of his gang than any other hunter.'

He grabbed me with his free hand, so fast I gasped with shock and found myself lifted off the floor. OK, what was it about tall guys always doing that to me? Pick on the small girl, why don't you . . .

He slammed me against the wall, pinning me like a butterfly. Or a moth.

I saw the truth in his eyes: he was going to kill me.

'You're a pathetic excuse for a monster, girlie,' he hissed, pushing up close and getting right in my face.

Girlie? Now I was really pissed.

'You're monster enough for both of us, Murdoch, so I guess that's cool.' I swung my legs out and wrapped them around his waist, taking him by surprise. His grip relaxed – only slightly, but it was enough.

Clinging around his torso, I squeezed his wrists until I felt bones grate together. He cried out in pain and released me, but I was still attached to his waist and he didn't seem to know what to do with me. Which suited me fine. I head-butted him so hard that I saw stars and he howled with rage – and what was hopefully a good amount of pain. The agony shooting through my own skull was almost worth it.

Jace was standing by the shattered door, keeping watch in case any neighbors heard the ruckus we were making. The last thing any of us needed was the cops to get involved. He pointed his gun in our direction but, apart from that, didn't seem to know what to do with us.

I used Murdoch's tall body as a living climbing-frame, pulling myself up by his shoulders, then up once more until I was standing *on* his shoulders. I made sure to snatch his crossbow on my way up and he grabbed my ankles, trying to dislodge me.

'Get the hell off me, you freak of nature!'

I leaped, ninja-style (or so I liked to think), and landed right by the window. My feet and knees were killing me from the impact, but nobody needed to know about that.

I waved. 'I'd love to stay and chat, but I really should get going.'

Murdoch roared something surprisingly creative and vaulted over the couch. For a big guy he was fast.

But I was faster.

'Dad, just let her go!' Jace yelled, finally opening his big dumb mouth.

Fat lot of good he was doing. Not that I could really blame him. This was his father. I understood the pull of family – in more ways than one.

'Oh, don't worry on my account,' I said breezily, using the butt of Murdoch Senior's crossbow to smash the lock off the window. He'd surely have a warding charm on it to keep the undead out – that kind of protective magic existed if you knew where to find it – but would it work both ways? What about a vampire already *inside* the apartment who was trying to escape? It looked like we were all about to find out. I just hoped that, if I was wrong, I didn't end up fried like an *actual* moth that flies too close to the flame.

I'd just gotten the window open when the man himself grabbed a handful of my hair and pulled me back. Kyle had warned me about how my hair could be used against me in hand-to-hand combat. I'd sort of blown him off, figuring that I wouldn't really get into many fights – especially considering how good at running I am. Looks like Kyle was right about something, after all.

'Dad, stop!'

Oh goodie, there was Jace 'talking' to my rescue again. Because *coming* to my rescue was clearly way too hard for him.

My neck snapped back as Murdoch dragged me away from the window and I dropped the crossbow. Luckily, it didn't go off. I let all my weight go, sank to the floor and let him think he'd beaten me, then twisted and kicked him in the shin as hard as I could while he was off balance. It felt like a huge chunk of my hair had been ripped out at the roots. Do you know how much that hurts?

Let me take a moment to tell you something. You're probably thinking: Moth's a vampire. She's super-strong and super-fast, and she should be able to beat a human (even a big guy like Murdoch) with one hand tied behind her back. But it's not that simple. Having special abilities doesn't make you an automatic expert in using them. I was a new vampire with *new* abilities. I was still getting used to being in a body that was mine . . . and yet not mine. Sometimes I'd do something as simple as opening a bottle of Coke and I'd break the whole top off, shattering the glass rather than just twisting off the cap. I couldn't always control things like strength and speed. I mean, I'm getting better at it, but I still surprise myself.

So that's why an incredibly well-trained, battle-scarred man like Papa Murdoch can hurt me. Or, at the very least, stop me from hurting *him* too bad. Give me a few more years, I could probably wipe the floor with him. With *both* hands tied behind my back. But that time hadn't come quite yet. And I certainly couldn't kill him. That was meant to be *Theo's* task. I couldn't do it for him, even if I was able to . . .

Jace ran toward us, finally acting against his father and kicking the crossbow out of *Daddy's* hands as he tried to grab it off the floor.

My, how impressive, I thought groggily. I shook my

head, tried to get to my feet, but everything was spinning. I could feel blood running down my face where the hunter had smacked me into the broken window. I'd heal, so I tried not to worry. It wasn't like I could look in a mirror to see how bad the damage was. I wiped blood from my face and used the window ledge to pull myself to my feet. I contemplated the open window, then glanced back at Jace.

The Murdochs were having a family disagreement. Murdoch Senior had snatched the gun off his son and now whacked him across the face with the butt of it. Jace's face was stricken, and I didn't think that expression had anything to do with the *physical* pain of being pistol-whipped. He looked . . . shattered. Blood was running from a badly split lip and he stared at his father with a mixture of shock and hatred.

'Screw you.' I was glad to see Jace standing up to his asshole of a dad. The effect was slightly ruined by the fact that his voice was kind of muffled from all the blood in his mouth.

I hesitated by the window as they faced off. I should leave them to it, but the reason this was happening was me. It was my fault Jace was taking a beating from his old man – I should stay, just in case he needed me. I shook my head slightly, almost smiling. Oh, how times change.

Also, it was vaguely entertaining – in a car-crash sort

of way – listening to Murdoch Senior talk about me like I wasn't standing right there.

'Jason, you're defending one of *them*. It's a monster and you're hanging out with it like it's the most normal thing in the world. Maybe next week you'll be going on dates and buying it ice cream.'

Hmm . . . I like ice cream. That didn't sound so bad to me, although the mention of 'dates' freaked me out just a bit. Or maybe a lot.

Jace used the bottom of his T-shirt to staunch the steady flow of blood from his lip. Maybe this would help change his mind about going into the family business.

Murdoch Senior glanced at me. 'Go on, get out before I change my mind.'

I tried to catch Jace's eye, but he was too busy staring at his father with an unreadable expression on his pale face.

'I won't tell you again, Dead Girl. Get out.'

Fine. I had the information that I needed, and now all I wanted to do was go looking for my sister. I could leave the boys to play happy families.

As I slipped out of the window – and yes, I was right, the warding charm clearly only worked one way – I couldn't help feeling guilty for leaving Jace behind. His father was more of a monster than the vampires would ever be. I needed to tell Theo that Murdoch was back.

I ignored the needle of guilt that told me I was handing Jace's father over to my Maker – to the vampires. But even if we were working together all of a sudden, that didn't mean Murdoch Senior got a free pass. He had to die. My life *depended* on it.

If Theo didn't kill Jace's dad, then he might just have to kill *me* . . .

Chapter Fifteen

The minute I got home all thoughts of the Murdochs, revenants and even Theo slid away. Caitlín was waiting in the hallway outside the apartment. A mixture of feelings washed over me: love, relief, anger . . . I couldn't put my finger on any one of them, simply noticing the confused tangle of emotions and trying to focus on the most important fact: *Caitlín was OK. She was here.*

My younger sister was sitting like a tired sentinel on the worn carpet opposite the apartment door. Her head rested on her knees, long red hair a flame flowing down her legs. I often wondered why it was that both Sinéad and Caitlín had inherited Dad's coloring, while I was the only one who had followed our mother. We all had the O'Neal pale skin but mine had always been more smooth and creamy, lacking the freckles that plagued my sisters every summer. Sometimes it struck me that I'd never seen a vampire with freckles, but I suppose that made sense – especially the older and more sun-sensitive they got.

Caitlín raised her head. 'Sis!'

I pushed aside all thoughts of Theo and dead kids; even the possibility of my own death if my Maker didn't succeed in his task.

'Oh my God! Cait, what are you *doing* here? Why didn't you call?'

She shrugged as she stood and pulled her curls back with both hands. She had a green scrunchy in her hand that matched her eyes, and quickly twiddled it into her hair. 'I did call. You never answer your phone.'

'Oh.' I felt in my pockets – all of them. 'My cell phone's gone.' Had I dropped it at Jace's? Left it in the bathroom? I couldn't remember.

'I've been waiting here for ages, Marie,' she said. Just hearing her voice pushed away all concerns about my stupid phone. Who cared about that? My little sister was OK! She was *here*.

Caitlín was almost as petite as me, standing only an inch taller. We were both small-boned, but that's where the similarities ended. The hair was the obvious difference, although the way we dressed was another. Cait was all about the colors; today her bright pink sneakers clashed wildly with her hair, and the emerald-green

T-shirt with multi-colored miniature fairies on it was classic Caitlín.

She grabbed me in a hug and held on like she never wanted to let go. I felt my frozen heart expand in my chest. God, I loved my sister so much it hurt. I held on tight, but not too tight for fear of crushing her shoulders. Dropping my head to Caitlín's shoulder I took a deep breath and let her scent wash over me, grounding me. Reassuring me that she really was OK.

'Hey,' she said, pulling away. 'You're sort of damp, dude. What happened?'

'Got caught in the rain, but forget that. What' – here I fixed my sister with a mock-serious look – 'are you even doing here?'

'Oh, well that's just lovely. Thanks, sis, it's good to see you too.'

I rolled my eyes. 'Shut up. Of course I'm happy to see you – I was going crazy with worry when Sinéad turned up here earlier today telling me you'd gone missing.'

'Sinéad came *here*?' Caitlín's pretty face flushed. 'God, she's such a dick.'

'Hey, mind your language.' It was a joke between us, me telling her off for cursing. I loved how easily we slipped into the familiar banter. It felt almost as good as sliding on a favorite pair of comfortable slippers and putting your feet up. By a warm fire. In winter.

Caitlín scowled, but my eyes must have been shining

with the cheeky humor I loved. Only she probably couldn't tell because of the contacts. She said, 'You can talk. Every other word out of your mouth is "freakin' this" and "freakin' that".'

I shrugged. 'That's not even real cursing. I'm a good Catholic girl.'

'Riiight.' Caitlín stretched out the word far longer than necessary, waggling her eyebrows at the same time.

Laughing, I unlocked the apartment door. I felt light-headed with relief. 'So, are you coming in or did you want to camp out in my hallway for the rest of the night?'

I still had the apartment to myself, since Holly would have gone straight from Subterranean to her shift at the courier company. God only knew what she'd say if she knew I had yet another member of my human family at the apartment. I was grateful for the reprieve. For the space and time with my little sister.

After I'd taken a deep breath and called Sinéad from the landline to let her know Caitlín was safe, we curled up in the living room, one at either end of the couch.

I also made a quiet call to Theo, to let him know I'd spotted Thomas Murdoch. Because my luck is what it is, I got Kyle instead. He tried to cover his surprise, but I could tell he wondered how I'd gotten the information about Murdoch. Theo had already left to go hunting, but his Enforcer promised to track him down and pass on the message. He told me I had done well. I wished Theo had a cell phone, but that was one modern gadget he refused to carry.

I tucked my feet under me and pressed my cheek against the purple velvet cushion behind me. I wrapped my hands more tightly around the mug of hot chocolate, irritated that the color reminded me of Jace's eyes. Jesus, I was turning into a total sap. Thinking about his eyes reminded me that he was going to look totally worse for wear tomorrow, but I pushed my sympathy to one side.

Caitlín was in the middle of a tirade against Sinéad. 'And then she told me that I was in danger of turning into a dropout like . . .' Her voice trailed off and she glanced guiltily at me. 'Well, like you.'

'What a surprise,' I said dryly. Like I cared what my uptight older sister thought of me. It wasn't as though I was getting new information.

Caitlín squirmed against her own pile of cushions. 'Yeah, sorry sis.'

I couldn't resist smiling. 'No worries. I'm not exactly surprised.'

'So?' Caitlín said.

'What?'

'So what did Sinéad say when you called?'

'I already told you; you just weren't listening.' I rolled my eyes. 'She was relieved. Honestly, Cait, she was practically crying.' She rolled her eyes but I ignored her.

'Sinéad wanted to pick you up right now, but I convinced her that we'd get you home in the morning. She wants you on the first train we can manage tomorrow.'

Caitlín leaned forward. 'I'd far rather live here, in the city.' The words came out in a rush and she flushed as she said them.

OK, this was new. I frowned. 'Really? Since when?'

'Hello? Since forever. I hate being stuck with Dad. Martha Stewart I can almost put up with, but him? He's really starting to bug me.'

'Bug you, how?' Much as it worried me to think of my little sister wanting to run away to live in the big city, I didn't want her to be unhappy.

She shrugged. 'The usual. You know . . .' She paused and we shared a moment of empathy. Yeah, I really *did* know. Dad could drink with the best of them.

'But, Caitlín . . . what about school?'

'What about it? It's the same stupid city. I can commute. I could even transfer. I've only just started Junior year anyway, so maybe it would work out.'

'But what would you do here?' I tucked my chin against my knees.

Caitlín was absent-mindedly picking at her already chipped nail polish. 'I could get a part-time job, stay with you, pay my way . . .'

I felt myself deflate. 'Oh, Cait. You really wouldn't want to do that.'

'Why not?' She lifted her chin in a gesture that was all too familiar. With a stab of sadness, I pictured Mom doing the exact same thing – the stubborn set of her jaw when she was pissed about something.

'What about Oscar?' I tried appealing to her love for the family dog, knowing I was probably fighting a losing battle. Oscar (named for Oscar Wilde) was riddled with arthritis and on his last legs. Despite her fondness for him, my sister was a realist. 'Cait, you're better off with Dad and Sinéad.' I hated saying it, but it was true. How could my sister live with me? It was impossible. Even if Caitlín knew and accepted all there was to know and accept about my life – the monster hiding in the shadows, and the unspoken truths between all the lies – it just wasn't *practical*. A human teenager living with vampires? No way. And where would we live? Not with Holly, that's for sure.

'It's not just that,' she confessed, looking away.

'OK.' Why did I get the impression that I wasn't going to like this?

'I'm worried about you. You never come to visit and I don't understand why. Something's changed – and I'm not just talking about Mom. I mean, something else.'

I fiddled with my mug, trying to think of what I could say. I hated lying to Caitlín, I really did. But what if I contemplated, even for a moment, telling her the truth? What would it mean?

'See?' Caitlín said. Her tone was accusing. 'You're thinking up more lies to tell me.'

'Cait! I . . . I'm sorry. There are things I just can't talk about.' I knew how lame it sounded as soon as the words left my mouth.

She fixed me with that familiar stubborn expression. 'I followed you today, you know.'

I froze. 'What?'

'Yeah,' she said, warming to her subject. 'Followed you across Boston Common and watched you climb a wall like you're Spider-Girl or something.'

I swallowed, trying to come up with an excuse that would make sense. Failing miserably. I *knew* someone had been following me! Now I sincerely wished I'd taken the time to investigate.

But it was too late now.

'Are you, like, some kind of superhero?' Caitlín had the good grace to blush. It sounded ridiculous, sure, but the truth was actually even stranger. *My* truth was a hell of a lot more scary, and I wondered if she was ready for it.

I rubbed my face, trying to scrub away the sadness and regret. I sat up straight, fixing my sister with the most serious look I could. I was exhausted – worried about all the crap going on right now – but this was my sister. The only human being I loved this deeply. I had to make Caitlín understand that her place wasn't here in the city; at least, not with me. It would be like introducing a rare and delicate flower into a bed of weeds, and then waiting for it to choke.

Now, Caitlín was giving me a strange look. 'What's wrong with your eye?'

My stomach clenched. 'What do you mean?'

She leaned forward and reached out a tentative hand. 'Your left eye, it looks funny.' She squinted. 'Hey, are you wearing contacts?'

Oh. Crap. I stood up, far too quickly, and began moving in the direction of the bathroom. 'Um . . . yeah. I told you I was getting old. I've got glasses but hate wearing them.' *Liar, liar.*

But Caitlín wasn't my sister for nothing. When she got hold of something that she found interesting, she was implacable. I suddenly flashed on an image of her asking Mom questions about her cancer. It had taken all my strength not to scream at fourteen-year-old Caitlín to just *leave Mom alone. Can't you see what you're putting her through?* But our mother had patiently answered all of her youngest daughter's questions with her usual grace.

Unfortunately for me, Caitlín had that look in her eye now; the fierce expression of a cat watching an injured bird trying to escape, while preparing to go in for the kill. 'Let me see,' she said, touching my arm and trying to look past the long strands of curly black hair that were hiding my eyes.

I wanted to push Caitlín away; it would be easy. So easy to twist out of her grip and escape to the bathroom, the only room with a lock on the door. Fix the contact lens, go back out and come up with some bullshit that might placate my sister.

I felt my whole body sag. No amount of lying would convince Caitlín that there wasn't something bizarre happening.

'Holy crap, you've got silver eyes!' Caitlín yelled. She took a step forward and stared. Her eyes were round with . . . *shock? Disgust?* I couldn't tell for certain. All I knew was that I felt ridiculously weak, as though I might faint at any moment.

'Wait, let me explain—'

'You're not getting out of this, Marie. No way. I saw what I saw earlier, and now this. I've had some crazy suspicions about you for way longer than you probably realize.'

I tried to turn away from her. Tried to fix the stupid contact lenses.

'Dude, you look so *beautiful.*'

'It's not what you— Wait. What did you say?'

Caitlín's whole face was alight. 'I said, you look amazing. OK, sort of weird but totally stunning. Beautiful.'

I swallowed. This was actually going a lot better than I'd expected. I didn't know what to say so I stood there, nervously squeezing the ruined lens between the fingers of my right hand.

'Marie . . .' Caitlín's voice sounded more grown up. 'Don't tell me this is just a trick of the light, or you're wearing contacts underneath your contacts.' Her pale face was composed and strangely dignified.

I knew my eyes were shimmering wildly; it really was difficult to hide my emotions with eyes this expressive. 'Caitlín, there's so much you don't know about me. And it's not what you think. It's not something . . . good.' I bowed my head. 'I'm not a superhero.'

'I don't care. You can tell me *anything*.'

'I'm not even sure where to start,' I said.

'Start at the beginning,' Caitlín replied, a gentle smile on her face. 'Isn't that usually the best place?'

The beginning . . .

He tells me everything I thought I'd never hear.

Mom is gone and I hurt in ways I never even knew were possible. I am eighteen years old. For real: eighteen. I've barely started my first semester at college after Mom died. I don't know if I even care about school anymore, but it gives me something to focus on. And I do care about art. I care about drawing comic books. That's what I tell myself.

Then I see Theo. He is talking to a group of Goth kids and they are all completely in love with him. The girls and the boys – though he seems more interested in the girls. OK, if I'm being honest, he is mostly interested in me.

I can't figure it out. Me. Quiet little Marie, who still hasn't come out from my older sister's shadow; who is still afraid of her father's temper.

I am drawn to him like . . . well, like a moth to a flame.

I think he is lonely . . . Theo singles me out. Something about my blood sings to him, he tells me. I can't decide if this is weird or romantic. Weirdly romantic? He calls me m'anamchara *because he knows I'll understand it, coming from good old-fashioned Irish stock.* My soulmate. *Theo always knows exactly what to say.*

I want him so much. He is so beautiful. I love how his black hair shines under the moon when we sit in 'our place' on some benches by the Charles River. I dangle my legs over the edge while he laughs at me. I love the curve of his lips, just a little too full to be as masculine as his biker clothes would have you believe. His nose is just like a hawk's, but so noble; I love to trace the curve with my finger and watch as he smiles with those white, white teeth.

Oh, and his eyes . . . when we are with the others they are gray, cool stone after rain. But when we are together they shine as silver as the stars. I think I am imagining things because I am so in love with him.

I know he isn't human, even though I have no real idea of what he could possibly be or what that might mean. It is like a sense of something — intuition of the most basic kind, no more than that. But no human could be that beautiful.

I don't care, anyway, even when he scares me, because simply being with him makes me feel free.

He listens to me too. Listens like he really cares about what I have to say. Just to sit with him, to talk with him – those things make my heart soar . . .

As the memories flooded through me, I began to talk softly, to tell Cait how I'd first met Theo – how my want for him had gone so much deeper than I'd ever thought possible.

'Back then, I had nothing to compare it to,' I said. 'Now I know what that stomach-wrenching desire really feels like. Sorry. This is sort of heavy.'

She reached for her cold tea and wouldn't quite meet my eyes. 'It's OK. Go on, I want to hear this – I want to know about this guy. Theo. What was he doing at school, hanging with teenagers? Sounds kind of gross to me – he looks way older than you.'

I almost laughed at the understatement, but managed to restrain myself. I didn't want to risk sounding hysterical.

'He made me feel so freakin' special, Cait,' I said. 'He never actually used the word "love". He simply told me that he needed me – that I was a part of his soul he'd been missing for more years than he cared to remember. He'd been empty, fractured.

'He called me *anamchara* again and again. Said that I

reminded him of somebody else – although he didn't tell me back then that he meant his wife. But I'm getting ahead of myself again. And this is *my* story, not his. It was the most significant thing that had happened in my tiny life. Who was I that this god-like being would look at me and want me in this way? I could hardly believe it, and it wasn't long before we were kissing. The thrill of kissing someone – a *man* rather than a boy – a guy who would be considered completely unsuitable in Dad's eyes was, of course, a part of the attraction. But the majority was all Theo. I'd only kissed one boy before him, and imagined that the difference would be like canned Guinness compared to the real deal on-tap in Dublin.

'It was dizzying, Cait. The taste of him totally intoxicating as we kissed in the moonlight. It reminded me of those Victorian romances you love so much – and don't start protesting, you know you can't stop reading them. Only my Mr Rochester had a far darker secret hidden in the attic than a crazy wife. That would be child's play for Theo.

'We went to his house and I was overwhelmed by its beauty. Theo lit candles that he seemed to produce from out of nowhere. In the flickering flame, his dark face looked more like a pirate's than ever. I didn't care about whether he was just using a line on me, one he'd used on other girls so he could get them to sleep with him. The only thing I cared about as I looked into his shining silver eyes was that he'd said he wanted me.'

Cait leaned forward, eager to hear what was to come. And I didn't disappoint.

'He made love to me,' I murmured. 'On a beautiful ornate rug, right in front of the fireplace. Corny, right? But I still remember how he pulled down cushions from the couches and placed them beneath my head. He took my hair out of its braid and told me how gorgeous I was as he spread it out on our makeshift bed. It was my first time, but he was gentle. More gentle even than I'd hoped he would be. I would've done anything for him. Anything at all. Afterwards, when he was still lying on top of me with his face buried in my neck, I felt so at peace. I touched the back of his head, revelling in the fact that I could run my fingers through his dark curls – so much like mine, and yet more filled with velvet than mine would ever be. He was otherworldly in his perfection. I didn't know how right I was. About the "otherworldly" part, I mean.

'Then he growled, his whole body suddenly tense against me. I tried to look at his face, but it was half hidden behind a tangle of hair. He raised his head and I looked into the eyes of a predator . . .'

Caitlín reached forward impulsively and clutched my hand for comfort. For me? Or for her, hearing this story – hearing how I had become a monster? And it was as if I was back there once again, back on those cushions, fighting and scratching at Theo as he pinned me down with such ease.

'He begged me to stop struggling,' I continued, 'told me that I was making it worse, but of course I didn't understand what he was talking about. Not right then. But now I know that once a true predator's instincts kick in . . . well, it's almost impossible to just switch them back off. That's not the way it works. And that night, I hurt him pretty good, driving my knee into his crotch, making him howl with rage . . .'

Theo shoves me back down with one hand, while his other grips a clump of my hair and forces back my head. I think my neck might snap under the pressure, and almost hope it will.

His teeth – those razor-sharp fangs – plunge into my throat, below the ear and directly into my jugular . . .

'The pain was bad, Cait,' I said. 'When he bit me. Really bad. It was . . . the sort of pain you have to blank out, you know? It's something that I can't ever talk about. I used to wake up crying every single morning, for weeks after Theo brought me back, and I didn't know what had woken me. I think maybe my body remembered the pain and was somehow processing it at night.

'And what happened after that? After the terror and the pain had all but erased the beautiful? What then?

I don't remember, not clearly. There are . . . feelings, impressions; a confused dream that only comes back in pieces. But nothing concrete. Nothing I can grab hold of to anchor me in the past and force myself to remember how Theo made me into a monster.

'He says he was forced to Turn me. I believe him when he says he never meant to change a living human as young as I was back then. Theo lost control – something he'd not done for more than a century. He prided himself on the tight leash he kept on the vampire's bloodlust. Especially a vamp as old and powerful as he was. It surprised me to learn that the older they got, the stronger the bloodlust – almost as though the number of kills and the more times they feed somehow made them more susceptible to bloodlust, not less. Theo says that when a vampire feeds, they take more than just blood. They take energy too: *chi*. It's addictive.

'Anyway, he lost control and then came to his senses. Realized he was about to murder a human – and not just any human, but a human he supposedly had feelings for. I wonder how many men try to rip out the throat of the girl they love? I mean, really? Apart from serial killers.

'So Theo brought me back, which means he had to revive me enough to force me to drink his blood. He had drained so much from me that I would have died if left for even a few more minutes. Apparently, I was *that* close. Instead, I did it. I drank Theo's blood and became one of his eternal Family. He will forever be my Maker – no amount of physical distance will change that. I belong to him, because he made me. Our souls really are connected now.

'The first thing I saw when I opened my eyes, several days later, was Theo's face. He said: "Welcome to eternity, little Moth." I looked at his devil's face: his beautiful eyes and hair, his wicked pirate lips that hid those deadly fangs, and there was a part of me that was glad. Glad to be spending eternity with the monster that had killed me and saved me, all in the space of a single night . . .'

Chapter Sixteen

The morning was cold and bright, the sort of morning that I would have loved when I was alive. Now it made things difficult. Contacts or sunglasses? Or both? The sun hurt my eyes, but the contacts hurt them more. Theo didn't like it when I went out in public *sans* lenses, but whatever. *Theo isn't even around*, I thought, my chest tightening with what I hoped was anger but felt more like anxiety. He'd be sleeping now, having been out hunting Murdoch last night. Hunting the hunter – after I'd left that message with Kyle.

Sinéad had, of course, called the apartment at oh-my-God o'clock to make sure we were awake. But no matter how worried she might be, it would never enter her head to skip classes for a family emergency. It 'wasn't really an emergency, once we knew Caitlín was safe,' as Sinéad had reminded me in that superior tone I hated. She was going to meet Caitlín during her break that morning.

We were up early anyway as I wanted to get Caitlín out before Holly came back in. We took a cab to the station so that Caitlín could get a really early bus. When I hugged her goodbye, I kept my sunglasses on to hide my tears. It always amazes me that I can still cry, although there's no salt in my tears now. I know, because I've tasted them.

We'd barely spoken last night after I had told Caitlín the truth about who I was now, why she couldn't stay with me. Why everything was different. But now she had questions, which wasn't exactly a big surprise.

'Are you unhappy?'

'What kind of question is that? Of course I am!'

'But it can't be all bad, being what you are.'

My gut went cold. 'Don't get any ideas.' I glared at her. 'Seriously, this isn't something that I'd wish on anyone.'

She watched me for another few moments. Then: 'Is he awful to you?'

'Who? Theo?'

She nodded.

I sighed. 'It's not that. It's just so . . . stifling. As a vampire in a Family, you have no freedom. Everything revolves around the Master. Everything has to go through

210

him – he gives permission or he doesn't. And if he doesn't? That's it. How am I supposed to live like that?'

Caitlín's lips twisted into something approximating a smile. 'Sounds like Dad.'

'God, it does, doesn't it?' I'd traded one set of restraints for another. That's how it felt.

Caitlín held me tightly and whispered in my ear, 'You're still my sister. That won't change, will it?'

'No, of course not. How could it?' I pulled away, keeping my hands on her arms. I looked at her for a long time, wishing we could stay together somehow. *Maybe someday*, said a voice in my head that sounded a little like Mom's. 'You're not scared of me, are you, Cait?' My throat hurt.

'Of course not.'

'I mean, I guess I couldn't blame you . . .'

She put her hands on my shoulders, shaking me slightly. 'I told you that I'm not afraid, OK?'

'OK,' I whispered.

'You had this done to you,' she said, sounding far older than her sixteen years. 'You don't want it. You didn't ask for it, I get that. It's a terrible, terrible thing, but you're still you. You have to hold onto that.'

'I keep thinking of all the things I can't do now.' I shrugged, trying not to sound too pathetic. Failing. 'I want to go back to school, you know? I never even got started.'

'There's always night school,' Caitlín replied, a slight smile on her lips.

My throat was almost too tight to get the words out. 'You will always, always be my little sister.'

'Even when I'm older than you?' my sister asked, flashing a lopsided grin that almost broke my heart.

'Even then.'

Afterward, Caitlín stood on the platform, a lonely figure wrapped in my leather jacket on top of her own thin denim one. She was cold, and it's not like I really needed it.

'But you love this jacket,' she said.

'I love you more,' I replied.

At least she hadn't run away screaming when I'd shown her my fangs – she'd begged me for a peek, of course. But now I had to leave my sister to find her own way back to the O'Neals' suffocating embrace, and return to my life as one of Theo's Family.

The Boston Common murder made the front page of all the newspapers. The police made no official comment, but that didn't stop over-zealous journalists from speculating in all kinds of ways. Some were even calling the murder the work of a serial killer, despite the call for calm from the police. One newspaper was naming him – or her – the Boston Ripper. Originality wasn't exactly their strong suit.

I walked to the corner of the common where Erin's body had been found. Without the police vehicles surrounding the area, and the barriers holding back the morbid curiosity of the crowd, the place looked almost normal again. Something about that made me feel sad: a girl had died, but the world still turned just the same. There were a few limp bouquets of flowers scattered by the roadside, but they'd been pretty much pulped by last night's rain despite their cellophane wrappings.

I couldn't help hoping that Erin really *was* dead, wherever they'd taken her body. Who knows how long it would take the police to give her back to her family; how would they find closure without that? Any violent death was bad enough, but when a very young person was involved it made everything ten times worse. I sniffed the air, trying to pick up the same scent from last night. I didn't want to believe that Theo really was involved in this, but what else was I supposed to think? Every time my tired mind wandered back to that screwed-up possibility, it felt as though something cold was clutching my heart and I found it difficult to draw breath. Even more difficult than normal, I mean.

I was just about to walk around the perimeter of the area that had been cordoned off yesterday, when I caught sight of someone watching me from the nearest clump of trees. Leaving the sidewalk and entering the Common I slowly approached him, all the time trying to get my irritation under control. This was the last thing I needed.

Byron Castle Jr glared at me as I approached. 'Who the hell are you?'

Nice guy. 'Oh, I'm sorry. Is this private property?' I made a big show of looking around.

His eyes narrowed. Their color almost matched the arsenic-green streak in his black hair. 'Hey, I remember you.'

My stomach dropped. 'What? From where?'

You mean from when I practically tripped over your girl-friend's body and . . . sniffed her? Why would you remember that?

'Don't screw around. I saw you skulking around Erin when they . . . took her.'

'I don't skulk,' I said.

'You were skulking,' he replied. 'Probably a loser fan of my dad's, trying to get some kind of sick memorabilia.'

I wanted to ask him about his girlfriend, but couldn't think of a way to do it without coming off as a total ghoul.

Ugh. Why did I have to think about 'ghouls'?

'I'm sorry for your loss, Byron,' I said. I was sincere, and I hoped he heard it in my voice. 'I'm not a fan. I knew Erin.'

He glared for a moment, and then his face cleared and it was a relief to see a less hostile expression. 'Oh! I really

214

do know you, don't I? You disappeared from college last year. Rick noticed.'

He had? My heart squeezed in my chest and I closed my eyes for a moment.

'Come to pay your respects?' he asked.

I nodded. 'Something like that. Byron, I really am sorry. Was Erin—?'

'My girlfriend.' He looked like he hadn't slept for a week, but that was probably just the tear-smudged guyliner shadowing his eyes. 'I'm sorry, I don't remember your name.'

'Marie,' I said, the name feeling strange on my own tongue. It was OK when I heard it from others, somehow.

We stood shoulder to shoulder, watching the rain-flattened flowers and pulped messages as they stood guard over the site of Erin's death. Or at least, I amended, where her body had been dumped.

'Do the police know anything at all?' I felt awful digging for information, but I still had a nagging fear that this girl could rise again – Unmade. Would we even find out if that *did* happen? Perhaps the 'Spook Squad', whoever they were, would deal with it. Cover it up or something. But surely I shouldn't actually be hoping for that. Wasn't it better for the truth to come out?

Byron was shaking his head in reply. 'No. They've got squat. Not that they're telling us, anyway.'

215

'Do you know where they took her remains?'

He stared at me. 'Why would you want to know that, if you're not a freak who just wants a piece of her?'

Um . . . Because I'm a vampire and I want to make sure she doesn't turn zombie?

I cleared my throat. 'Just curious.' I cringed. God, that was lame.

'Fuck off,' he said. He turned on his heel and walked away. His long black coat floated behind him like a cape.

It wasn't like I could blame him.

Maybe it was a rogue vampire moving in on Theo's territory; we'd had those before. Perhaps someone wanted to cause a stir for the vamp community as a whole, by threatening to 'out' us in some way. Two innocent kids were already dead – both of whom I'd come into contact with myself – not to mention poor Nurse Fox's horrible end.

I got home and found my cell phone had been left in the mailbox. *Jace*. I smiled to myself. There was no note, nothing to indicate how he might be coping now that his dad was back.

The phone rang, and I almost dropped it in shock. Expecting it to be Jace, trying to be clever, I was surprised to see a number I didn't recognize.

'Hello?'

'Marie, it's Detective Trent. We need to ask you some

more questions and would appreciate it if you'd come to the Department's headquarters this time.'

I'd hoped they would have forgotten about me, but that was naïve at best.

I sighed. *Now what?*

Chapter Seventeen

The Boston Homicide Unit was all large windows, vaulted ceilings and potted plants. There were even cubicles, like you see in regular offices. The walls were blank of any decoration – white, smooth, and dull as hell. It was weird to think that my dad used to work here. I wondered if anybody remembered him anymore, of if disgraced cops were simply shuffled under the pastel blue carpet like a dirty secret.

I sat in an interview room in the stifling heart of Boston's main Police Headquarters, meaning I'd been forced to drag my butt all the way across town to Ruggles Station in rush hour. Well, let's be honest: every hour during the working day is 'rush hour' in Boston.

When I found out that Alison Trent was based out on Tremont Street, I'd had a minor freak-out. The building was an architectural monstrosity: a huge mass of ugly blocks made out of steel and glass. Lots and lots of glass. Hardly the ideal place for a vampire to go hang out with the local PD. It was pretty hard to miss. Every time I walked past another section of polished mirrored windows, I cringed and sort of ducked as though I could make myself even more invisible than I already was. It earned me some strange looks from passers-by, for sure, but I didn't care if it meant nobody noticed the tiny Goth chick with no reflection.

I'd changed into clean black jeans, a black T-shirt (with a silver logo that said, 'The Meaning of Life is: Whatever'), and my favorite steel-toe-capped boots. I was also wearing a fitted black satin coat that fell in elegant folds to my knees. Caitlín needed my leather jacket more than I did, but I couldn't help missing it – there was something comforting about the weight of it across my shoulders, and I liked the way the zips rattled when I walked. Maybe I'd get it back next time I saw her.

The whole place smelled dusty and cold.

Trent had put me in a featureless room, with faded yellow walls and blue plastic chairs. She got me a coffee and sat opposite me, resting her elbows heavily on the table. There was no sign of Denmark Smith, her partner, and I half expected him to walk in and join us every few minutes. I was on edge, almost jumping out of my skin.

I tried to chill, not wanting to look any more

suspicious than I already did – I'd already caused problems getting in here. *Not my fault, I swear!* Inside the main entrance of BPD headquarters, there had been a line of people waiting to go through the metal detector. The overweight, middle-aged officer running the show had little-to-no sense of humor, so I kept it dialled way back and just followed the lead of those before me. He demanded to see my driver's license (I never learned to drive), made me remove my sunglasses, then my coat, before sending me into the walk-through metal detector.

The steel toe-caps of my boots set off the alarm, and I cringed.

That involved a five-minute delay and lots of glaring. I tried to make myself as small as possible. Eventually, they let me through to a lobby with a vaulted ceiling and I faced another uniformed officer behind a reception desk. She had freckles, hair as dark as mine, and a no-nonsense attitude. I asked for Detective Trent.

'Do you have an appointment?'

Cops made appointments? 'Um . . . I don't know. I mean, she asked me to come in.'

'Name?'

'Marie O'Neal.'

'Hold on and I'll give her a buzz.'

At least she didn't look at me like I was a potential terrorist. Maybe my Irish roots appealed to her. The name on her badge read 'Hannigan'.

I waited while she picked up the phone, wondering what Trent wanted with me now. Wondering if I'd have the right answers or not. I could at least use the opportunity to find out whatever I could about Erin Doyle.

Officer Hannigan indicated that I should wait at the doorway at the far end of the lobby so that Detective Trent could collect me. She flashed me a quick smile, told me I was 'all set' with her distinctive Southie twang, and I felt marginally better.

Five minutes later, Detective Alison Trent was watching me across the interview-room table as though I might jump up and bite her at any moment. Of course, she wouldn't be thinking that *literally* – more fool her – but she still looked incredibly wary. I wondered if I was giving off crazy vampire vibes or something. I wasn't trying to look threatening and, for me at least, I was dressed quite conservatively.

'I've run a check on you, Miss O'Neal,' said the detective. 'My sources say that not only did you drop out of college weeks into the course, you've also never had a job. Who's supporting you?'

'My pimp,' I said, batting my lashes.

Trent fixed me with tired blue eyes. 'Listen, Marie, I could do without the attitude.'

'But it's my best attribute,' I muttered.

She just stared at me, clearly not impressed, but I

221

shouldn't have to justify myself to this cop. She was judging me, and she didn't even know me. And it wasn't like I could tell her the truth, was it?

Trent opened the manila file beside her and placed two black and white photographs on the table. 'Do you recognize either of these people?' she asked. 'People seen with Rick not long before he died.' After my initial panic that maybe she had been about to show me something gory from a crime scene, I realized that they were just surveillance photos. Well, that's what I assumed they were. Taken from a high vantage point, like the position of a camera – hidden or otherwise – and capturing a front and side view of a tall man wearing some kind of long trench coat.

Or a cowboy duster.

Thomas Murdoch. The pictures showed him outside an unmarked building talking to another person, but I couldn't make out who that person was because in both photos Murdoch's companion was blurred. Like a ghost. A vampire? It looked a bit like . . . Kyle. Kyle? Surely not. I dismissed the thought, but felt certain that the blurry figure was a vampire. Just like in mirrors, we didn't show up in photographs properly. Was it perhaps one of the visiting vampires? That would make more sense, right?

I couldn't, however, imagine Murdoch Senior knowingly working with the monsters. No, he might be involved, but that didn't mean he was the one actually pulling the strings. Perhaps whoever was behind the murders just didn't want to get his or her hands dirty? Could the hunter be under a powerful vamp's *persuasive* brand of magic?

Which of course gave me a crazy idea.

I kept my gaze trained on Detective Trent, and as soon as I caught her eye, I chose that moment to push my sunglasses up onto the top of my head. I tried to relax and let my eyes draw her in. *Don't push it,* I remembered Holly telling me one night when she was in a sharing mood. *Let* them *come to you.* Whatever I'd done to Jace the other day had been a total fluke; now I needed to make this vampire 'gift' work for me. And I needed whatever was going to happen to happen *fast.*

'Detective Trent, I can understand you're upset but if you'll just give me a chance to—'

'Don't tell me what to do, kid,' Alison Trent replied. Her voice was huskier than mine – that probably had something to do with the menthol cigarettes she chain-smoked.

She tapped her fingers on the desk, a nervous movement that gave me what I hoped was an opening. Something in her was reacting to my ability to capture her in my gaze. I knew my eyes must be glowing crazily, and yet the good detective wasn't saying anything about that. I was getting to her, I could feel it.

I kept talking. 'The newspaper today mentioned

another murder over the weekend, one where the victim's name hasn't been released yet.' *Erin.* 'Is that true? Was it like Rick's?'

Trent froze. 'I can't discuss that with you,' she replied, but her voice held a note of uncertainty.

I leaned forward. 'Could I see her body? Is it still an active crime scene?'

'Crime scenes aren't tourist attractions,' she snapped. Her gaze fully met mine. I thought I could see the silver disks of my eyes reflected in her own, kind of like twin moons reflected in deep blue pools. Trent stood up and then sort of stumbled. 'What are you—?' Her voice trailed off.

'It's OK, Alison,' I said softly. I still didn't know how to make this work, and yet part of me seemed to be taking control of the situation. It was almost as if my inner-vamp was coming out of hibernation. It wasn't the same as that time with Jace; now I felt more in control, as though I wouldn't fall into her mind and get lost in some random memory.

At least, I hoped that wasn't going to happen.

Detective Trent stood in front of me, not moving or speaking. Her eyes were fixed on mine, and I wondered what would happen if I broke that contact – would our connection end immediately? I wasn't about to risk it so I had to talk fast; someone else could walk in at any moment.

'Alison,' I said. I cleared my throat. 'Detective Trent, can you tell me if anyone else has been to see you?'

'Yes,' she replied. 'I gave Byron Castle – Erin's boyfriend – my card yesterday; told him to contact me if he thought of anything that might help us with the investigation.'

Trent frowned, although her gaze remained fixed on mine. I was surprised she was so forthcoming, but she looked totally exhausted – maybe that helped this whole coercion thing to work better.

'And where is Erin's autopsy taking place?'

The detective frowned. 'At the OPI's headquarters in New York.'

Crap. *New York City?* I thought quickly. 'What's the OPI?'

Her face twisted and perspiration beaded on her forehead. *Dammit, I was losing her.*

I narrowed my eyes. 'Detective Trent? The OPI . . . what is that again?'

Someone knocked on the door, making us both jump. In the space of a single second, I lost my grip and the link between us snapped like a fine cobweb being swept aside.

Being the spider at the center of that web didn't feel so good. My head ached, and my eyes burned almost as badly as the time I'd rubbed them with chilli-coated fingers. I took slow, deep breaths as I regained my composure.

Alison Trent looked as shaken as I felt, but the presence of one of her minions forced her to regain her own composure and listen to what the young uniformed officer was saying. I'd slipped my shades back in place as soon as he came in, hoping desperately that he hadn't seen anything suspicious.

The police dude cleared his throat. 'Spook Squad are here for you again, Detective Trent.'

She scowled. 'Hey, I've told you guys about calling them that.'

The cop shrugged, not looking even slightly embarrassed to be told off in front of a civilian. 'So what are we supposed to call them? Next thing we know they'll be opening up the basement and giving Mulder his own damn office down there.'

I examined my fingernails, trying not to look so interested in what he had to say. *Spook Squad?* Something told me this might be the very same organization as the mysterious 'OPI'.

He nodded his head in my direction, a crooked smile on his handsome face. 'Sorry for cursing, miss.'

I stifled the urge to laugh. 'No problem, Officer . . .' I leaned closer and squinted through my shades to make out his name badge. 'Officer Delaney. Ah, I love an Irishman in uniform.'

Detective Trent looked as though she was busy trying to figure out what she'd spent the last few minutes

226

talking about. She massaged her temples and, for a moment, exhaustion slipped through the cracks in her professional mask. 'Miss O'Neal, don't forget to let me know if you have any information that might help us.'

I took the card she handed me and slipped it into a back pocket. 'Sure. Thanks for listening, Detective Trent.'

As Officer Delaney directed me out of the precinct I couldn't resist flirting with the guy. Apart from being sort of cute, he might have information I could use. Back when Jace and I had been escaping from Rick's final resting place at the hospital, the 'Spook Squad' had been mentioned by whoever had been on the other side of the door.

I smiled at Delaney, peering over the top of my shades briefly before pushing them back up. 'That Detective Trent is pretty intense, isn't she?'

He shrugged as we stood by the entrance. 'She's good at her job.'

'Right. And dedicated. We talked about the work she's doing for the . . .' I screwed up my face. 'The *Spook Squad*, I think I heard you call them. The OPI . . .' I let my voice trail off and turned my head as though more interested in the squad car pulling up to the doors outside.

He snorted. 'Office of Preternatural Investigations. They're a bunch of freaks if you ask me, always chasing shadows. Though you didn't hear me say that.' He looked guilty for a moment, probably wondering why he was even telling me this. 'I think "Spook Squad" suits them better.'

'Yeah,' I said, nodding earnestly. 'Definitely.'

He escorted me all the way back downstairs. At the bottom of the stairwell, he held open the metal door to the lobby. I exited the glass doors, grateful to avoid the stupid metal detector this time, and welcomed the chill winter air on my face. The sky had turned to granite while I'd been inside and I headed for the nearest T stop, trying to figure out my next move as I prowled through the afternoon crowds.

I couldn't help feeling bad for taking advantage of Alison Trent, but I was also surprised at how easy it had been to influence her mind. Did this mean my abilities were getting stronger? She was clearly a dedicated cop – a good person – but it sounded as though she was under pressure from the so-called Spook Squad. Who knew there really *was* a modern-day X-Files? So, the Office of Preternatural Investigations was on to the case of these murdered kids. Maybe I shouldn't be surprised. Boston had some serious supernatural activity hidden away; it was only a matter of time before we attracted official attention.

I had to tell Theo about the Spook Squad (if he didn't already know they existed) – and about the photo – but I couldn't do that until he was up and awake. I glared at the sky, willing night to fall, but there were at least two more hours to go. Impatient, I called Jace but it rolled over to voice mail. I resisted the urge to throw my phone in frustration. Where next? Where might Kyle be? Or the visiting vamps? My lips curved into a smile. Where else but Subterranean?

Chapter Eighteen

Subterranean was cool, hip – all of that good stuff. I hadn't been inside before, but Holly had told me all about it. I think she'd been trying to scare me off, but there was a little part of me that thought it was sort of cool.

I'd been home, grabbed a few hours' sleep, then waited impatiently for the club to open, and now a group of young people crowded in with me, hooting laughter and pushing each other. Drunken shouts of, 'Duuude! Let's get a beer.'

Bass thrummed against the soles of my boots. Loud music filled my ears and my head, and I concentrated on that rather than on the scent of humanity. Kids were jumping and dancing to the heavy sounds pounding from the speaker system. They didn't know they were prey just waiting to happen.

Vampires didn't usually kill when they fed. Why would they? Random, blood-drained bodies would draw way too much attention, and vampires were all about the secrets. No, feeding was a seductive thing – that's why places like Subterranean existed. It was full of youth and beauty with more than enough blood to go around, without anyone having to die for it. All the vampires had to do was come up from the sub-basement and take their pick. And when the victims rejoined their friends, it wasn't exactly unusual to look out of it at Subterranean . . .

At least, that was the way it was supposed to work.

I'd left a message on Jace's voice mail to tell him that I might stop by the apartment if I found out anything from Subterranean. I couldn't believe I was actually checking in with the guy who only days before had been trying to kill me. My lips tightened and I headed with new determination through the nightclub. *People changed.* Sometimes for the better and sometimes for the worse. I hoped that I was right about which one applied to Jace.

I suspected that if he'd been around to take my call he would've wanted to come with me. But the son of an infamous vampire hunter walking into a known vampire haunt was worse than suicide. I had to be careful not to bring the young hunter anywhere near my Maker: if Theo got hold of Jace, he wouldn't give the kid a merciful death and be done with it. No, he'd probably torture him until his *real* target – Thomas Murdoch – came riding to the rescue. Theo still figured he had a score to settle with Jace for the way he'd treated me six months ago. But the scars on my arms were fading and, more importantly, the memory of that night seemed almost to belong to another person.

People can change, I told myself again. *I'm evidence of that.*

I craned my neck over the eclectic crowd, checking out the bar area and getting bumped by a black-clad couple as they gyrated past. Perspiration flicked onto my face as I got too close to a lanky blue-haired boy rocking glaze-eyed to the beat. The music was a fist, punching into my heart and making me feel alive.

I'd been there barely fifteen minutes, had seen nothing or no one of note, and was heading over to the bar when I was shoved in the back. Hard. I stumbled against one of the ebony pillars that surrounded the dance floor. I half turned, only to be grabbed from behind, my face shoved against the cold stone. The faint grain of the pillar scratched my cheek, and I could feel the thrum of the bass beating all the way down to my toes.

'Well, well, what have we here,' hissed a nasty voice in my ear. A voice I was unfortunately familiar with. 'Looking for someone, *little Moth*?'

I tried to dig my elbow into the skinny ribs pressed

against my back, but it felt like my wrists were being crushed in a steel trap. 'Get off me, Kyle.'

'Say please,' purred that irritating voice in my ear.

'Go screw yourself. Theo won't be happy when I tell him about this.'

Kyle loved to mess with me; it was one of his hobbies. 'Sorry, kid, but the boss isn't here tonight. I'm keeping an eye on things. And what are *you* doing here? I didn't think Theo had given you permission to come in here yet.'

I tried to rein in my temper. 'I was looking for Theo, OK? If he's not here, I'll just leave. Is he at home?'

His eyes glittered, and his smile was as sharp as knives. 'He's out hunting, little Moth. Same as me.'

Theo was hunting again? He hardly ever went out on a hunt by himself, let alone this regularly. He'd already been out on Saturday – when I'd found him almost glowing with fresh blood. *Erin's blood.* A horrible thought wormed its way into my mind, but before I could focus and try to unravel it, Kyle grabbed my chin and forced my head up until our faces were almost touching. His talons dug into my flesh, forcing a gasp of pain out of me. Kyle's nails were more like claws – just another weapon he could use in combat. His eyes spat burning silver.

I tried to twist out of his grip, while nervously looking around at the human patrons nearby. 'Put a lid on it, Kyle, you're *sparkling* all over the freaking place.'

I couldn't believe it was *me* having to tell *him* that. What had gotten into him? 'Listen, I know this is our territory but there are still humans around.'

'Ah yes, all the lovely sheep. So many tasty snacks wandering around.'

He moved next to me, pressing his hip against mine as he leaned against the pillar. He slid his arm around my waist and kept hold of me, gesturing at the spinning dancers with his other hand.

'See how they move, little Moth. Can you smell it?' His stance was watchful, focused, and his gaze was hungry. His presence seemed like a jagged rock in a stream. Wiry and feral.

I was starting to get seriously pissed. If I didn't know better I'd say he was high, but vampires weren't affected by narcotics – especially not the older vamps, and Kyle had more than a century under his tasteless studded belt. And just what was with his outfit tonight, anyway? He was dressed like a blond version of Russell Brand: all skinny jeans, unbuttoned shirt and guyliner.

'What are you talking about?' I tried to move away from him but his fingers dug into my side, those long nails like small needles piercing my skin even through the material of my coat.

'Take a good, long sniff, my dear. Breathe it in. Life . . . The scent of the living.' He pressed his face close –

so close that his long hair tickled my cheek. He opened his lips, showing the tips of white fangs. '*Food.*'

'Get a grip,' I snapped, trying to sound braver than I felt.

'I'm perfectly in control,' he said. 'Just speaking the truth. Don't tell me you haven't felt it too. It's what we are. It's the darkness inside all of us, giving us the chance to lose ourselves in really bad places. I mean, *really* bad shit, you know? It's being bad and liking it. You can pretend all you like, but you want to watch them bleed as much as I do.'

It was the way he said it that turned my stomach to lead. A weird sort of precognition, intuition or one of those fluke 'feelings' . . .

'Get your hands off me and maybe I won't tell Theo.' Yeah, right. Because I really *wasn't* going to tell Theo that his unofficial right-hand man was a total freak just waiting to flip out and go on a murdering rampage. I glared at him, seriously tempted to kick chunks out of his shins with my steel-toe-capped boots.

'Theo doesn't care what I do.' He ran his tongue along his teeth, flicking it between razor-sharp fangs. 'The boss is getting soft in his old age. Maybe he's losing his touch – maybe *he's* the one losing control, eh?'

OK, now this wasn't good. Not good at all. My mind raced as I pictured Erin's lifeless body and Rick's transformation from emo-kid to Zombie Boy from hell. Kyle had been the one to look into their deaths for Theo, hadn't he . . . ?

Of course, we only had *his* word for whatever he had or hadn't done to investigate these vampire-related deaths. Did Kyle really have anything to do with all this crap? He was probably the right age to create revenants – that book had said vamps were usually under two hundred years old in order to screw up a Turning enough to *Unmake* the victim. *Was* that him in the photo with Murdoch? I shivered. What was I getting myself into now?

'Ah, Moth. I'm surprised you haven't noticed anything . . . wrong with the boss lately. Considering all the *quality time* you spend with him.'

'Stop talking crap, asshole, and get your stinking hands off me.' I grabbed a handful of his stringy blond hair and yanked down on it. OK, so hair-pulling was kind of beneath my dignity, but whatever worked in a tight situation was fine with me.

Kyle growled and pushed me away so hard that I stumbled and banged my hip on one of the chairs tucked behind the pillar. I hissed with the sudden burst of pain but jumped up onto the chair, giving me the high ground – and a good view of the dance floor. All the way across to the exit, which was flanked by what looked to me like two vampire doormen. I wondered if the human manager of Subterranean knew that the silent owner of the club, Theo, was providing more and more of the staff. Most of the muscle was undead, although Holly had told me that the bar staff remained human – for some reason vampires couldn't mix a good cocktail. Not like Augusto, who reigned supreme at the main bar.

'Ah, so you don't want to dance with me tonight,' Kyle said, his voice dripping with fake disappointment.

'Thanks,' I replied with a not-so-sweet smile. 'I think I'll pass.'

He shrugged. 'Yeah, because I really give a rat's ass about a runt like you.' He shrugged and half turned away. 'My work here is done, anyway.'

I frowned. Now what was the stupid idiot talking about? 'What work? Collecting glasses?' Then understanding dawned hard and cold. He'd been playing with me – holding me up for some reason. Keeping me from . . . from what? I jumped down from the chair, hating myself for going to him but needing to know what had just happened. 'What are you talking about?' I grabbed his arm. 'What have you done?'

His face was suddenly empty of emotion. Even the gloating smile had slipped away, leaving a blank mask. 'You didn't come here alone, child.'

Confusion washed over me, making it difficult to think. The flashing lights and pounding bass weren't helping. 'But I did come alone. You're not making sense.'

The older vampire looked thoughtful for a moment

and then that slow smile spread across his face again. 'Maybe one of your little human friends has been following you, then. What a pity for him . . .' He let his voice trail off in mock sorrow as he shook his head.

Oh God, no. Please don't let Jace have been dumb enough to come after me. Why the *hell* had I left that stupid message? I licked my lips and stared at Kyle, fury waging war with terror in my gut. 'If you've hurt him, I'll make you sorry.'

'Ah, so concerned about the human boy.' He spat on the ground and then fixed me with cold, cold eyes. Eyes that had gone the color of flat steel.

I didn't wait around to ask more questions. If Jace had followed me here, surely he would've brought weapons – he was potentially crazy, but not crazy enough to arrive unarmed at a place like this. I had to find him. He'd be out back in the alley; I might not have been here before, but I knew how the vampires dealt with unwelcome visitors to Subterranean. Holly's stories had *some* uses.

Running through a small crowd of clearly underage kids on the edge of the dance floor, I pushed someone out of my way and ignored the girl who yelled something at me. I couldn't hear anything above the beat of the music, the bass making time with my pounding heart. I was almost too overcome with fear to notice how hard my inhuman heart was suddenly trying to beat – something that would normally make me bizarrely happy.

I slammed through the fire exit so hard that I left the imprint of my hand on the metal bar across the door.

The cold air hit my face and brought me to a sudden stop. The night was still and the rain from last night had already frozen into icy puddles dotting the alleyway, making it difficult to stay upright. I looked left, toward the main street: nothing.

Turning my head, I held my breath as I looked to the right. At the end of the alley a crumpled shape lay on the ground. It was too dark to make out any detail, but it looked like a guy-shaped body curled into a foetal ball. Shadows danced as an overhanging tree was caught by a sudden gust of wind, its empty branches making spidery trails on the alley's high wall.

I walked slowly toward the body – no, not the body, I wouldn't think like that – toward the *shape* on the cold ground. I trod carefully on the light covering of frost as I knelt down beside the young guy who lay so very still.

It took me a moment to register the fact that he was wearing a long black coat and heavy black boots. Camouflage? A disguise of some kind? I frowned as I gripped his shoulder and turned him over.

'Oh no,' I said. 'No.'

His stark white face glowed in the darkness. His sludgy green eyes were wide open and blood still seeped from the gaping wound in his throat. The blood seemed leached of color; it was almost black in the surrounding gloom as it slowly dripped into a growing puddle beneath him.

'Byron,' I whispered. 'You *idiot*.'

It wasn't Jace at all. The whole time that Kyle had been tormenting me – delaying me and playing for time – Byron had been lying out here in the cold, slowly dying. All alone. A sob hitched in my throat. He was just a dumb kid whose only 'crime' was to love his girlfriend and try to find out what had happened to her. Tears ran hot down my frozen cheeks, taking me by surprise.

Now there was another murdered kid to deal with. Murdered by Kyle? How else might Theo's Enforcer be involved? And what about Theo's scent on Erin's body? I rubbed a hand across my tear-stained face. Whatever else was going on here, I knew one thing for certain: this boy was dead because he'd been following me, probably desperate for the answers that I'd held back this afternoon. He must have waited for *hours* outside my apartment.

I swallowed bile as I looked at the bloody mess of his throat, knowing that I'd cost him his life.

Chapter Nineteen

Byron's eyes were half open, glazed. I brushed his streaked hair away from his face, gently, as though I might disturb his peace if I moved too quickly. Grief closed around my heart like a fist. And the scent of blood took me back, back to that earlier time. Those first few days . . .

'I can smell it from here,' I say. I want to cry, but the tears won't come. 'Why can I smell it from all the way out here? Why does it smell so good?'

Theo kisses my forehead. He casts no reflection in the window. 'Because you're hungry,' he says, so softly I almost don't hear him.

'But I'm always hungry,' I whisper.

'Yes.'

* * *

I couldn't leave Byron's body here. Much as I wanted to make an anonymous call to the BPD and let Smith and Trent come out here to do their thing, I couldn't take that risk. Not right behind Subterranean. And what if Byron went the same way as Rick? His girlfriend hadn't – or not that I'd heard – but it didn't mean that this boy would be so lucky.

Lucky. What a word to apply to a murdered teenager.

'Screw it,' I said under my breath, reaching for my cell phone. Then I cursed loudly. I shouldn't use my own phone. Not here. What if calls could be traced? I didn't need my name coming into *another* murder investigation. I forced myself to take a breath to steady myself, then dug through Byron's pockets. It felt wrong, gruesome, to disturb him in death, but I needed a phone and his had to be here somewhere.

Of course, Byron's cell phone had a cracked screen. *Crap*. I held my breath and hit the 'on' button. Waited what felt like an eternity. But finally the graphics shuddered into view. I didn't know where Theo was, and he didn't carry a phone anyway. I couldn't call out the vampire security – not while Theo was trying to convince them I was nicely under control. Who was to say I wouldn't be blamed for this death? So there was only one person I could call for help. I punched in the number still stashed in my jeans pocket. Thank God I hadn't dumped it, or left it in my leather jacket –

which was safe and sound with my sister.

After two rings Jace picked up.

After a brief explanation he was on his way.

And that's how it came to be that it was *Jace* who helped me lift the body into the back of his father's van.

'So,' Jace said, his casual tone hiding something darker, 'is this kid going to vamp out on us?'

I swallowed and shook my head. 'No, you're safe from that.' I couldn't quite keep the bitterness from my voice. 'They didn't make him feed from them. Either he's dead or he's coming back as Zombie Boy Mark Two. But he won't be a vampire.' For a horrible moment I thought I might start to cry again. What was *with* me and all the tears lately?

Jace nodded as he moved the body's legs so he could shut the doors. 'Good.'

Hot fury warmed me. 'Why? Because it's one less monster for you and Daddy to dust?'

'No, of course not.' His voice was quiet and he didn't quite meet my eyes. 'Because I didn't want us to have to kill another one of your friends.'

'Oh.' I paused, gathering my scrambled wits. 'He wasn't my friend. I only met him properly today.'

Jace whirled his silver-edged blade between his fingers, making it glitter like a sharpened shard of moonlight. It was making me nervous.

'Moth, I've seen a newly risen vampire before. If

243

there's no Maker around to control it . . .' He looked away for a moment and I couldn't help wondering about the things this kid had seen in his life. How old had he been when he first knew that the monsters were real?

'It's OK,' I said. 'At least we only have to worry about the whole Unmade thing.' I shook my head. 'I can't believe I just said that.'

Jace's mouth was set in a grim line as he pulled a huge sheet of plastic over the body. It was thick, black, and looked perfect for hiding corpses in the back of his dad's van. The vehicle stank of death and decay, and I knew that wasn't only thanks to *this* body. Gross as it was to even think like that, Byron was too fresh to smell this bad.

I watched Jace tuck everything out of sight and swallowed. 'What are we going to do with him?'

A muscle flickered in his jaw and he shot me a dark look. 'What do you think?'

I grimaced. 'I just—' I shook my head. Dammit, this was *hard*. And I didn't even know the guy. Well, hardly. 'I was hoping there might be something we could do.'

Jace barked a laugh that echoed with bitterness. He turned his back on me and climbed between the front seats, sliding into the driver's position and hunching his shoulders as he fiddled with the ignition. He put the car in gear, tapped the accelerator and drove down the street. He banged a left at the first intersection, weaving around pedestrians and motorcycles and other cars running the red light.

I frowned and followed him, leaning over the seat backs and trying to catch a glimpse of his face. 'What's wrong? What did I say?' I clambered into the passenger seat. It was covered in cheap nylon that was worn in several places.

'Why do you guys care about him all of a sudden?'

By "you guys", I assumed Jace was referring to the vampires that existed under-the-radar in the city. I tucked my feet underneath me on the seat and clasped my hands in my lap. They were shaking and I didn't want Jace to see. 'So what's your big plan for dealing with this, then? Especially as I have no idea if he's going to come back the same as Rick.'

'We have two options. Either we take him to your Maker or we deal with him ourselves.'

'There's no way we're going to Th—' I stopped and glared at him. 'You asshole, you almost had me there.'

Jace's mouth quirked very slightly. 'It was worth a try.'

'I'm not telling you anything about him, so you can just go screw yourself.'

'You say that so often, and it's not getting any more appealing.'

I pouted and stared out of the window. I wasn't interested in looking at anything outside – I just wanted a break from Jace Murdoch and his irritating know-it-all posturing. I glanced out of my window and watched the road blur pass, black and endless as the night itself.

'Moth?' His voice was low. Insistent.

'*What?*' I practically growled, still gazing out of the window.

'You're steaming up the damn window. I can't see shit.'

Oh. I'd been breathing without even thinking about it. That was sort of cool.

The guy who wasn't supposed to be in my life touched my arm. 'Moth, are you listening to me?'

'No.'

'Good.' He shifted in his seat, as though uncomfortable with what he was about to say. 'If you don't want my help that's cool. I'll be honest with you, I don't particularly want to be here dealing with this. I've had enough of it in my life already.'

'So why didn't you leave me there? Why did you even bother to come in the first place?'

'I came when you called because I wanted to see what crazy drama you'd gotten yourself into *this* time.'

'I thought you didn't trust vampires.'

'Sometimes, you don't seem like a regular vampire,' he said.

'What am I supposed to be like?'

'I don't know. Just . . . not like you.'

I raised my eyebrows, wishing my vamp-abilities

extended to reading his mind. He probably thought female vampires were femme fatales, sultry seductresses who wanted to drink the blood of every man they met. A siren. Someone who radiated menace. I almost laughed. That was so far from who I was it was laughable. I was tough, rather than dangerous. Needy, rather than sexy. And my total geekiness pretty much ruled me out of the seduction stakes (no pun intended).

But Jace wasn't done talking. 'I didn't leave you there in the alley because . . .' His voice trailed off as he concentrated on a stream of traffic and we pulled out onto a busy road.

I continued to knead my fingers together in my lap. It reminded me of the way my mother used to make bread. 'Well? You can't just say something like that and stop.'

He glanced at me, then focused back on the dark road stretching ahead. Headlights zoomed past us on the other side, but Jace handled the van effortlessly. He zigged and zagged along side streets I wasn't even sure I knew had been there, dodging triple-parked cars that were common sights in Boston.

Finally, he said, 'Why do you think I didn't leave you there, you idiot? I always said you were a freak.'

If my heart could race, I knew that's what it would be doing. But I could still feel its ghostly beating, as surely as I could feel the warmth from the van's heater beginning to thaw out my frozen cheeks. An echo of humanity.

Jace said, 'OK, maybe this will help. When you saw that body in that alley, did you think it might be me?'

I bit my lip. Maybe if I didn't say anything, I couldn't get myself into trouble. I turned and watched him as his dark eyes reflected back the lights from passing cars.

'For a minute, yes. When I saw him lying there. And I couldn't stand the thought that something had happened to you.'

He didn't say anything, but I watched that familiar muscle pulsing in his jaw. Then he nodded. 'Yeah, that's what I thought.'

Oh, please don't say he's going to be smug about this.

'Moth, are you really so dumb that you need me to tell you that I came here for the same damn reason? *That's* why I came when you called me – and you're just too stubborn to already know it.'

'Why can't you just say what you mean?' I pouted. 'You're so confusing.'

'Maybe . . . maybe I like you.'

He *likes* me? Did threatening me and pointing sharp weapons at me count as liking me? I snorted. Yeah, maybe if you're in third grade. But then again . . . I glanced at the bruises on his face. Bruises from his father. Bruises he got sort of (lamely) defending *me* . . .

Jace stared through the windshield, fingers drumming

on the steering wheel. He laughed, but it came out sounding strained. 'You gonna leave me hanging here?'

Silence filled the van, the only sounds filtering through the thick glass from outside. The wheels bumped over a patch of gravel on the freeway; the engine grumbled under the hood as we made our way to the cemetery.

I slumped down in my seat and leaned my head back, gazing at a smear on the ceiling directly above my head that looked a lot like dried blood.

I sighed. 'Jace, how was I supposed to know how you felt until you told me? It's not as though we're the most natural of . . . friends.'

His lips curved into a tantalizing ghost of a smile. 'I thought you vampires could read minds.'

Dammit, I didn't want him to make me smile. 'Is that what your dad's books say?'

Finally he glanced over, locking eyes with me for dangerous seconds before returning his attention back to the road. 'Nope. I figured that one out all by myself. When you pulled that number on me down in that hospital storeroom.'

I laughed. 'I'd go back to what you do best, genius.'

'What's that?' Jace asked.

'Hunting the bad guys. Being a pain in the ass.'

He glanced at me, his face tinted green by the van's dash lights. I couldn't read the expression in his eyes, and before I could even try, he returned his attention to the road.

We travelled the rest of the way in silence, but my vamp-hearing could still detect his heartbeat and it didn't make me hungry – not even a little. At least, not for blood.

Chapter Twenty

The Granary Burying Ground was the last place on earth I wanted to be.

Seriously, would you want to be sneaking around a freaking cemetery at night? I shivered. Just because I'm a vampire doesn't make this my natural habitat or anything. Shadows shimmered like dark water, and in between, crumbling stones lined the path. Grave markers were haphazardly arranged so that they looked like broken teeth scattered around.

It was spooky, and no amount of fake Egyptian gates and obelisks would make me think any different. I looked around nervously as we checked it out for a suitable spot to bury Byron, half expecting to see a ghost creeping between the grave markers. I let out a muffled squeal as something that felt like cold fingers touched the back of my hand.

Oh, I thought. It had felt like chilled fingers because that's exactly what it was. Jace had touched my hand and his fingers were frozen. Wow, I was totally lame tonight. If Holly saw me jumping at shadows and shrieking like a girl, she'd never let me live it down.

I shrugged and whispered, 'Sorry, you made me jump. Didn't know what that was for a minute.'

Jace thrust his hands into the pockets of his army jacket. His breath puffed out in little clouds as we trudged back to where we'd left the van. He glanced at me, but his expression was difficult to read under the dim light of the mist-cloaked moon. 'What else would it have been? We're the only people out here.'

'Um . . . nothing. Nothing living, anyway,' I muttered. I kept my eyes down, concentrating on not tripping over a stray tree root winding across the narrow pathway.

'No, really,' he said. 'I'm curious. What did you think it was?'

I let out a dramatic sigh. 'A ghost, OK? I thought maybe a freaking ghost touched me.' I kicked a rock out of my way, taking childish pleasure in the sound it made as it hit a gravestone.

'Don't tell me that you, of all people, believe in ghosts.'

'Vampires are sensitive to this kind of stuff.' I eyed

him to see if he was taking me seriously. 'It's like, that first near-death experience brings us closer to those who live in between. Or something.'

Jace nudged me with his elbow. 'Sounds very technical.'

I stifled my smile and gave him a mock-angry look. 'Well, I don't know how it all works. I've not exactly done a ton of research on this, you know.'

'But . . . surely this concerns you. I mean it's part of who you are, right?'

I barely had time to freak out when a dangling tree branch brushed across my face. I pushed it irritably out of the way. 'Sure, it's part of my life now – this whole being undead thing – but I don't make a habit of studying the phenomena. It's hard enough adjusting to all the crap that comes with it. The last thing I want to do is read about what it means to be undead, or the difference between ghosts and wraiths—'

'You mean, there's a difference?' Jace deadpanned.

'Shut up,' I said. 'You know what I mean. Come on, think about it. If you were in my shoes, would *you* want to spend any free time you had immersing yourself in occult nonsense?'

We arrived back at the van and Jace leaned against the back doors. 'First of all, I wouldn't be seen dead in the sort of footwear you seem to love.'

He held up a hand as I opened my mouth indignantly. 'Secondly, yeah, I probably would read up on all of that "nonsense". I always like to know what I'm dealing with. Information helps with that.'

Whatever I was about to say froze on my lips as the back doors of the van flew open, crashing into Jace and throwing him to the ground.

No, I thought. *Please, this isn't fair. Not again.* But if anyone was listening to my silently offered prayer, there was no evidence of it as the boy – or what remained of him – climbed out of the van on unsteady legs.

Jace had already pulled himself together and was up and running, heading for the van's cab.

'Where are you going?' I yelled.

Jace didn't reply, but I was pretty certain that after all the sappy sharing we'd done tonight it was unlikely he was running out on me. Even if he *would* consider leaving me alone to face the newly risen, there's no way Jace would run from a fight. Especially not one that involved kicking undead butt.

Whatever he had planned, I wished that he'd hurry up. The zombie had focused its sickly white eyes on me and was sniffing the air in my direction. No matter how blind these things seemed, I couldn't help wondering how true that really was.

I may not know too much about revenants, but I was a fast learner and this one looked hungry – extremely hungry.

I tried to remember that the monster stumbling

toward me had, only recently, been a screwed-up kid. I backed away as it advanced on me, trying to figure out a smart plan of action that didn't involve just running the hell away. I darted behind a nearby tree and peeked out as it shambled unsteadily across the uneven ground. I dived out from the sparse cover and was heading back toward the van when Jace shouted.

'Duck!' His voice carried across the little clearing and I didn't need to be told twice.

I threw myself onto the hard ground, inwardly cursing as I felt something sharp dig into my left leg. The *whoosh* overhead, and then the *thunk* as a crossbow bolt hit the tree behind me, reminded me that there were more important things than ripped jeans and a scraped knee.

I raised my head and scowled. Amazingly, the zombie had gotten out of the way in time and managed to reverse direction. Either it wasn't as slow as I'd first thought or Byron's body was adapting to zombification a lot faster than I'd thought possible. He had certainly gone from dead body to walking zombie quicker than Rick had. Chalk up another reason to do more research. Not that I'd admit that to Jace, of course.

I could hear Jace cursing as he struggled to reload the crossbow. Wincing with pain, I climbed to my feet and rubbed my knee. It felt like something was still embedded in the flesh, but I didn't have time to worry about that – not with the creature sniffing the air and turning slowly in Jace's direction.

'Moth, go to the back of the van – Dad's sword is in there,' he yelled. 'Be careful – it's silver.'

I resisted the temptation to comment. *Dad's sword? What kind of life had Jace Murdoch really led?* I shook my head and jogged in a wide arc, careful to keep Zombie Boy in view, even though Jace seemed to be keeping the creature busy by taking aim and firing the crossbow again.

The zombie howled and I thought I could see the bolt protruding from its shoulder. And then I was at the van, leaping into the dark interior as my eyes already began scanning the piles of weapons.

Surely it couldn't be too hard to find a freaking sword.

But just as I was lifting more heavily worn tarpaulin, hoping I'd find something useful underneath, there was a bone-jarring crash and the van shook.

I stumbled, but managed to stay on my feet. 'What—'

Another shockwave cut me off and I found myself on my knees as I grabbed for something – anything – that might help keep me upright.

What was going on out there?

Struggling to stay on my feet, I wavered toward the doors. I couldn't see anything. Whatever had been pounding on the side of the van had also caused the buckled doors to swing shut.

Gritting my teeth, I pushed my way back out into the graveyard—

And came face-to-face with the blank-faced Zombie Boy. Its hand shot out much faster than I expected, grabbing my throat and lifting me off my feet.

I gripped its wrist in both hands and kicked wildly with my legs, using every bit of my not inconsiderable strength to get free of the implacable creature dangling me like a puppet. The muscles of my neck and shoulders were killing me, but I still managed to look around desperately for Jace.

It didn't take long for my eyes to focus on his prone body crumpled on the ground next to the van. The cross-bow was snapped in half and Jace was face down on the hard earth. Kicking more violently, I refused to think about how badly he might be hurt. I tried to catch my breath as the revenant's fingers dug into my windpipe. Panic began to claw at my chest when I realized I could no longer take in air.

I mentally gave myself a good slap. Much as I didn't want to admit it, I didn't really *need* to breathe anymore. At least, not all the time. It was just a habit. A bad one, according to Theo, but still nothing more than a necessity in human company – something that made vampires fit in when we hung out with mortals. Immediately, the pressure in my lungs eased and I felt more at peace than I could remember feeling in a long time. Sure, my throat was being crushed and it felt as though my head might come off at any moment, but this thing couldn't kill me. Not really, and certainly not by strangling me.

Not that the revenant knew that. My mind felt sharp and the cold air helped me to think straight. Getting free was going to be a lot easier than I might have thought.

I let my body go limp, making exaggerated choking sounds to keep things as convincing as possible. I had no idea how much awareness the Unmade had, but I was pretty certain it would recognize defeated prey if I made it convincing enough.

And, of course, I smelled dead anyway.

My supposedly lifeless form hung like a scarecrow, and the zombie gave me a final shake, almost as though it were making sure I was done for.

It threw me against the side of the van. The impact jarred all the way through to the roots of my teeth and I slid to the ground next to Jace's still form. Playing dead in those next few moments was one of the hardest things I'd ever done. Those precious seconds when I could've been checking on Jace seemed to take a lifetime.

The monster reached down to us, prodding at me with the toe of a heavy boot and then crouching down next to me. My hair covered my face and I peeked out at the milky white eyes that swept over my body. It was almost as though it was deciding which part of me looked the tastiest.

Ugh, that was possibly the grossest thing I'd ever thought.

As the zombie wrapped cold fingers around my wrist, I allowed myself to take a breath. OK, so it was going for the arm, just like Rick had done with Nurse Fox. Must be a zombie delicacy or something.

I let the monster get a firm grip and coiled my body, preparing to spring and use my fangs as a weapon—

And then Jace jumped to his feet, plunging his dagger into the creature's neck until a fine spray of blood showered me with warm salty drops.

Zombie Boy staggered and released my arm as it clutched at its neck, trying to find the source of the attack. The knife didn't seem to be causing it too much pain, although it did swipe at the hilt a few times with wildly uncoordinated hands. The gash in its throat gaped obscenely at us.

'What were you *doing*?' Jace yelled. 'Waiting for it to snack on your goddamn arm?'

I rolled over and pushed up onto my feet. I ignored the hand that Jace held out to me. 'I thought you were dead! Why didn't you move sooner?'

Meanwhile Zombie Byron turned slow circles as it tried to see what was sticking out of its neck.

'I was just *playing* dead.' Jace had a cut on his fore-head which was already blooming with a multi-colored bruise around it – he was building up quite a collection of injuries – but apart from that he seemed OK.

I flashed him a quick smile and held up two fingers. 'How many fingers?'

'Cute,' he muttered. He watched the still-spinning revenant with something like fascination shining in his brown eyes. 'Wow, this guy must've been particularly dumb as a human being.'

My stomach contracted and the smile slid from my face. 'Don't talk about him like that. He's dead – long gone.' I gestured at the shambling thing.

Jace shrugged and looked down at his destroyed cross-bow. Regret flitted across his face. 'Damn, that's the second bow I've lost when you've been around.'

'I couldn't find your dad's sword,' I said. 'How are we going to, you know . . .' I made a cutting motion across my throat.

Jace raised an eyebrow. 'We'll burn it, like before.'

I dodged a flailing white arm. 'With what, Einstein? The lighter's long gone and I don't have any matches.' I fixed Jace with a hopeful expression. 'Unless you used to be a Boy Scout? Maybe you could rub two sticks together and we could make a fire.'

Jace patted down his pockets, cursing as he came up with a box of matches that turned out to be empty.

I gazed at him for a moment, trying hard to focus on our predicament and not on how beautiful the angles of his cheekbones were.

'Oh,' I said. 'I know!'

'I know—' he said.

'*Dashboard lighter*,' we shouted in unison.

I raised my hand. 'High five!'

Jace shook his head and ignored me. 'Keep it busy – I'll be back in a minute.'

I watched Zombie Boy stagger in the direction of the tree line. There was something incredibly sad about the way it struggled to negotiate the terrain; I had to swallow a sudden dryness in my throat. Guilt hit me; how dare I see ending a kid's life as a victory. That's what this thing had been, once upon a time. Yeah, it had tried to kill me, but *he* hadn't known what it was doing. It was sort of pathetic seeing him like this – seeing *it* like this, I reminded myself. It seemed like something crucial had short-circuited in its brain. The revenant was stuck in a loop of trying to figure out what was jammed into its neck, but no matter how hard it tried it couldn't get its hands on the dagger's hilt.

So it kept turning those slow circles, looking for an opponent that didn't even exist. I didn't have to do a thing to keep it occupied – it was managing just fine all by itself.

Jace ran back brandishing the lighter in one hand, and a beer bottle with a rag sticking out the top in the other. The shining tip of the dash lighter shone clear in the darkness that blanketed the cemetery. I let my attention wander, for a second almost hypnotized by the orange glow.

A gunshot rang out, echoing in the silence like a thunderclap.

Jace stopped in his tracks. 'Get down!' He hit the deck, and I spared a thought for the gear he was carrying. I hoped he didn't set *himself* on fire.

I had already thrown myself onto the ground, instinct taking over. *Holy shit!* Another shot exploded into the night and I cringed.

I rolled beneath the van, feeling the warmth from the recently started engine. Crawling on my stomach to the back of the vehicle, I tried to pick out Jace lying on the ground, but it was difficult to spot him in his army jacket. I hoped that meant that the shooter would have trouble targeting him too.

That's if we even *are* the targets, I thought. I could see the zombie's feet shuffling left and then right in a bizarre sort of dance, and had a horrible suspicion about who – or what – the real target was.

Crap. Who was out here taking pot shots at zombies? As if I couldn't guess.

The explosive crack of another bullet made me grit my teeth. If Papa Murdoch had somehow followed us, he clearly didn't care too much about drawing attention to what was going on out here.

Catching sight of movement in the overgrown patch

of dying shrubs over to my right, I sighed with relief when I saw the pale glow of Jace's hair. He really needed to wear a hat when he went out on night-time missions. I rolled my eyes. Here I was, grovelling in the dirt beneath a van in a graveyard, while some crazy person used a revenant for shooting practise, and I was worried about Jace's lack of appropriate 'special ops' clothing?

Another shot and Zombie Byron jerked back a step. And then another and another, each sharp report of the gun causing the creature to shudder. Its long black coat jumped in multiple places, again and again, as though tiny creatures were burrowing beneath it.

But it wasn't falling. It – the *revenant* – wasn't falling down. I knew that silver bullets could cause the undead pain, but I didn't know how much harm they would really do to a zombie. There's no way they'd kill a vampire – not unless several rounds were pumped directly into the heart, anyway. Was the shooter even using silver bullets?

The creature finally collapsed and lay twitching – whatever he'd been hit with, it was enough to incapacitate if not 'kill'.

Jace began crawling toward me, his eyes fixed intently on mine as he made for the underside of the van. I tried to read his expression, but he reached me before I could think about it for long enough.

'Budge over,' he grunted as he pulled himself alongside me and lay panting for a moment. He rolled onto his back and I was suddenly aware of how close we were. His hip was pressed firmly against mine as we lay beneath Thomas Murdoch's Batmobile.

I was still lying on my front, my nose almost poking out of the precarious metal shelter. Jace was on his back, his head by my feet and his legs bent at an awkward angle to ensure all of him was tucked beneath the van's chassis.

I wriggled until I was pointing the same way as him. My face was inches from his and I could feel my eyes glowing like twin full moons in the darkness.

'You might want to turn the light down a bit, you know?' Jace's voice was mock-serious, but I could see he was making a sensible point by the way my shining eyes cast reflections in his.

'I can't help it,' I said, my voice laced with defensiveness born of habit. 'They do that sometimes when I get stressed.'

A strange expression crossed his face. 'Are you stressed, then?'

I frowned. 'Sure. Your dad's out there acting like he's in the middle of a warzone.'

'That's not my dad.'

'How can you say that? Of course it is. Who else would be out here shooting at everything in sight?'

'He didn't give me a signal,' Jace whispered, shaking his head. Stubborn. 'Maybe it's the "Spook Squad" – that's possible, right?'

'I guess . . .' Yeah, like I was really convinced. Let Jace live in denial if he wanted to. Some of us had to deal with reality.

He seemed about to reply but then closed his mouth, gesturing for me to be quiet. Whoever had been shooting was approaching the still-twitching body in the clearing.

I hadn't even noticed the footsteps. In the cool quiet of this little capsule with Jace, I'd allowed myself to forget the danger – just for a moment. But a moment was all it might take for something *else* crazy to start happening.

'What—' I whispered, but had to stop when Jace put two gentle fingers against my lips. His skin smelled of dust and dried blood, an earthy combination mixed in with his natural human scent.

'I think he's going,' he mouthed.

I listened and could easily make out slowly retreating footsteps, accompanied by a heavy dragging sound that seemed ominous. Was what remained of Byron being dragged away? Was he dead – *really* dead – or simply injured?

Whatever he'd done since his transformation, it wasn't the kid's fault and I felt fear rise up in my gut. Where was the body being taken? I had sudden visions of a lab and horrifying experiments. Maybe Jace was right. Maybe a squad from the Office of Preternatural Investigations really *was* out there. I let my imagination run riot for a few moments, not liking what I saw in my overactive mind's eye.

'We can't let him be taken, not like this,' I hissed.

I could hardly make out Jace's features in the gloom, but there was no mistaking the eyebrow-raise and the accompanying glint of silver from his piercing. 'He's dead anyway, Moth.'

'So am I,' I whispered. I'd meant it to sound more forceful, but somehow it came off sounding sort of pathetic.

'No you're not,' Jace replied. 'Not like that. You're just about the most alive person I know.' And then he did the last thing I would ever have expected from him: he kissed me.

His lips were gentle but insistent – at least, to begin with. The sensation sent a flutter of many-winged butterflies into crazy flight around my stomach. I pressed myself against his warmth, not caring that we were beneath a van in the middle of a graveyard, with who knows *what* out there. I had enough presence of mind to hope he didn't cut himself on my fangs, but it didn't stop me kissing him back. I kissed him as though my life depended on it – which maybe it did. In a weird sort of way.

I wanted to feel alive. I wanted to feel *human*.

He crawled on top of me, pushing me against the ground with the full length of his body. Heat radiated from him and I could feel every muscle, every movement. My head spun and I felt dizzy, even lying down, as instinct took over and I wrapped my legs around him. I'd only ever been with Theo before, and he had felt cold – any warmth hadn't been real. It was all illusion, after feeding, and his big mistake had been not feeding enough before taking me to his house that night.

But Jace was warm and alive, really alive. Not only could I hear his heart beating, I could feel the steady flow of blood pumping through his veins.

I pressed my face to his neck and took a deep breath. He smelled so good. He would taste even better—

His whole body went rigid. Oops. I probably shouldn't have done the sniffing thing.

Jace looked down at me. 'What do you think you're doing?'

'Um . . . sorry?'

'Jesus.' He was still lying on top of me, but he held most of his weight on his arms. He closed his eyes and took a shaky breath that was warm against my face. 'What am *I* doing?'

I didn't know whether I should feel upset or angry. I wanted to be angry – that was easier. But as I looked into his now open eyes, it was too easy to lose myself in those velvet-brown depths. Here was a guy who had suffered loss and pain; someone who knew what it was to survive in a terrifying world, and yet who still managed to hold onto his humanity. Just about. It was difficult to hate someone like that, even when he was rejecting me.

'If you hate what I am so much, why did you even kiss me?' I wondered if he could hear the breathless hitch in my voice.

He just stared at me, looking so lost that I wanted to hold him despite my anger.

'Jace?'

He ignored me and rolled over. He poked his head out from under the van. 'Hey, I think they've gone.'

The butterflies in my stomach turned into black-winged bats. *Crap*.

'You only kissed me to give him a chance to get away, didn't you?' I didn't care that my voice had suddenly risen well above the acceptable volume for 'covert operations'.

Screw covert operations.

'Stop saying dumb shit like that,' he replied, but his tone sounded way too defensive. I could practically smell the lie on him.

Humiliation replaced all the other feelings I'd experienced only moments before. 'You're such an ass-hole. I knew it! That's your dad out there, isn't it?'

I pulled myself forward and prepared to crawl out from under the big hulk of metal that was beginning to feel disturbingly like a coffin.

Jace gripped the top of my arm and pulled me back.

He wasn't gentle anymore. 'Stay here, I'll check things out.'

'I will *not* stay here. I'm going to find out what happened to Byron. And I want to know who was shooting at us.'

Jace sounded tired; way too old to be nineteen. 'He wasn't shooting at *us*.'

'Who was it, Jace?' Like I didn't already know. I just wanted to hear him say it. 'You'd better tell me or—'

'Or what, girlie?' The voice was gruff and deep and dangerous.

Murdoch. I shivered.

Jace slowly lowered his head to the ground and let go of the death-grip he had on my arm. I had almost lost the feeling there because he'd been holding on so tightly.

'I think you two can come out of there now,' Thomas Murdoch continued. 'Coast is clear.'

Jace lifted his face but refused to look at me.

'You knew it was him all along, didn't you?' I demanded as betrayal curled in my chest, making me feel as though I might choke.

'What do *you* think? I was trying to protect you, OK?' He glared at me before sliding out from beneath the van. 'Stay close to me and try to keep your mouth shut for once.'

Chapter Twenty-one

Jace had been quiet since we had crawled out from beneath the van, keeping his eyes fixed on the ground and doing everything he could to avoid looking at me.

I swallowed. This wasn't good. It was very far from good, especially as there didn't appear to be any sign of the authorities riding to the rescue. And even worse, Byron had disappeared. I couldn't help morbidly speculating about what had happened to his remains.

The cold expression on Murdoch Senior's face made me suddenly hope that whatever was left of the kid was well and truly dead.

I thought about how Jace had kissed me underneath the van. He'd been so tender; surely he couldn't have faked it. *But then again*, said that treacherous inner voice, *it was only to stop you noticing what was happening.* Jace must've known his father was out there and wanted to avoid the situation we were in now.

But that didn't mean it hadn't been real. Did it?

Murdoch spat on the ground, close to my feet. 'I told you what would happen if I saw you again, girl.' He was still holding a powerful-looking gun.

'It's not my fault you've been following me.'

His laugh sent shivers down my spine – and not the good kind. 'Following my son, freak. Keeping an eye on him, ever since you got your claws into him.'

I rolled my eyes. 'Oh, please. I'm hardly a femme fatale. Jace has a mind of his own.'

'Not if you're compelling him against his will, he doesn't,' the hunter replied.

Jace stepped forward. 'Hey, I'm right here. Stop talking about me like I'm not.'

I shook my head. I didn't have the energy for this. I had far better things to do than play referee between these two screw-ups. 'I'm out of here.'

Jace grabbed my arm. 'You're staying right here.'

'Get your hands off me. I think I'll leave you and your father to . . . catch up.' I shook myself free and was relieved when he let go; I didn't want to have to use my strength against him.

I turned my back on Thomas and Jace Murdoch. I had only managed a couple of steps when Murdoch Senior called after me.

'Hey, Dead Girl! Where d'you think you're going?'

'Dad—'

'Shut up, Jason. Dead Girl, I'm talking to you!'

My shoulders tensed and the longing to smash Jace's dad in the face was so strong, so *visceral* I could taste it as surely as I'd tasted Theo's blood just two nights before. I rolled the desire around my tongue as I slowly turned and faced the older man.

'Where's Byron?' I demanded. My silver eyes swept over Thomas Murdoch, as though I could divine the answer simply by looking at him. If he would just stop avoiding my gaze I might even be able to do it. My experience with Detective Trent had given me new confidence in my skills.

Murdoch ignored me and turned back to continue an argument with his son.

Jace's hands were held in loose fists at his sides. 'How did you even find us here? Have you been following me?' He frowned.

'Grow up and think, boy,' growled Murdoch. 'The van has GPS; when I got home it was gone so I tracked it.'

Scowling, I stomped back toward them. I didn't care about interrupting their oh-so-touching father–son re-union. Let's see the big bad vampire hunter try to leave without telling me what he'd done to the kid.

Murdoch flashed me a nasty look. 'Come any closer,

little Dead Girl, and I'll stake you before you even know what day it is.'

'You talk a good fight, Murdoch,' I said, working hard at keeping my tone even. 'Let's see you back it up when you're not hiding behind a gun.'

'Dad—'

This time it was me who interrupted Jace. 'Shut up. This is between me and him. If you want to protect your father from me, I guess I can't blame you.'

Jace's father squared his shoulders. 'Frankenstein's monster is gone, you don't have to worry about him anymore. I've got plans for a nice bonfire later on, so you'd better walk away now unless you want to join him.'

'No,' I said. 'I want to know what happened to him. You shot him full of enough silver to do a lot of damage to most vampires. I'm guessing that's the same for . . . whatever he's become.'

Murdoch wiped his mouth with the back of his hand. '*Revenant*. I think that's the word you're looking for. That friend of yours turned into a zombie after one of your kind tried to turn him – and failed.' He glared at me as though I was personally responsible.

I swallowed, trying to get rid of the bad taste in my mouth. This guy was a total freak – forget vamps or the Unmade. Men like Thomas Murdoch were the reason the supernatural community stayed underground and, if they had any sense, wouldn't even dream of coming out of the coffin any time soon. At least, not for another century or two.

I ignored him. 'Let me see his body – we heard you moving him. I just want to make sure.'

'OK,' he said, a nasty grin flashing across his face. 'He's over there, on the edge of the clearing. Follow me.'

This was a sudden change of heart that I wasn't exactly buying, but I needed to make certain that Byron was actually dead. *Really* dead. For his sake as much as for the safety of local residents, because nobody deserved to be left to the sick whims of a stone-cold hunter like Murdoch.

Jace stepped in front of me. 'Leave it, Moth. Get out of here and I'll catch up with you later.'

His father sneered. 'Jesus Christ, son. You're breaking my heart here.'

'Dad . . . shut up for a second, will you?'

I couldn't help raising my eyebrows. Score one for Jace standing up to Daddy. Finally.

'I told you already not to speak to me that way. I think we need to talk about what they did to you at that god-damn school. Those places are filled with bleeding-heart liberals – makes me sick.'

I held up both my hands as though trying to stop traffic. 'Both of you, stop arguing and let me see him. Then I'll go.' I glared at Jace and tried to pretend I didn't notice the guilt in his eyes. 'I won't bother you again.'

'That's right,' Murdoch cut in. 'Because if you do, you're going to end up like the corpse you should be.'

I gritted my teeth and didn't give him the satisfaction of a reply. I was furious with Jace too – way to stand up for the girl who'd watched your back more than once now. The girl you'd just *kissed*. Let your psycho father insult and threaten her. *Nice one, dude. Totally smooth.* If I was ever going to talk to him again, I was going to give him a few lessons in basic manners.

Jace frowned at me and looked like he was about to say something when the sound of sirens stopped him. He closed his mouth and scanned the area.

His father cursed. 'You take the van – we'll put the body in there. I need to ditch the car I stole.'

'You *stole* a car?'

'I had to track my van in *something*.'

The sirens were getting closer. There was no time for anything and I didn't know what to do. I hesitated, watching as Murdoch leaned inside the car and began tossing equipment to Jace.

'Put these in the van. I'll bring the body.'

Jace fumbled a rolled tarp, then had to put it down when his father threw a jacket at him next. I stepped forward automatically to help Jace before his father tossed something heavy and smacked him on the head with it. My hands reached for the item on top of the pile. The jacket.

My jacket.

The jacket I'd given to my sister when I said goodbye to her at the station yesterday.

I clutched the leather in my fingers and held it to my chest, watching as Murdoch moved beyond the car and bent down to what I assumed was Byron's body. I couldn't see properly beyond the vehicle – and the crimson veil that swept across my vision.

Caitlín's scent was still on my jacket. What was Thomas Murdoch doing with it? Where was my sister?

I didn't even realize I was moving until I stumbled, my legs buckling beneath me. Jace had returned from dumping equipment in the van and reached out to stop me from falling.

'What's wrong with you? You look as though you've seen—'

'A ghost?' My lips felt numb. I could hardly work my mouth.

'Moth, what is it?' Jace filled my entire field of vision, holding my shoulders and shaking me.

Static filled my ears, blocking out the sound of sirens as they passed us by. They weren't even coming for us, but I didn't care about that anymore.

Only my little sister mattered.

I shrugged Jace off as though he was nothing. He staggered back as I pushed him aside using my full vamp strength.

Byron was in the van. They'd burn him and that would be the end of him. No more shambling revenant – no more Unmade vampire. Even that meant nothing to me.

I moved to the car. Murdoch had just started the engine. His eyes widened as he saw me appear beside his window. It must have looked like magic. I'd show him magic.

I punched the window so hard that the skin across my knuckles split and blood sprayed. I hardly noticed. Murdoch ducked as glass caved in and covered him. I reached through the jagged hole and grabbed him by the throat. He made satisfying gurgling sounds as I attempted to pull a fully-grown man through a gap the size of my fist.

His face grated across the broken glass like cheese. The smell of human blood awakened the predator in me. I pulled harder and he screamed—

And then I was on the ground with Jace on top of me.

'What is *wrong* with you? What happened?'

I shook my head, trying to clear it of the desire for blood. Trying to shake myself free from mindless rage.

'My sister.' I glared at Jace, expecting him to understand.

'Huh? Where?' He looked around, half expecting to see another girl in the clearing.

'Her jacket,' I said. '*My* jacket, I mean.'

'You're not making sense. Like, at all.'

Murdoch crawled out of the car, blood covering the entire left side of his face.

Jace leaped to his feet. 'Dad! Are you OK?'

'Do I *look* OK? Kill that thing.' He slipped a crudely carved stake from somewhere inside his coat and tossed it to his son. 'Kill it now.'

Jace instinctively caught the length of wood and I forced myself to stand and face him. I didn't think he'd attack me – not now, not after everything we'd been through together in the past week – but it didn't hurt to be cautious. Not where families were concerned.

I still clutched my leather jacket under one arm. I held it out, exhibiting it like a piece of evidence. 'What is your father doing with *this*?'

Murdoch snorted, mopping blood from his cheek with his sleeve. '*That's* what this is about?'

Jace looked between us in turn, clearly confused.

I took a step toward Murdoch Senior. 'Where is my sister?'

He smiled, the expression even nastier than usual thanks to his lacerated face. Blood pumped from a particularly deep wound by his left eye. 'She's your *sister*?' He whistled, as though impressed. 'The vamp's got balls, I'll give him that.'

I saw Jace's mouth begin to open, but I cut him off. 'Whatever you're about to say, save it. This is between me and him.'

Murdoch shook his head. 'He said she was insurance, but I didn't realize you actually knew her. Like the first three kids were all connected to you in some way. Don't you understand now? They were to frame *you* – so that your boss would be held responsible. But the new one?' He nodded at my jacket, still crushed between my frozen hands. 'I thought she was just another piece of collateral damage.'

'"Collateral damage"?' I stared at the hunter, trying to fathom what kind of a person calls a teenager something like that. He was a *father*, for God's sake.

Jace tucked the stake into the back of his jeans. 'If one of you doesn't tell me what's going on—'

'The guy I'm working with took another kid. Said it would make sure Dead Girl here didn't get in our way any more than she already has.'

I swallowed. 'Kyle. You're talking about *Kyle*, aren't you?' I'd been right! Kyle was involved, right up to his skinny little neck.

Murdoch shrugged. 'Yeah. So?'

I glanced at Jace. 'He's a vampire, you know. Part of my vampire Family. *Theo's* Family.' There. I'd said my Maker's name and the world hadn't ended. At least, not quite yet.

Jace stared at his father like he didn't recognize him. 'Wait, you're working with a *vampire*? How can you justify that, given everything you've always said to me? After what happened to Mom . . .'

Now it was my turn to stare at Jace. His *mother*? The vision I'd had – that brief and terrible glimpse inside his head – flashed into my mind. Horror took hold of my chest and squeezed, but I didn't have time to examine the possibilities any further because Murdoch Senior was walking toward the van.

I headed him off. 'What are you doing?'

'Screw the car,' he said. 'I've got somewhere to be.'

'You're not going anywhere until you tell me where my sister is.'

He shook his head. 'Where do you think? Tonight's the night everything ends for your boss.'

Theo? I forced out a breath, just to steady myself. 'This is all about killing Theo?'

'It's more complicated than that. At least, it is for Kyle.' Murdoch's lips twitched into something resembling a smile. His teeth were coated with blood. 'For me, I'll just be happy to take down the Master vampire of Boston, but you'll have to ask Kyle about *his* plans.'

Jace had his hand on my shoulder and I shook it off. I hadn't even noticed him move. 'I don't give a crap about Kyle,' I said. 'I just want my sister. Where's Caitlín?'

The hunter opened the driver's side door. He nodded his head toward the back of the van. 'Right about now she's probably joining the kid in zombie land.'

My eyes widened and I clenched my hands into fists.

I'd kill them all if they hurt Caitlín. I didn't know how I'd do it, but I would. Somehow.

'Come on, son,' Murdoch said. 'You don't want to miss taking down a Master vamp. Her boss. *Theodore Fitzgerald.* We need to get over to his house on Beacon Hill.'

I had to help Theo. What was I going to do? Was Caitlín at Theo's house? She must be – if that's where Kyle was intending to put his plan into action. Whatever that plan actually was.

Jace stood shoulder-to-shoulder with me, but I couldn't find it inside myself to care. Not anymore. 'I'm not going anywhere with you,' he said to his father.

'Stop arguing and get in the van.'

'Not without her,' Jace replied, his face pale and set in hard lines.

'The only way *that* gets in *my* van again is with a stake in its pretty little chest.' Murdoch fixed his son with a cold stare. 'Your choice.'

'Jace,' I said, carefully keeping my tone neutral. 'Thanks for the *support*, but I've done just fine by myself so far.'

He held out a hand. 'Come with me – let me help you.'

I shook my head, feeling sorry for him. 'Your daddy's made the decision for you, Jace. Just make sure that Byron's truly dead – that's all I ask of you.' Surely I could trust him to do *that* much. I could get to Theo's by myself.

Time to make use of my vampire abilities. Time to turn them into a *strength*.

I turned and ran back toward the heart of the grave-yard. The distant rumble of traffic reached my ears as I almost flew beneath the branches of skeletal trees. Hardly watching where my feet were falling, I trusted my instincts to guide me safely and not let me run into grave markers half hidden by brambles and dead foliage. I hurdled a fallen branch and made it to the far side of the grounds. But I didn't stop there, simply using my momentum to leap at the iron bars of the fence, swing-ing my legs up and over.

I slid down the other side and landed lightly on the sidewalk opposite the shining white façade of the Law School, no longer caring if a passing human saw me. What did I care about that when Caitlín was in danger? And Theo, too. There were worse things that could happen right now than discovery.

If I could save her, I wouldn't even care what the Council did to me for telling her the truth about what I was.

Gritting my teeth against the aching desire to scream, I put down my head and ran.

Chapter Twenty-two

Theo's front door was unlocked. That was my first clue that things were way beyond screwed and on a fast-track to oh-shit-we're-all-gonna-die.

The place was dark, feeling empty. I didn't hear any breathing, but then vampires didn't have to breathe. I moved up the stairs, attempting silence. I took the stairs two at a time. I reached the top floor, grateful for the vampire lungs that meant I could run up four flights of stairs without getting out of breath.

When I reached the top, Theo's cathedral-like eyrie spread out before me. I stopped and stared, trying to process what my eyes and brain were telling me. Shadows flickered, pinpoints of light from the few candles that remained standing, like cats' eyes watching and waiting at the edges of the room. Desperately, I searched for my

Maker among the signs of struggle and violence: chairs overturned; one of the beautiful stained-glass windows smashed; even Theo's plants torn apart and scattered, as though destroyed in a petulant fit of rage.

And blood . . . so much of it. Too much to possibly belong to just one person.

Caitlín! Her name filled my head like a mantra. I had to find her, to make sure that the blood didn't belong to her. To make her safe.

Something inside me broke, shattering alongside the multi-colored glass that covered the floor like confetti:

There is blood everywhere.

For a moment, I think that's all there is to see – a roomful of blood and pain. The floor gleams wet. The whole room reeks of death.

Kyle. I grit my teeth against fear and anger, the alchemy of emotions making me feel like a shaken-up Coke bottle.

Where is my sister? And Theo?

Terror threatens to make me careless, but I force myself to step carefully over the threshold, my feet slipping and sliding on the wet floor. I wonder how there can be so much blood. The carpet is spattered with it and I can't help but turn away—

Which is when I see my wounded Maker in a crumpled heap at the side of an overturned chair. I run to him, trying to keep my balance but no longer caring if I end up on my ass; I have to reach Theo. My hand closes on the back of the chair and I jerk it away, my fingers slick with cold blood.

I am too busy falling to my knees beside Theo to notice anything else. I am overwhelmed with panic and shock; fear for my Maker and how badly he might be hurt. I hate him at times, it's true. But I still belong to him.

And what does this mean for Caitlín? He might have protected her, but I can't see any sign of my little sister. I'm wearing the jacket which still carries her scent, meaning that I can't trace her that way. She's all around me.

Not that I can smell anything much besides blood.

I see the stake shoved through Theo's chest, close to his heart but not quite all the way there. Not quite enough to end him. I wonder whether Kyle missed, or did he leave our Master 'alive' for a reason.

I grab the blood-stained stake and yank as hard as I can. The broken length of wood slides free, and blood gushes hot and dark – so dark it looks black. I drop the stake, only vaguely aware of the wet sound it makes as it hits the floor.

Theo stirs under my touch, his many other wounds already beginning to heal. His eyes flutter open and then widen. He opens his mouth to speak – to warn me – but it is too late.

I'm too focused on helping him to notice somebody moving silently behind me.

Something cold and hard strikes the back of my head hard enough to split my skull, and I go down and down into darkness . . .

* * *

Silence. The world came back in a rush and I blinked. Suddenly there was a bed beneath me.

I was no longer alone. Jace was standing at the foot of the bed, looking down at me.

'How did *you* get here?' I said, watching him blearily. My brain felt like a wad of chewed gum.

'Dad told me where to come. He was getting ready, but I wouldn't wait. Oh, and the front door's wide open.'

'Oh.' Had I left it like that, or was it Kyle? Or Murdoch? I tried to sit up. 'I need to get out of here. I have to find Theo—'

'Don't be stupid, you're bleeding all over the place.' Jace passed me a glass of water. I drank and drank, making myself feel sick. 'Slow down,' he said. 'Easy.'

Water sloshed onto my hand and memory clawed at me with sharp fingers.

I look at Theo over the glass of water, try to read his mind just by watching his beautiful face. 'How did you die?'

He strokes my hair, hums gently under his breath. Something Gaelic. It makes me smile, but I notice that he doesn't answer me.

'What was it like?' I ask him. 'Who held you, when you came back? Who brought you water and took care of you?'

He doesn't reply. Just kisses my cheek and lays me back down on the bed, covers me with a blanket and walks out.

I don't know if he has somewhere he needs to be, or if he is angry at my questions.

I curl up under the covers and wait for him to come back. I don't have anything else to do.

Jace was watching me like he thought I might collapse at any moment.

'Someone hit me,' I said. *Way to state the obvious, Moth.* 'Theo . . .' I continued. Agitation forced my limbs into action. I tried to push against Jace. 'Where's Theo?'

'Your Maker? On the roof,' Jace replied. His tone was flat, all expression leached from it.

I tried to focus on what he was saying. If I could just stop feeling *sick*, that would help. A lot. '*Where's Caitlin?*' I tried to *move*, using all my speed to propel myself up and out. Only my legs weren't working right and I stayed exactly where I was. 'My sister—'

'I didn't see her, I'm sorry. Now stop struggling and take a minute to rest. You're no good to her in this state.' Jace handed me one of Theo's towels. It was black, of course. At least it won't show the bloodstains, I thought, as I dabbed at the back of my head. I felt crazy – light-headed. I shouldn't feel this bad, should I? What happened to my vampire super-fast healing? I probably needed to drink some blood.

As soon as that thought crossed my mind, I became

aware of Jace sitting close to me on the bed. Hyper-aware.

I kept seeing everything in shades of red. It felt like when I'd first been turned.

'I need—'

'This?' Jace was holding a familiar-looking bag filled with hospital blood.

I bit my lip, my stomach contracting with hunger at the sight of the glowing ruby liquid, but at the same time filled with disgust that Jace should see me like this. 'No, I think I'm OK,' I said.

'Don't be stupid. You need it.' He thrust the clear plastic container at me, pushing it into my hand and making me take it from him before it fell onto the bed. 'Come on, drink it up like a good—'

'Jace,' I growled, 'I'm fine.'

'I'm not leaving you alone till I know you're really all right. That bastard tried to bash your skull in with a silver candlestick. Some tall, skinny blond dude. Sort of ratty-looking.'

Kyle. Not that I was surprised. I tried to focus but still couldn't think straight, and I was just so *hungry*.

I tried my best to fight off the gnawing need, but I was beyond tired and it was all I could do to keep from tearing into the blood bag right now. 'What happened to him? The blond vamp?'

'Ran out when I shot a crossbow bolt into his shoulder.'

I screwed up my face. 'His *shoulder*? Even with silver bolts, you should really be aiming for the heart.'

Jace scowled. 'I missed.'

'Oh.'

'And then your Maker . . . *Theo* . . . just got up and followed him. Looks like he heals fast from a stake through the chest.'

'It wasn't in the heart. I pulled it out.'

He nodded. 'Right. So he told me to check on you and went up to the roof.'

Theo was OK. Relief blazed all the way through me.

Trying to piece events together was getting easier, but I was still pretty groggy. I remembered Byron. *Poor Byron* . . . 'What happened to Byron? Was he really dead?'

Jace's mouth tightened and I saw something hard in his eyes. 'He is now.' He turned away. 'But Dad's coming, you know. To kill your Maker.'

But the pain in my head was beating a rhythm in time to the sound of Jace's heart; hunger combined with weakness made it increasingly difficult to keep control. Jace was so warm – and sitting so close to me that I could almost taste his pulse on my tongue. I flashed back to our kiss under the van.

'It's OK, I don't mind if you drink it here,' Jace said. He shrugged and gestured at the blood bag again.

Moaning softly, I pulled up my knees and buried my face against them. 'Jace, please . . . you don't get it.'

I didn't want the stupid bagged blood. I had to get away from him. Away from *his* blood. I pushed him away and ran across the room. My eyes wouldn't focus properly, but I knew the door must be here somewhere. If I could just get away I wouldn't hurt him.

But, oh Jesus, the smell of him and the beating of his heart in his warm chest while he'd sat by me on the bed.

'Moth! What's the matter with you?' Jace was striding toward me. He had the bag in his hand again, but I wasn't focused on that. No, I was looking at the gash I'd only just noticed in his arm, and how blood oozed out of the wound and trickled down the muscle of his bicep. I remembered the taste of his blood; that tiny taste six months ago. It had only been a single drop, but it was enough to remind me that not all human blood tasted like crap.

Luckily for Jace it seemed as though he was wising up to the situation. Finally. *Maybe it's not too late*, I thought.

He was taking slow steps backward, his brown eyes wide as he stared at me. The dawning realization on his face would've been funny if only I weren't so *hungry*.

I was growling under my breath; softly in the back of my throat, more like a purr than anything. I hoped he couldn't hear it, but no matter how hard I tried I couldn't stop. I was exhausted, scared and stressed out – it was no wonder I was losing control.

I tried to fight the craving, told myself it would pass.

Heard Theo's voice in my head, from another time and place: *Hold on. Calm. Be calm.*

The air was so brittle I felt like it might crack. The twisted feeling in my gut got worse. Calm was beyond me. Holding on was no longer an option.

I sprang at Jace, and he was lucky that he already had his hands out or he wouldn't have had a hope of stopping my fangs latching directly onto his throat. We crashed against the far wall, my momentum carrying us both the length of the room. Jace was back-pedaling like crazy, trying to stay on his feet but losing the battle when his shoulders struck the wall.

We went down, me on top of him, and all I could do was see him through a haze of the deepest crimson. I was strong, far stronger than him. Even injured, the bloodlust gave me a new burst of strength. My legs clamped around his hips and I held him in place, pressing myself against him. My mouth watered. God, I wanted . . . what? What did I want? *Him?* Or his blood . . .

'Moth!' He had his hands on either side of my face, but his fingers were anything but tender. His white-knuckle grip would've left bruises on anyone human.

But I wasn't human.

I was so close to his flesh now, I could almost taste the blood pulsing through the taut arteries of his neck. I tried to dig my nails into his eyes but he shook his head violently from side to side. He was trying to flip us over, but my knees were locked in place on either side of his waist as I clung to him like the deadliest ivy.

The door crashed open and a familiar scent washed over me. My hesitation was all Jace needed and he managed to get his forearm across my throat, pushing me back until I thought my neck might break.

Theo strode across the room and plucked me off my prey as easily as if he were picking fruit. He had me by the scruff of the neck and shook me, then threw me onto the huge bed.

'Get a hold of yourself, Marie!'

Why did he have to do that? I hated it when he called me Marie. I shivered on the expensive bedding I hadn't noticed when I'd first come to in Jace's arms.

Of course, I thought, *Theo* would *have black silk sheets*. It was almost a relief to hear my familiar snarky voice peeking through the inferno of need that raged through me.

Jace was struggling to his feet, and I couldn't help noticing the flash of silver as he pulled the dagger from its hidden sheath. *Huh*. So he'd gotten it back.

Theo held me down with one hand and, without even looking, flung his other arm out behind him to block the young hunter's attack.

'Let her go,' Jace replied. He sounded almost as calm as the Master vampire, a pretty good trick to pull off under the circumstances.

Theo still had me pinned to the bed, but twisted to face what he no doubt considered a young upstart. 'If I release her, she'll only go for your throat again.'

I tried to dislodge my Maker's hand. 'I'm fine, Theo. See? All back to normal. Just hungry.' I ducked my head as hot shame filled the emptiness in my chest.

He laughed. 'I don't think you're *fine* at all, my little Moth.' He raised his left wrist to his lips and tore into the veins with wicked sharp canines. A single deep slash marred the newly healed perfection of his pale skin, and he held the dripping blood to my mouth.

I struggled against him, trying desperately to be free of the dark temptation he held just out of reach of my lips. 'No, you're too weak to give me blood.'

Theo climbed onto the bed with me and pulled me into his arms so quickly I didn't have time to realize he'd released me for a couple of precious seconds. He cradled me against his chest and I craned my neck to see his face. He was still watching Jace with that hawkish expression I knew so well.

Jace took a furious step forward. Spots of color blazed high on his beautiful cheekbones. 'What are you doing to her?'

'What does it look like? I am feeding her. If you'd prefer to donate your own blood, be my guest.' He laughed softly. 'I was under the impression that you were trying to escape doing that very thing.'

I wriggled so that I could see Jace over Theo's insistent arm. 'Just get out while you still can, Jace.'

Theo stiffened against me. 'Jace? I wonder if that's the same "Jace" the hunter mentioned while he was begging me for his life . . .' He let his voice trail off.

'*What?*' Jace had retrieved the knife from the ground and was gripping it so tightly I could see the white of his knuckles. 'What did you just say?'

Theo smiled – I could hear it in his voice even if I couldn't see it. 'Thomas Murdoch, the man who took it upon himself to *end* several vampires under my protection.'

'That's his job,' Jace said, his voice trembling with an emotion I couldn't name.

'A job that involved slaughtering innocents.'

Now it was Jace's turn to laugh. The sound came out ugly and strained. '*Innocents* . . . I don't think so.'

'You know nothing, boy,' Theo said in a quiet voice. 'But this one was right.' Here he nudged me. 'If you value your pathetic human life, leave now and I won't send anyone after you. Maybe you have helped my Moth these past few days, and for that you get to live. For now.'

I began to shiver. 'Please, Jace, just listen to him. Get out.'

Jace looked from Theo, to me, and then back at Theo again. His brown eyes were wide in his pale face. Darkness shadowed them and he looked exhausted.

I licked my dry lips. 'Go on, Jace. Go find your dad.'

'Or whatever is left of him,' Theo said.

For a horrible moment, I thought that Jace might really attack my Maker. He wouldn't stand a chance.

But then he turned and ran from the room.

I slumped back into Theo's arms. 'Did you really kill him? Murdoch, I mean?'

Theo stroked my hair and it felt so comforting, so tender, that I didn't even care about the blood he must be wiping into it. He whispered in my ear, 'Not yet. That would be far too easy.'

I sighed. 'But you have to . . . The Council . . . your challenge.'

'That's true.' Theo sounded amused.

'Wait, I'm totally confused.'

'I've left the hunter fighting with my *Enforcer*.' I couldn't miss the bitter irony in his voice. 'Though he is badly injured, Kyle is carrying out his final job. And then *I* will finish *him*.'

My brain creaked under the strain of trying to figure things out. But I was too tired to think about it now, and Theo had pushed his wrist back to my mouth.

'Hurry, before the wound begins to close.'

I tried to push his arm away. 'No, there's a bag of blood here somewhere. Give me that.'

Theo was having none of it. 'You will drink from me. *Now*.'

We locked eyes and I felt something inside me crumble; a barrier I'd been trying to erect to keep him out of my heart. Out of my *soul*. Was he doing this to me? Influencing my thoughts while I was so vulnerable? I didn't think he would do that, but maybe I didn't know him at all.

And what did any of it matter? I was stuck in this so-called life and couldn't see any way out.

So I drank from my Maker. Even though he was weak and had been drained to the point of collapse. Even though he knew about my 'friendship' with his enemy's son. Theo gave me his blood to revive me.

I wanted to ask him why he would do such a thing, but I didn't really need to. I knew his reply even before he gave it:

You're mine, he would say. *You are part of me always and forever, for better or worse.*

Chapter Twenty-three

After I'd fed, just a little – just enough to get me back on my feet, and to prove to Theo that I was well enough to go look for Caitlín – we headed up to the roof. My Maker couldn't have stopped me even if he'd been at full strength himself.

My sister was up there and she needed me.

The iron steps leading to the roof angled sharply in a zigzag up the side of the building. Even in our injured states, it was no trouble for either of us to climb. I was running on a mixture of my Maker's blood and my own adrenaline, but where *he* got the strength from I was honestly beginning to wonder. He was the Master of Boston – he had to be strong enough to hold together dozens of vamps, so I guess being stabbed through the chest couldn't hold him back for long.

Theo had assured me that a lot of the blood on the floor had actually been Kyle's, but I didn't believe him until I caught sight of the lanky blond vampire fighting for his worthless 'life' against Thomas Murdoch.

'Wow,' I whispered, 'you weren't kidding about how messed up Kyle was.'

Theo tried and failed to hold back an unbearably smug expression. 'When have I ever lied to you?'

'I'm taking the Fifth on that.'

He raised his brows. 'Moth, you wound me . . .'

I shook my head. 'You'll get over it.'

I pulled myself up next to him on the very edge of the roof. I could smell the oily scent of the Charles from up here, and the distant sound of traffic reminded me that life was going on as normal far below us. We were crouched next to a low wall that gave the illusion of safety for anyone choosing to 'sunbathe' in Theo's rooftop garden. The irony of this setup amused him, but at least he knew that there was only one other way on and off the roof: the main access from an enclosed staircase that led back down to the house. The hatch was located roughly in the center of the rectangular roof.

I couldn't see Caitlín or Jace anywhere.

Theo leaned his head close to mine, his black curls touching my face. 'Kyle has been working to unseat me.' His lip curled. 'Fool.'

'I know.' I could hardly believe it myself. Surely Kyle

wasn't that dumb. 'It still doesn't sit right with me – he's way too young to lead a Family, so what's the point?'

'It seems he tried to set me up, regardless.' Theo's beautiful eyes met mine, and I felt the familiar tug of power in my gut. He looked sad. 'There was a human girl I fed from, not so long ago . . . He took her away for me . . .'

'Theo,' I whispered urgently, interrupting him and grabbing his arm as my attention was suddenly drawn to the battle. I was glad of the distraction; I didn't want to hear about Erin's death. 'Look!'

To our far left, Kyle had Murdoch Senior forced backward over the surrounding wall and seemed to be gaining the upper hand. Murdoch's right arm hung uselessly by his side and the sword he had been wielding only moments before lay on the gravel. Blood slicked the long blade – it looked as though the hunter had added to the vampire's already significant injuries.

Kyle was moving slowly – he had too many open wounds that weren't healing fast enough – but he still had Thomas Murdoch beat. The vampire's eyes were furious disks of white fire in the night, and his hair shone under the half-moon.

I turned to say something to Theo, but he'd disappeared.

Crap. I hadn't even felt him move. I looked over my shoulder, searching the roof for him. *Where had he gone?*

299

Back down, inside the house? What was he doing? I stared into the gloom but couldn't see any signs of movement.

I also couldn't see any sign that Cait had been here and was beginning to think Murdoch had tricked me on that front. He had her/my jacket, but that didn't mean he actually had *her*. I began to allow myself to hope – which is a dangerous thing when you know how harsh life can be.

The battle continued to unfold. Kyle had Murdoch Senior pinned on his back like a butterfly now, his arms flailing out over the edge as he came precariously close to falling.

It was at *that* moment that Jace practically *flew* out of the roof hatch and skidded to a stop before running into me.

'Moth, are you OK?' His voice was hoarse and I could see fresh blood on his face. Maybe *I'd* done that to Jace while I was stuck in that stupid bloodlust. Hot shame overwhelmed me, and for a moment I couldn't say anything.

'Jace, I'm sorry about—'

He waved me away, looking around wildly. His wide eyes finally came to rest on his father on the other side of the roof. 'Dad!'

Kyle's clawed hands latched onto Murdoch's shoulders, holding him in place so that he could get at the man's throat. He burrowed deeper, ripping into flesh.

Murdoch went down without a sound, not even a scream of shock or pain. Kyle dragged him to the ground and straddled him. He sat on the hunter's torso, pinning his arms to the concrete, feeding, swallowing mouthfuls of blood.

'*Dad!*'

Jace ran.

'Wait—' I gave up and went after him. There would be no stopping him, not when his father was on the verge of death.

Jace picked up his father's sword and hefted it, one-handed, as though it was something he'd done before.

'Let him go.' I'd never heard Jace like that; his voice sent chills down my spine, and not in a good way.

Unfortunately, Kyle only laughed. 'You've got a lot to learn. Stick around and I'll show you a few things – *after* I've taken care of your daddy.'

I cringed as I watched the murderous rage in Jace's dark eyes. He was going to take out the vampire – or die trying.

Thomas Murdoch chose that moment to lock eyes with his son. His throat and chest were a mess of blood and torn flesh. His voice bubbled up from somewhere deep and painful. 'Get out of here, boy. Remember what I taught you: it's OK to run when you're outnumbered by the monsters.'

Jace was so white I thought he was going to pass out. Murdoch Senior was bleeding from countless wounds, blood mixing with the saliva pooled at the corners of his thin mouth.

I put my hand on Jace's arm, carefully, as though approaching a wild animal. 'He's too dangerous; leave Kyle to me.'

Which of course made the vampire laugh even more. I gritted my teeth and swore to make sure Kyle didn't leave this roof tonight – at least, not until I'd made him tell me where Caitlín was.

Thomas Murdoch struggled weakly under the vampire's hands. And then Kyle moved quicker than the human eye could see. He lifted Murdoch by the tattered collar of his shirt with one hand, while slashing across his throat with the other. I'd experienced the touch of Kyle's talons before, but this was something else. This was a killing blow.

The vampire cut what remained of the hunter's throat in one swift movement, smiling as Murdoch's lifeless body slipped out of his arms and crumpled to the cold concrete.

Jace screamed and swung the silver-edged sword at Kyle, but his emotions made his attack clumsy. The vampire spun quickly and caught the sword between his palms. Kyle's devious mind translated amazingly well to fighting. This was the true reason he held a respected position in Theo's Family – not many vamps were stupid enough to challenge Kyle in combat.

Heedless of the blood that ran from his hands, the vampire *twisted* the sword and forced Jace to let go or have his arm snapped. His foot lashed out, a vicious kick that caught Jace in the stomach.

He staggered, doubling over and fighting for breath.

Kyle spun the sword casually in his hand and kicked Jace again – this time in the face. I winced as Jace went down and out.

With a grin of triumph the vampire tossed Murdoch's sword aside. 'Looks like you won't be needing Daddy's toothpick.'

Theo stepped out of the shadows. 'Let's see you face *me*.'

But it wasn't Theo I was focused on. Not the expression on his face or the fire of his eyes. I was staring at who he carried in his arms.

'*Caitlín!*' My chest expanded with a dizzying combination of hope and terror.

Theo met my gaze with compassion. 'She is alive.'

I ran forward, making the huge mistake of turning my back on Kyle. He grabbed me by my hair and pulled so hard I thought my neck would snap.

'Told you about your hair, Moth. Far too useful for your opponent.' His tone was conversational.

'Go screw your—'

Kyle smashed my head into the nearby wall, effectively silencing me as my legs turned to dental floss and I sagged against the hard concrete of the roof. I was conscious, but barely. I looked up at him and my gut froze when I saw the expression on his face. His eyes were empty, like a robbed grave. Like the abyss. He punched me in the stomach as I tried to rise, grabbing my hair again and banging my chin on the ground. Pain exploded in my jaw and I felt a rush of copper in my mouth.

Theo's voice broke through the pounding in my head. 'Release her, immediately!'

His Enforcer chuckled, as though he was having a fine time out here, killing humans and beating the crap out of me.

Still, it was enough to see my little sister lying unconscious in Theo's arms. There was a part of me that was grateful she was out of it. She looked peaceful. Too pale. Too still. But she was alive, and at least she didn't have to face the monsters. I watched the steady rise and fall of her chest, taking comfort in the fact that she was with Theo and not Kyle.

A feeling of false security that slipped away within moments.

Kyle kept me on my feet, one arm wrapped around my neck and the other across my stomach, holding me against the front of his body. His fangs were so close to my throat that I could smell Murdoch's blood on them.

He ran his tongue down the side of my face. It was like a large slug, leaving a hot, bloody trail across my skin.

Theo's hands tightened against Caitlín's body. I could see his knuckles go stark white and, for a moment, I worried he might break something. My little sister was so fragile. So . . . human.

Kyle pulled me with him over to the wall. I would have fallen were it not for his pseudo-lover's hold on me. I couldn't seem to control my body, but that probably had something to do with the dent in my skull. That one was going to take a lot more blood to fully heal and I'd already taken more than my Maker could give.

'I have a proposition for you, *boss*,' Kyle said. His voice was pitched low and steady, as though he was in control and had all the time in the world.

'I don't deal with traitors,' my Maker replied. 'Release my fledgling. Now.'

'Can't do that, I'm afraid. There's more at *stake* here than you know.'

Kyle punctuated these words by removing his right arm from around my neck – still holding me up with his left – and smoothly pulling a stake from one of his sturdy biker boots.

He spun it in his hand and pressed it against my heart. 'Thoughtful of Murdoch to bring these with him.'

Mention of the dead hunter made me glance in his son's direction. Jace was still out cold. I hoped he wasn't too badly hurt, but Kyle was inhumanly strong. He didn't look much like he was holding back when he put his boot into Murdoch Junior's face.

I felt the tip of the stake pressing against my shirt and wondered if this was really the way my second life would end. I swallowed my fear and tried to turn my head so I could at least catch a glimpse of the man holding me. Look into his eyes one more time before he did it.

'You killed the man you were working with,' I said. 'Why would you do that?'

'He got squeamish when I killed the second kid. After Theo had taken his fill of her first, of course.' Kyle pushed the wickedly sharp point through my T-shirt so that it pricked my flesh. Directly over my heart. 'Wouldn't let me try turning her.'

'You're telling me that Murdoch had a conscience?' *Interesting*. And Erin wouldn't be doing the zombie thing in New York – that was good to hear. 'What possible use could you have for him, anyway?'

Kyle bit my ear, drawing blood. 'Hmm? Daylight was a problem. I needed to dump the bodies in the morning – draw attention away from the vamps, while sending a message to Theo. The hunter would do *anything* to take down a Master vamp.'

I nodded, confirming the information to myself. It made sense.

'No more questions,' he said. He released the pressure

on the stake for a moment, then pressed it back into position again with a wicked smile.

'Stop!' Theo moved forward, still carrying Caitlín. He seemed to suddenly remember that he was holding her and bent over to lay her on the ground.

'Don't do that,' Kyle said.

Theo hesitated. Kyle shifted his grip on me, forcing me to follow him as he stepped up onto the ledge that overlooked the side of Theo's home. One of my feet hovered just over the edge, and I wondered how much it would hurt to hit the ground below. We were directly over a narrow street – lots of pavement, lots of parked cars. Lots of attention too. If Kyle intended to stake me first, I probably wouldn't feel a damn thing anyway. I swallowed, trying desperately to get a grip on my senses. My head throbbed and, despite Theo's earlier 'donation', I was still weak from earlier.

Theo stood up straight again. He shifted Caitlín's weight in his arms. I knew she couldn't be too heavy for him – perhaps he was preparing to make some kind of attack.

Oh, God, I hope so, I thought. *As long as Cait doesn't get caught in the crossfire.*

Theo smiled suddenly, his stance relaxed and easy. My sister's hair swept down his shoulder and over his arm. Could I trust him to care about whether or not she got hurt? Why would he protect her? He wouldn't necessarily see Caitlín as an extension of me, however important 'family' was to him. He pinned his Enforcer with an expression filled with disdain. 'Fine. Let us hear this . . . proposition.'

I couldn't see Kyle's face, but I could hear the answering smile in his voice. 'Ah, good. Now you're being more agreeable.'

Theo growled, long and low and dangerous, deep in his throat.

'Sorry, boss. I forgot how impatient you can be.' Kyle tightened his grip around my throat. 'So here it is: I'm going to end your little pet unless you do one simple thing for me. Just one. It's only a small favor.'

'Get on with it,' Theo snapped, his eyes flashing silver fire.

'That human girl you're holding – turn her, the way you turned our Moth here. You can do it. Give me my own pet vampire.'

Theo took a step forward. 'You go too far—'

'Not really, no. But we're hoping that it'll look like *you* have.' Kyle smiled unpleasantly. 'And just as a nice little incentive, if you don't do it in the next sixty seconds, I'll stake this skinny bitch of yours and toss her dead body off the roof.'

Chapter Twenty-four

My brain struggled to take in what he was saying. Turn Caitlín? Why? Why would Kyle want Theo to do that? What could he possibly hope to gain?

I struggled, not caring when the razor-sharp wooden tip broke my skin.

'Ah, back with us?' Kyle breathed into my ear. 'Keep fighting me like that and you'll stake yourself, precious.'

I ignored him and continued to thrash wildly, forcing him to lower the stake and hold me with both arms again. I managed to free one arm, but only for a moment. Kyle clamped down on my hand so hard I felt one of my fingers break.

I gasped, tears of pain burning my eyes.

Theo, meanwhile, had laid Caitlín gently on the ground. Oh, God, I wanted to go to her so much. It was like my vision had narrowed to the point where all I could see was her. Her red hair was lank and she looked sickly-pale, her face practically glowing in the darkness.

Kyle moved one hand so quickly I didn't even notice he'd half released me. He punched me hard enough to crack ribs and I gasped, trying to focus past the pain.

'I said, stop wriggling. Next time I'll snap your neck.'

I forced myself to be still. He'd really do it, and then I'd be as near to death as a vampire can get. And I didn't doubt Kyle, not for a second. He'd break my neck in front of my Maker – his 'Master' – and he wouldn't blink. The ruthless efficiency that made him one of the best Enforcers in the country was the very thing that made him such a dangerous enemy. Who would have guessed that he was ambitious too?

Theo stood in the gentle breeze, last night's rain long gone and an autumnal chill in the air. His black clothes and black hair made him seem like a slender shadow – apart from the dangerous glint of eyes and teeth.

'You are in no position to make demands,' he said.

He sounded calm, but I knew he was furious. Beyond furious. His rage was something that was a tangible thing, almost as though he could make it a weapon and cut out Kyle's heart with it.

The object of all that anger simply laughed. 'You've always had a subtle kind of humor. I like that about you, Theo. Of course, I am in the perfect position to make demands – you'll do what I say or watch your "little Moth" take her final flight.'

I stared at Theo, wondering what we could do. He met my eyes and blinked, slowly. His eyes were almost completely silver, so bright I wanted to look away . . . only I couldn't.

For the first time since he'd turned me, I wished he could be inside my head and tell me what his plan was. Did he have one? He must have a plan, right?

But what if he didn't.

I licked my lips and tried to push strength into my shaking legs. I needed my own plan, just in case.

Theo shook his head. 'Kyle, have you lost your mind? What will turning this one human achieve? You cannot beat me, you know that. I am older than you. Stronger than you.'

'I may not be strong enough to kill you, but I'm smart enough to discredit you.'

Theo took another step. 'That's what this is about? For what purpose? Perhaps you want my place as head of the Family. Perhaps you have your eye on a greater prize – unseating Solomon . . .'

I felt Kyle's arms stiffen. 'Your position is the very least of this. Do you really have no clue? I think you've grown complacent. Look how you handed that other girl over to me to return *safely* to her life, her friends – handed me weakened, easy prey, covered in your scent.'

311

Theo ignored the taunt. 'Why stage a coup after all this time? Do fifty years of partnership mean nothing to you?'

'*Coup?*' Kyle shook his head. 'You're not listening to me, old man.'

So weird to hear him call my Maker that; but then, Kyle was half his age.

Theo bared his teeth. 'You don't possess enough years to depose me. You clearly don't have enough years to successfully Make a vampire.'

'I don't need centuries, not when I have you.'

'Wrong,' Theo said. 'Without age, you cannot take my place.'

'I don't want to take your place. I just want you *gone*. I'm part of a group that believes the time is right for a change in the status of the vampires of this world. Masters like you – those who want to stay in the shadows – are only holding us back. Keeping us locked in the Dark Ages.'

'You're talking about announcing our existence? Integration into human society?' Theo's voice held disbelief.

'Well,' Kyle said, 'not so much integrating as ... governing. And I needed to prove that Moth wasn't your only slip in self-control.'

This had gone far enough. I couldn't stay out of it any longer. 'You're jealous of him, aren't you, Kyle?'

'Shut up,' he growled, almost breaking my windpipe.

'I always knew you were secretly jealous,' I croaked. 'Is it because he's got bigger . . . fangs than you?'

'Stop. Talking.'

'Why, when I'm so good at it?'

Theo closed the distance by another tiny step. He gestured at Caitlín's still form. 'Why involve this girl? She is an innocent.'

Kyle barked out a laugh. '"Innocent"? That didn't stop you before. I thought you had a taste for O'Neal girls . . .' He stroked the hand holding the stake across my belly, tightening the other around my throat. 'That one behind you is even younger than the first. You can never have them too young, right, boss? In fact, why don't we take turns with her first? We could turn her together. I've always liked redheads.'

Terror parched my mouth. Not for me, not any more. I was beyond something as pointless as fear. I was dead already. But . . . Caitlín. My baby sister. The thought of Kyle hurting her made my whole body weak, hollowed out. I wanted to kill him. I wanted to rip off his head and pull his heart out through his neck.

Bad thoughts piled into my terrified brain, washing away the fear with a welcome black-hearted fury.

'Don't you touch my sister,' I said. 'I'll kill you, you sick bastard.'

'You didn't call your precious Maker that, did you,

hmm . . . ? I bet you begged him for it. I bet he made you scream.'

Yeah, but not in the way you mean, you perv, I thought.

Theo took one more step forward. 'Nobody gets Made tonight.'

'That's far enough.' Kyle pointed the stake at Theo to punctuate his words.

And that was his mistake. Well, that along with threatening my baby sister.

I slid my left arm free in the split-second I had and snatched the stake from Kyle's hand. I sensed, rather than saw, Theo *blur* forward as I spun and ducked Kyle's strike. His fist grazed my temple. He'd recovered fast and now I was off-balance.

I gripped the deadly stake and wobbled on the ledge, gazing down four floors below. I'd survive the fall, but it sure wouldn't be pretty.

Everything went into freeze-frame.

Jace was still on the ground beside his father's dead body. Caitlín lay behind Theo, ghostly pale. Theo was moving toward us, super-fast – vampire fast – but in my mind's eye he moved in slow motion. Kyle seemed torn between finishing me off – all it would take was one push over the edge of the roof – and facing his former Master.

I dropped to my knees and threw myself to the side, missing out on my potentially messy swan dive by millimeters. As Kyle's fist shot out again, Theo reached us and he grabbed the back of my jacket. He yanked me off my feet and I went down, dropping the stake over the edge of the roof, scrabbling to save myself from following it into the wide open space below.

Baring his fangs, Kyle *moved*, diving at Theo. I flinched as they clashed, seemingly in mid-air. It was all too fast, too brutal. Blood flowed and splashed to the ground.

Theo and Kyle began fighting, Master and Enforcer, in a whirl of faster-than-the-human-eye-can-see punches and kicks. Even *I* had trouble following the action.

I rolled off the ledge and limped toward Caitlín. My whole body hurt and I wanted to curl up in a ball and not get up for a week, but this wasn't over. It was very far from over, and I knelt beside my sister and checked her breathing. Everything seemed normal. Her heart beat in a comforting rhythm against my hand and I could feel her breath on my cheek. It seemed that Kyle had simply compelled her to sleep, which meant she would take a very long time to wake – unless another vampire broke the compulsion first. It would need a stronger vampire than the one who had placed it, so I was out of luck until Theo finished with Kyle.

He now had his Enforcer pinned face down on the roof. It looked like one of the Kyle's arms was broken.

'Moth.'

I spun, surprised to see Jace looking at me. The

emotion on his face was like a raw and open wound. He'd dragged himself back to consciousness while I'd escaped from Kyle. I touched Caitlín's silky hair one more time, just reassuring myself that she was really there, and crawled toward Jace. I didn't think I could stand up again and didn't have the energy to try.

Jace was bent over his father's body. Murdoch Senior was dead, and although I was glad he was gone, I couldn't hold onto that feeling for long. Not when I had a full view of the ragged grief and shock on his only son's face. Thomas Murdoch hadn't been a very nice man. At all. But he was still Jace's dad, and since the death of his mother he was pretty much all Jace had.

'What?' I said, as I came up close to him and the bloody remains of his father.

I approached cautiously, as though Jace was a wild animal who could be spooked by sudden movements.

'Help me with him. I can't carry him down those stairs on my own.'

'Jace,' I whispered. 'I'm so s—'

'Don't,' he said. 'Just . . . don't.' He paused. 'I saw you fight Kyle, though. You took his stake and seemed fine.'

I couldn't help feeling defensive. 'I think that must have been adrenaline.'

'Because he threatened your sister.'

'You heard that?' I shrugged. 'Yeah, I guess. Anyone

hurts her – or even thinks about it – has to go through me first.'

'I get that,' he said, his voice so quiet I had to lean forward to hear him. 'I would have been the same – had my sister lived.'

'What?' I searched his face. 'You had a sister?'

He turned away. I wondered if he regretted the revelation. 'I would have done. My mom was pregnant when she died.'

A lump rose in my throat and I had trouble swallowing past it. 'Oh, Jace . . .'

His shoulders were rigid. Then he stopped moving, stared across the roof and cursed. Loudly.

'What?' My head jerked up and I looked in the direction of his shocked gaze. How could I have forgotten that Theo was fighting for his life? Was it that I had simply assumed that he would win easily?

But Theo had been weakened before fighting Kyle, and that could be the only possible explanation for the scene I saw before me. Kyle had gotten hold of Thomas Murdoch's sword and my Maker was impaled on the end of it. The weapon had gone all the way *through* his body: piercing his stomach, with several inches of bloody blade protruding from his back. Theo hung on it, eyes blazing and mouth open in a silent scream. No way would he give Kyle the satisfaction of hearing him actually make a sound.

Theo was made of strong stuff, but this was bad. This was really bad. The silver must have been causing him unbearable pain.

I pulled myself up on shaking legs, using Jace's shoulder for support.

'Moth, what are you doing?' He grabbed my wrist and I glared at him.

'Don't try to stop me.'

'You're crazy! You can't even walk.'

'This is my duty,' I hissed, shaking him off and staggering in Theo's direction.

Jace looked like he was considering trying to stop me, then his shoulders slumped. He glanced down at his father's still face.

'Whatever,' he said. 'It's your funeral.'

'It wouldn't be the first one,' I said, and began a limping jog across the roof. 'Keep an eye on Caitlín for me.'

Kyle was so focused on making Theo suffer as much pain as possible that I managed to catch him in an unguarded moment. I snuck around from behind, conveniently downwind so that he wouldn't catch my approaching scent, and used the last of my determination to power my failing body. Theo saw me coming – I know he did – but he didn't blink. Not even while impaled on a sword.

Without a second thought, I threw myself onto Kyle's

318

back. No reason to fight fair any more, not after the bastard had almost crushed my skull with silver while my *own* back had been turned.

I grabbed his face and dug my nails into flesh. He roared, grabbing my arms and shaking wildly in an effort to dislodge me. My back hit the wall and the pain almost made me let go, but I managed to hold on. I gripped with both arms and legs and my fangs extended. I wanted to bite him. I wanted blood.

Kyle twisted around, trying to buck me off, but I hung on and forced him down onto his knees. He let go of the sword's hilt and Theo sank to his knees, still skewered.

I didn't know what to do, now that I was here. I was simply trying to buy my Maker time, but had no weapon other than my fangs and Kyle was moving too violently for me to have any hope of biting him.

Movement out of the corner of my eye made me hesitate.

Jace approached, wiping blood from his face. I stared at him, shock leaving me momentarily frozen. I'd thought his father's death had broken him – thought that he'd left me to pick up the pieces of this battle alone. But, once again, the young hunter surprised me.

He gripped the hilt of his father's sword and, without warning or any sign of squeamishness, pulled it out of Theo's gut.

Theo fell back and lay on the roof, blood-soaked, but still . . . alive. Still here.

Jace spun the sword once, single-handed, in a flamboyant gesture that almost made me smile.

Almost. There really wasn't much to smile about in Jace's expression. His eyes were the darkest I'd ever seen them.

Kyle elbowed me in the stomach, and the sudden sharp pain brought tears to my eyes. But I wasn't about to let go of him. I had a pretty good choke-hold on him – even though he couldn't exactly choke – and I'd managed to wrap my legs around his waist to stop him taking another shot at me. I was determined to hang on until Jace did what he had to do.

The sword trembled almost imperceptibly in the younger Murdoch's hands, whether from exhaustion or fear I wasn't certain. *Had Kyle noticed?* I hoped not. Beheading a vamp with a sword wasn't the easiest way to end our existence. Jace's father's sword had better be sharp. Just thinking about it made me want to throw up, but it wasn't like Kyle didn't deserve it.

Of course, Theo chose *that* moment to – impossibly – rise to his feet.

He looked amazingly calm and collected for a guy who'd been stabbed twice in the same night. He also had a set of chains in his arms.

Kyle thrashed in my grip like a shark rolling its prey.

Luckily for me, he didn't have teeth quite as deadly as a shark's and we weren't anywhere near water.

Theo ignored Jace and continued to approach Kyle – and me – with the chains. His expression was grim. 'Why don't we restrain him in a more . . . appropriate way?'

I had to admit, my arms were freaking killing me. I'd been thrown in every direction for the past couple of minutes, including being rolled on the ground and smashed against concrete. Letting go and leaving Kyle in Theo's capable hands seemed like a pretty good plan to me, although I wasn't sure that Jace would agree.

My eyes were irresistibly drawn to the chains that Theo cradled against his chest. He held them awkwardly, and I realized that it was because they were made of silver. *Oh, nasty*, I couldn't help thinking. Kyle was in for some bad times.

Jace had other ideas. 'Back off, he's mine.'

Theo narrowed his eyes. 'You're mistaken.'

'That monster just murdered my father. Nobody ends him except me.'

'No, child.' Theo was using his extra-soothing voice – the one that left a thrill of pleasure running through his willing blood donors. 'Kyle belongs to me, and only to me. Your involvement is . . . unfortunate.'

'*Unfortunate?* My father is dead.' Jace made it a statement, his voice ice-cold and controlled but his face twisted with hate.

'This one disobeyed me and tried to remove me as the head of Boston's Family. He risked uncovering our existence to the world at large. That is a far more serious crime than the death of a *hunter*.'

Fury poured off of Jace in sickening waves. Kyle had frozen in my arms, waiting for judgment. I released him and backed away, shaking my arms to try getting some feeling back into them. I touched Jace's back and he spun around and glared at me.

I shrugged, facing my Maker. 'We could stake him,' I said, 'but I dropped the one I had.'

'Staking's too quick,' Theo said.

I shivered at his tone, wondering what punishment he had in mind for the man he'd trusted with his life for almost fifty years.

But then, to immortal vampires, a decade is just the blink of an eye. Kyle had been biding his time – five decades must have seemed a cheap price to pay for gaining Theo's trust. Or perhaps his shift in loyalties had been more gradual. Perhaps it hadn't all been a lie.

Theo knelt by his fallen Enforcer and endured the silver-burn on his hands while he secured the chains around Kyle's chest and arms. The fact that he lowered himself to do the task himself held a significance I couldn't help noticing. He was showing Kyle a small measure of respect by doing the binding with his own hands.

I didn't think the disgraced vampire deserved even that gesture, but it wasn't exactly my place to argue. Theo would do as he pleased whatever my opinion, so for once I decided to keep my mouth shut.

It turned out that Theo's plan for Kyle was to truss him up, Thanksgiving-style, in heavy silver chains, and leave him on the roof to wait for sunrise. At his age, the sun would be intolerable – it would burn him to cinders. It was a harsh but appropriate judgment, and one I was certain the Elders would approve of. There would be no need to speak to Solomon first – Theo knew that there was no mercy for traitors.

To Kyle's credit he didn't beg for mercy and he didn't try to resist.

Sickened, I turned away and let my Maker finish securing the bonds.

Jace had walked away. He sat by his father's body with his back to me. I wanted to comfort him, but it didn't take a genius to figure out that he wouldn't want me to touch him right now. The tension in his shoulders and the way he held his body told me everything I needed to know. We'd locked eyes just once in the past few minutes, but he had turned away from me as though I was a stranger.

My stomach clenched with the injustice of it: *This was hardly* my *fault*, I wanted to scream at him. But that wouldn't matter to him right now.

I swallowed and took one more look at Kyle, wrapped in his silver cocoon like the victim of a giant spider. The sun would rise in a matter of minutes and Theo had already headed back down to his half-wrecked home. Kyle's eyes were open and I knew why. He probably hadn't seen the sun in at least half a century – this would be his last chance.

His only chance.

I shivered as a sharp breeze lifted the hair from my face. Thin fingers of sunlight inched their way from between gray clouds, pushing through nearly invisible gaps. I turned away from the shining aura that slowly began to surround the restrained vamp. His blond hair looked brighter than I ever remembered seeing it. The sun was already surprisingly intense; a few stray beams hit the glass of neighboring windows, and I winced in reflexive sympathy as Kyle screwed up his eyes against the glare. His skin began to blacken and shrivel, like meat on a barbecue. Bones cracked and melted. His body gradually collapsed in on itself, the decay of the grave taking minutes rather than years.

He burned under the sun, falling to ash in the first light of dawn.

Silence spread like a balm. Kyle was gone.

I crawled across the roof to Caitlín, reaching her after what felt like hours. I collapsed beside her, pulling her into my arms and propping myself up against the low wall. I checked her breathing again then rested my cheek against hers. I could take her downstairs when my legs felt like working again. Theo was most likely waiting for me before he slept; I needed him to wake her.

The morning sun on my face felt like a blessing. I didn't know how much longer I would be able to experience this – I couldn't take it for granted and I would need my shades on very soon, but for the moment I just felt human again as the sun stroked my skin. I held my sister tightly and thought about what might have happened, how bad things could have been.

We were lucky, I knew that.

I couldn't take *anything* for granted, and I didn't think I ever would.

Chapter Twenty-five

I felt Jace approach before I saw him.

His arm pressed against mine as he sat next to me, looking out at the slowly rising sun. We didn't speak for a long time, and there was a treacherous part of me that wished we could stay here forever. If we left the roof, I'd only have to go back downstairs to face Theo. I didn't want to have to live this life anymore.

While I could still survive under the sun – a winter dawn couldn't do more than hurt my eyes – I wanted to make the most of it.

'I'm so sorry about your dad, Jace.'

He took a deep breath; I felt it in the rise and fall of his body. 'Yeah, because he was such a great guy.'

I glanced at him sharply, but had to look away at the intensity of anguish written in his eyes.

'He was still your dad.' I thought of my own father, safely tucked away with his grief and his memories, picturing his drink-lined face and his fading red hair.

Jace stirred against me. 'Why did he have to be working with that . . . thing?'

I shivered and clutched Caitlín a little more tightly. 'Thing' was a pretty good word for Kyle, but was Jace referring to his being a vampire or just the fact that he was a back-stabbing, murdering bastard? I was sort of hoping for the latter, but if I was honest I couldn't be sure of anything right now. Least of all how Jason Murdoch might feel about me after everything that had happened.

'I don't know, Jace.' Wow, how much did I suck at the whole offering-comfort gig?

But it didn't matter now; none of it mattered anymore. Kyle was dead. Dead for real, this time – no coming back for another chance at existence. And more important than that, there would be no more innocent kids being taken and drained and then turned into shambling revenants. No more casual death for teenagers like Rick and Erin and Byron, or for innocent bystanders like Nurse Fox.

There was also the not insignificant detail that Theo had, by default, successfully completed his task for Solomon. His position of Master vampire in Boston was safe. We were safe – both of us. Although there was a job vacancy for a new Enforcer.

'Seems like Kyle was leaving a trail of bodies in the hope of framing your Maker,' Jace said. I kind of got the impression that he needed to talk about something – anything to delay the inevitable of dealing with his father's body.

My lips tightened. 'Yeah. Seems like it.' Theo had still drunk from an underage kid – Erin – but at least he wasn't a murderer. He hadn't gone rogue. That should make me feel a whole lot better, but somehow I couldn't find it in myself to be happy. Funny how that worked. Had Theo not fed from Erin in the first place, she would never have ended up in the hands of Kyle. Never ended up dead . . . I rubbed my eyes, wondering if I could somehow dislodge the unshed tears I knew were there. 'I'm sorry, Jace. Sorry he was involved in any of this.'

'It's not your fault. Looks like Dad was involved enough all by himself.' He lowered himself until he was sitting in the gravel of the rooftop, leaning against a low wall. 'He always hated the creatures he hunted. That was his mistake: getting emotionally involved.'

Emotionally involved. The words echoed inside my head. Was I emotionally involved with Jace? I looked at him, wishing I could say that I didn't care. For a moment, I seriously wished that I'd never met him. He was a human being, and one who had wanted to kill me when we first met. Not that I truly believed he would have followed through – not now that I knew him a little better. But after what had just happened to his father – and what Theo still had to do with Murdoch's *head* to complete his challenge – how could I know he wouldn't change his mind about me and put me right back at the top of his hit list?

I tried to wipe the blood off my face with my sleeve, but I only managed to smear it around. Oh, well. Healing fast had its uses. I glanced at Jace and found him watching me. My stomach dipped. I remembered the feel of his lips on mine, but the hard look in his eyes made it seem like a dream. I wasn't sure if it was a good dream or a bad one, but either way it was a long time ago. I wanted so much to believe it had happened. To believe in *him*.

I reached out, tentative, placed the tips of my fingers against his cheek. I felt his jaw tighten, but he didn't move away.

'Moth, I need to leave.'

His voice made me jump. I rested my hand back on Caitlín's shoulder and looked away from him. 'OK, I'm not stopping you. And Theo won't be outside again until sunset. I can deal with things here.'

He shook his head. 'No, I mean . . . I need to *leave*. Get away from here. Figure out what to do about my dad. I'll do what I have to do for him, make it right – and then lose myself for a while.'

Everybody leaves, I thought. Everyone goes away or I

leave them. Maybe that was my superpower: driving people away. My lip trembled like a stupid girl's. I laid Caitlín gently to one side and climbed to my feet. It felt like my body weighed a ton.

'Where will you go?' I asked. I thought of the OPI – they would be a natural home for someone like Jace. Would he join the 'Spook Squad'? Be my enemy forever? I cursed my vivid imagination. Surely he wouldn't do something like that. Jason Murdoch struck me as more of a natural loner.

'I don't know.' He answered me before I could say anything further, put any ideas into his head. 'Maybe somewhere in Europe. Dad has money put aside – I guess he won't be needing it anymore.'

I tried to push away the sadness that threatened to overwhelm me as Jace stood up and stepped toward me. I swallowed, wondering why I couldn't stop shaking and hating myself for it. He touched my face with fingers made sticky with his father's blood. I didn't care, for once hardly noticing the scent. All I could think about was how close he was to me and how much I wanted him to hold me. I wanted to ask him not to leave – not yet – but I couldn't speak past the confused emotions bunched together in my throat.

And then he pulled me against him, pressing my head against his chest and folding me in his arms. The feeling of safety reminded me of what it was like when Theo held me, only that was more like the embrace of a father – a father who loved me. Right now there was nothing familial about the desire warming my stomach. I felt a hunger I only vaguely remembered; not a hunger for blood, but for something so much sweeter. I buried my face into the rough material of Jace's jacket, took a deep breath so that I could remember his scent.

Jace rested his chin against the top of my head and I felt his jaw move as he spoke. 'I didn't realize vampires could be so sentimental.'

I could hear the smile in his voice, and for some reason that made the tears spill over. His father had died and I was the one crying. But of course, I wasn't shedding tears for Murdoch Senior.

Jace released me, holding me away from him and looking into my eyes. 'Will you be OK? I mean, with him. Theo.'

I nodded slowly. 'I have no choice.'

'Are you sure about that?'

I looked up sharply, but for once there was no judgment in his voice or on his face. I shrugged. 'Maybe one day,' I said. 'But that day is not now.'

'Don't let him control you,' Jace said. 'You're better than that.'

'Thank you.' My voice was huskier than ever. 'What about you? Are *you* OK?'

'I will be.' His gaze flicked over to where he'd dragged

his father's body and his jaw tightened. 'There's a lot of cleaning up to do.'

We both turned our attention to Kyle's ashes, stirring gently in the morning breeze. I shivered, but not from the cold. I avoided looking at Murdoch's body. 'Theo will sort it, Jace. All of it. He'll treat your father's remains with respect – he always respected him as a hunter. Just go . . .'

I didn't say anything about the Council, or about Theo needing Murdoch's head. It really wasn't what Jace needed to hear right now.

Much later, after Theo had done the 'cleaning up' he had to do, I walked into his bedroom, not bothering to knock. He should have been sleeping, recovering his strength, but I straightened my spine and fixed him with a serious expression.

'I need to know the truth. About that night.'

'Which night are we talking about? There have been many nights between us.'

Blushing, but refusing to back down, I continued to press him. 'You know which night I'm talking about. There has only ever been one quite like it.'

He visibly deflated. The expression on his face was loud and clear: *Here we go again.* 'You mean, when I turned you.'

'I mean,' I said, 'when we slept together.'

'Which was the same night, if my memory serves.' His

eyes narrowed as he clearly wondered where I was going with this.

'I want to know if you compelled me to sleep with you. If I was somehow . . . under your control.'

Anger flashed across his face, there and gone in less than a second. But I saw it and braced myself for his reply.

'Ah, my Moth. If you remembered that evening as well as I, you would not be so quick to claim I needed to compel women to my bed.'

Now my whole face was burning. 'Theo, I need to know.'

'You loved me,' he said, his voice rough with emotion.

'I still do,' I replied, surprised to find that I meant it. 'I always will. But that's not what I'm talking about. Recently, I've been remembering things. I remembered a lot of stuff from that time, and I can't help wondering how much of it was my choice – and how much of it was your . . . influence.'

'I didn't force you.' His voice was cold with anger.

'That's not what I said.' I took a step forward, expecting him to pull away and unbearably relieved when he didn't. I laced my cold fingers with his. 'I asked if you used your abilities – your vampire abilities, I mean,' I added hastily.

He smiled, but it was an unbearably sad expression.

'I did not. I . . . could never have done that to you, *m'anamchara.*'

Now my heart was pounding, and I felt suddenly afraid. 'Don't call me that. Not now.'

He brought my hand to his mouth, brushed my knuckles with soft lips and then held my hand against his heart.

A heart that had stopped beating a century and a half ago.

'You know that vampires have natural pheromones – a body chemistry that far exceeds that of our previous human form.'

'Yes.' I also knew that the older the vamp, the more powerful the pheromones. It's what draws our prey to us and relaxes them enough to enjoy the process of sharing blood.

'If I, to use your own word, "influenced" you in any way, it was something done without my conscious control. My pheromones would have convinced you that you were safe with me, but no more than that.'

I didn't know whether to feel anger or relief.

Anger won. 'But I wasn't safe, was I? That's the whole point.'

Theo bristled. 'I gave you eternal life. Many would be willing to die for such a gift.'

'And I did have to die for it, didn't I?' I couldn't keep the bitterness from my voice. 'You took my humanity.'

'You will only truly lose your humanity if you let it go.'

'That's not true. It's not something I can control – not entirely.'

He touched my hair, stroking it gently, almost absent-mindedly. 'Moth, I've been twenty-six for precisely one hundred and sixty-eight years. Do I get tired? Of course. Do I move further away from the person I was born as? Undoubtedly. But I still remember what it means to be human.'

'And that's why you could turn me in the first place?'

'I believe so, yes. I still possessed enough of my soul to share it with another.'

'With me?'

'Yes.'

My shoulders slumped and I shook off his hand. 'I can't help feeling angry at you. It's like . . . you took something that wasn't yours.'

'I don't know how many times I can tell you that I regret what happened.' He dropped my hand as though my skin burned him. 'I rarely apologize for anything, Marie. It is not what the head of a Family does. And yet I have apologized to you, many times.'

'Being sorry doesn't give me back my life. My real life.'

'Did you ever stop to think that perhaps this *is* your real life? Perhaps you were always meant for greater things.'

Greater things? Was my life, now, something greater? I wasn't convinced.

'So what you're saying,' I said slowly, wanting to make sure I really understood, 'is that although you didn't roofie me, you might have gotten me a little drunk.'

His expression was one of distaste. 'It is an unpleasant analogy, little one.'

'But it's the truth?'

'It will do. Are you satisfied?'

'No. But thank you for telling me the truth.'

He frowned. 'Perhaps you will forgive me, in time.'

'Perhaps.'

Epilogue

I have stared death in the face – on more than one occasion – and yet I still dread sitting at a dinner table with my biological family.

Strange how something so simple can feel so complicated. So *terrifying*.

I caught my younger sister's eye and her lips twitched. Caitlín's happiness made it difficult to worry about being here too much. I gave her a sickly smile in return.

Almost a week had passed since what had become known in Theo's Family as a failed coup. Kyle was gone. Thomas Murdoch too. At least three teenagers from my past life had died – plus an unfortunate, hard-working nurse called Stephanie Fox – during Kyle's attempt to unseat Theo from his position as Master of Boston's Family of vampires.

All along, he'd been part of the growing movement of vamps who believed it was time to 'come out of the coffin' and take their place alongside human beings in the world. Politics or violence, two pathways toward independence, and there were groups aligned on either side within the vampire community. Kyle was a member of the United Vampire Alliance, or UVA.

Yeah, the name was ironic. Never let it be said that the undead don't have a twisted sense of humor.

Theo was safe. The High Council had Murdoch's head, and that meant that I was safe too. I couldn't help but feel a warm glow at being fully accepted into the Family, no matter how much I wanted to deny it. There would be no more hiding for me. My un-life was opening up to new possibilities.

I glanced around the dinner table and tried hard not to think about Jason Murdoch. I especially hadn't given any thought to that one kiss beneath Murdoch Senior's van, or to the feel of his arms around me on Theo's roof the last time I saw him.

Well, OK, it might have crossed my mind once or twice. But, in all honesty, I was mostly thinking about that terrible, lost expression on his face as he sat by his father's body. Jace would be far away from here by now, taking the break he needed to get his head straight. Maybe even going back to school, but I doubted that somehow. He'd talked about there being a 'network' of independent hunters across the US. I worried about whether or not he might feel it was his duty to take on Daddy's mantle for real. I was glad he didn't know how his father's body had been mutilated before burial. It was probably for the best that he never found out.

Caitlín touched my hand and I glanced at her, dragging my attention back to the room. Jace was gone and I was here with my family – my real family. My little sister had finally gotten her wish: my return to the O'Neal home. And when she had awoken from her nightmarish experience, Theo had ensured she had no memory of how Kyle had trapped her. How the Enforcer had sent her into a sleep she might never have woken from were it not for my Maker's help. I'd begged Theo not to take her recently acquired knowledge of what I had become. Incredibly, he agreed – although there had been a price attached. I had to promise him I would embrace my role within my new Family, and let go of the old 'when the time came'.

Whenever that might be.

On the other side of the table, I caught Sinéad's eye and wondered whether she was as pleased to see me as she'd seemed. My arrival had been a surprise. Caitlín didn't give them any advance warning of my visit, partly because she wanted to catch them unawares, but also because she hadn't truly believed me when I promised I really would make it this time. No matter how difficult I found it – I barely touched the food on my plate, for instance, surreptitiously feeding titbits to Oscar, making him a very happy dog – I should try to come more often while I was still able, so that I could keep an eye on her. She was too precious and I had almost lost her.

My dad, Rory O'Neal, sat diagonally across from me. As usual, he only had eyes for his youngest daughter, but that was fine by me. The less attention he gave me, the less likely it was that we would clash or that he'd start spewing nonsense about what he thought I was getting up to in the city. It was two o'clock in the afternoon and he was already drunk. Sometimes he was better that way; others . . . not so much. Today was a quiet day, and for that we could all be grateful.

I looked at each of my human family in turn and was left, as I always am, with the question: How do I come to terms with being made into a vampire? How does a mortal adjust to immortality?

And, as usual, there was no answer. No *simple* answer, anyway. Caitlín stared at me, concern flickering briefly in her eyes. I forced a smile. It would be OK. We'd work things out and get through this – somehow. Sure, this wasn't the way my life was supposed to happen, and yet here I am. Trying my best to deal, mostly falling on my face – but always getting up again.

I raised my glass, nodding for her to do the same.

She held up her hand. 'Wait – let me make the toast.'

'Sure.' I shrugged, wondering if Sinéad and Dad would join us.

Their glasses were already raised, waiting.

Caitlín smiled at everyone, but there was a special message in her eyes for me. 'To new beginnings. *Slàinte.*'

I loved her more than ever in that moment and touched my glass to hers, tears shimmering in my eyes.

'*Slàinte*,' I replied.

The next day, I was surprised to find a package covered in foreign stamps resting on the floor outside my apartment door. It was too large to fit through the mail slot, and must have arrived while Holly was sleeping.

There was no return address. Any kind of delivery was bound to make me nervous considering how nobody was supposed to know where I lived. Apart from one person I could think of. I frowned, and if my heart could beat faster that's exactly what it would be doing.

I sniffed the parcel, wondering if I'd be able to sense something wrong with it. How would I know if there was something dangerous inside?

Screw it, I thought.

Tearing open the package before I could change my mind, my eyes widened when I pulled out the contents.

I shook out the bright green T-shirt. It had a badly screen-printed image of a four-leafed clover on the back and a pint of Guinness on the front. I glanced down and saw that a piece of brightly colored card had fallen out when I'd unfolded the shirt.

Scooping it off the floor, I realized that it was a postcard from Dublin. I smiled at the handwritten note on the back, wondering what it meant for the future:

I owe you one.
J.

Acknowledgements

Bringing Moth's novel to publication has been my dream since the first short story was originally published in the summer of 2009. Thanks are due to many people:

First of all, huge mega-thanks to Jessica Clarke, my editor. You saw the potential in this manuscript and helped me to craft a book out of it. Your patience is legendary!

To everyone at Random House Children's Books. I love being part of the Family – thank you for all your hard work on my behalf. Particular thanks to Sue Cook, who caught so many errors and inconsistencies that I wish you could copy-edit every book I write from now on.

To my agent, Miriam Kriss, who has believed in Moth for as long as I have – knowing that you're in my corner is the best thing that ever happened to my career. Thank you.

To the Deadline Dames – World Domination(tm) is just around the corner!

To Vijay Rana – life without you in it would be… boring.

Big thanks to all of my family and friends. There are simply too many people that I could single out by name, but then I'd no doubt forget somebody ... and then where would I be? (Clue: in trouble.)

Having said that, I really must thank: Uncle Rob and Aunt Eileen for always cheering me on; cousin Carole, for being generally awesome; Jo and Dean for putting up with my appalling track record when it comes to visiting, because I have yet another deadline; Tricia Sullivan for always being there; Stephanie Kuehnert, for showing me that writing alongside someone really can be fun; Brian Kell for being Moth's No. 1 fan; Candace Ellis for creative inspiration (#letsgoteamworkaholic); and Ana Grilo, who is just like a sister to me.

Last, but by no means least, to my mum – Mum, even though I'm supposed to be a writer, no words could ever do justice to how wonderful a person you are. I love you.